CHRISTMAS WITH THE SINGLE DAD

SINGLE DADS OF SEATTLE, BOOK 5

WHITLEY COX

ISBN: 978-1-989081-23-5

For Johanna and Alicia.
Whether it be constant messaging all day
long, wine and nachos at the pub,
or playdates with our kids, I know
that you will ALWAYS be there for me.
You are my people, my girls, my bitches
and I love you.

**Also, Jo, your birthday is December 25th, so you totally deserve an
extra shout-out!
Happy Birthday, you sexy thang!**

1

"CAN I TOUCH YOUR BICEP?"

Careful to hide his eye roll, and instead plaster on a big fake grin, Zak Eastwood pulled his earbud out of one ear and sat up on the workout bench, coming face to face with a camel toe in hot pink spandex exercise pants. Slowly, he let his eyes climb the petite frame. Past the bare midriff with the spray tan, past the fake boobs stuffed into a tight white sports bra. Past the makeup (who the fuck worked out while wearing makeup?) to finally see long fake lashes batting at him shamelessly.

"Rockin' Around the Christmas Tree" played on the speakers overhead, competing with the rap in his one remaining earbud.

The woman in front of him took a half step forward, forcing the camel toe even closer to his head. He kept his eyes on her face. He just had to.

"I've just never seen such big muscles," she purred, tossing her shoulders back so her big fake tits pushed out toward him. "I see you here a lot. It shows."

He nodded. "Yeah, spend a fair bit of time here."

Because I own the place.

She thrust her hand forward, revealing pointy, sparkly gold fake nails with little green and red gems glued to them. "I'm Shadley."

He shook her hand. "Zak. Nice to meet you."

She nibbled on her bottom lip. "I know who you are. *Everybody* knows who you are."

He cocked a single eyebrow but didn't say anything.

"So can I touch it?"

"Touch what?" He was quickly losing patience with this woman. He knew what she wanted—that was being screamed from the tallest mountain—he just wasn't interested.

"Your arm." She lifted her shoulder.

The rap music in his one earbud switched to something heinously filthy. "Sure, have at 'er."

He had to keep the customers happy. Keep the members coming back for more. Even if that meant he pimped himself out a bit and let the gym bunnies hop around him constantly, wiggling their little cottontails. Not that he ever did what bunnies do best with them though. No freaking way.

She bounced on her toes, then stepped forward, reaching out timidly as if his arms had teeth and would suddenly lunge out and bite her.

Her hands were cold. Like fucking freezing. A chill ran through him, and his nipples tightened beneath his black tank top.

"Wow." She squeezed. "These are amazing. And your tattoos are so beautiful."

"Thanks."

She wrapped her hand around and beneath his arm, gripping his tricep. "I don't live too far from here. Just a couple of blocks. Was going to head home, have a bubble bath and some wine ... "

His mouth flattened into a thin line as he fought the urge to smirk. "Sounds like a great way to relax."

"I have a Jacuzzi tub, too. It's so big for little ol' me."

"You should get a Great Dane. They're huge."

He snorted in his head. He was fucking hilarious.

Her brows pinched, then relaxed, and she smiled a bleached-tooth smile. "I was thinking something a little less hairy and a little more muscly and inked up might be better company. What do you think?"

Commotion at the front desk drew his eyes away from the bunny in front of him. A regular patron whose name he couldn't remember—but really should—was just coming in and shaking off a ton of snow from her coat and stomping her boots.

The bunny cleared her throat. "What do you think? Feel like coming over for a bath and wine? I can massage out the aches from your workout."

He pinned his gaze back on the woman in front of him, careful not to let his distaste for her come out on his face or in his tone. "Thanks so much for the offer, but I need to get home. I have my kids tonight." No, he didn't, but she didn't need to know that. Finding out he had two kids usually scared the majority of the bunnies away.

She released his arm and stepped back a couple of steps. "Oh, you have kids."

Ah, there it is.

That's right, little bunny, hop away now that you know I come with baggage.

He wiped his brow with his towel. "Two, a girl and a boy. Eight and ten."

Her smile was forced, almost grim. "How sweet."

Not into single dads there, little bunny?

She blinked her thick lashes, revealing what he knew to

be *the smoky eye* effect with her shadow. Seemed a bit over the top for the gym but whatever.

His ex had been big into the *smoky eye*. Once she'd figured out how to do it, that is. For the first bit, Loni would come out of the bathroom looking like she'd just been punched in both eyes. Zak would laugh. Loni would pout and then head back in and try again. Eventually, she figured it out. Though he always preferred her—preferred most women with subtle eye makeup rather than dramatic.

He didn't begrudge a woman who wore makeup, got her nails done, took care of herself. Not in the least. He liked when a woman knew how to put herself together and dress up but also wasn't afraid to go out in public looking like a hot mess because she'd just killed it at the gym.

Life was all about balance.

Fake nails were fine as long as when the weeds needed to be pulled, she didn't mind getting a bit of dirt on her hands.

Or didn't mind breaking a nail as she raked them down his back when he was showing her how he liked to get his cardio workout.

He just wanted a woman who didn't prioritize that shit over the stuff in life that really mattered—like health and family. Besides, there wasn't anything hotter than seeing a ring of bright red lipstick around the base of his cock after a really good BJ.

However, he could tell in the mere two minutes she'd been standing there that Shadley or whatever the hell her name was, had probably never pulled a weed in her life, and definitely wouldn't be caught dead out in public looking like a hot mess.

She tilted her head in the direction of the women's changing room. "Oh, I think I hear my phone."

Fsst. Yeah, okay then.

You sure it wasn't the K-word that scared you off?

Kids! Nearly as terrifying as the word prenup.

And he would never *ever* get married again without one that was ironclad.

Shadley cleared her throat, then cupped her hand to her ear. "Yes, yes, that is definitely my phone. I left it in my locker. I better go check to make sure it isn't work calling me. I run a nail salon." She backed up a few more steps. "Nice to meet you."

He put his earbud back in and reclined down to the bench again. "Yeah, you too."

She was gone in a flash, leaving Zak chuckling to himself as he picked up the dumbbells again and resumed his pec fly reps.

Yeah, he could get any piece of tail he wanted. But he didn't want any. Not right now. Not for a long time. Loni had burned him bad. And she continued to make his life hell with the way she used their children as pawns in her manipulation and games.

She was a liar too.

Always with a new scheme up her sleeves. Always with a new ploy.

Her boyfriend was a liar too.

Zak fucking hated liars.

If he ever found a good woman again, he'd state right off the bat that if she lied to him, they'd be done.

No second chances, no do-overs.

Liars were the scum of the earth, and no way in hell would he have them in his or his kids' lives ever again.

AURORA STRATFORD nearly face-planted into the garland- and holly-adorned front desk as she shook her coat and stomped her boots. The temperature in her cheeks was that of a volcano, but her heart was on the verge of shattering.

Why?

Because he was talking to Shadley.

He. Zak.

He was talking to Shadley Taylor, the most beautiful woman at the gym.

Her squats were unbelievable, her makeup flawless. Like crazy flawless. Did she even break a sweat when she worked out at all? Did she even work out? Or did she simply come to the gym to be seen and cruise the weight section for fresh meat to sink her sharp fake claws into?

Over the past few months, Shadley had been talking with her girlfriends in the changing room—whenever Aurora happened to be in there at the same time as them—about trying to hook up with Zak. Looked like she was finally making her move.

Aurora tried not to let it distract her, but her eyes were glued to the two gorgeous people over in the weight room chatting.

And then Shadley touched his bicep, and Aurora nearly passed out.

Why did she torture herself?

Because he's gorgeous, and loving him from afar is better than never seeing him at all.

True.

Staring at him a few times a week was her guilty pleasure. Her dose of happiness at the end of the day, in a world filled with loss and stress and loneliness.

Once she swiped her key card, she took her snowy self to the women's changing room and got dressed for a workout.

It was exactly what she needed after a long day in the bullpen at her law firm. After a white-knuckle drive across town to the gym.

Why was it across town?

Because Aurora was attracted to Zak, and she let her heart run roughshod over her practicality.

Because Aurora was a thin-dime recent law graduate, first-year associate who exploited the *free two-week trial* membership at nearly every gym in Seattle, rather than pay a fee, because her ass was broke. Until she stumbled into Club Z, that is.

At a twenty-five-minute drive from her home and a twenty-minute drive from work, she knew it was stupid. There were over a dozen other fitness facilities and rec centers closer—and cheaper—to either work or home. But none of them had Zak.

The moment she walked in to claim her free two weeks and saw him doing chin-ups, she signed up for a lifetime membership. A LIFETIME MEMBERSHIP.

She was still paying it off.

But he was worth it.

The man was magnificent.

Stunning.

A tattooed god with a beautiful shock of dark red hair, rippling muscles, sparkling blue eyes and a smile that would make an entire nunnery fall to their knees and chant a thousand Hail Marys.

And he had absolutely no clue who she was.

The clock on the wall said it was eight o'clock. She'd been pulling twelve- and fourteen-hour days all week. Today was the first day she left the office before 10 p.m.

She climbed onto the elliptical machine once she'd filled up her water bottle at the fountain and grabbed a complimentary club towel.

She just needed to zone out and do cardio for an hour or so. Normally, she'd do thirty minutes of cardio and then weights, but she was just too damn tired for weights tonight. It was all she could do to keep her eyes open.

But she needed to keep her eyes open. She had the perfect view of her fantasy paramour. The perfect view of his ass, that is. He was doing squats in front of the mirror now, and the way his hamstrings and calves bunched and flexed with each dip made her whole mouth go dry—because another part of her body was hella wet.

Aurora caught a glimpse of herself in the mirror. She wasn't ugly. She knew that. But she wasn't what you called a show-stopper either.

She was checked out and flirted with, asked out by associates at work, had drinks sent over while out for dinner with friends. She was attractive. But she wasn't Shadley Taylor. She wasn't in Zak's league.

Never would be.

So she resigned herself to loving him from afar.

Fantasizing about him as she sweat her ass off and watched his ass tighten with each pop up from a squat.

She knew every tattoo on his arm.

Didn't know what they meant or the significance of them, but she knew them.

Knew the flowers on his right arm and the way they twisted down from his shoulder around and under his tricep to end just above his wrist. A peppering of scripted words she had never been close enough to read filled out the rest of that arm, along with Roman Numerals in big, dark block letters. He had two different sets of very realistic flowers on either shoulder—she knew they probably held incredible significance—and more than once she caught herself tearing up as she stared at them.

It was harder to tell what was on his left arm, but even from far away she could tell the work was beautiful. More writing, crashing waves, a lighthouse, a fish, footprints. It was all in there. It was all stunning.

"You almost done?"

She blinked the sweat from her eyes, grabbed her towel and wiped her face.

"You've been on here for like an hour." A muffled voice interrupted the music blasting through her earbuds. It was Shadley, and she was giving Aurora a very odd look. "These machines are for everyone, you know."

Aurora nodded. Her eyes flicked up to the clock on the wall, where sure enough, it was almost nine o'clock. "Yeah, sorry. Lost track of time. Been a long day."

Shadley smiled tightly, though the corners of her eyes didn't move. Was that Botox or just a fake smile? "Don't forget to wipe down your machine when you get off, please. I don't want to touch your sweat."

Don't forget to wipe down your machine ...

Aurora wanted to wipe down Shadley's fucking face. With her fist.

She slowed down, hopped off the elliptical and went over to the paper towel and spray bottle station so she could disinfect the machine for Shadley.

Why did the woman need *that* elliptical? There were like eight others.

Why did Shadley pick Aurora to kick off the machine? Yes, they were all occupied, but why didn't she go and flaunt her camel toe at one of the beefcakes down the row and ask them to give her a turn? Was it because she saw Aurora as an easy mark? A wounded gazelle on the Serengeti, the easiest person to bully off the machine, take down with her talons. Kill swiftly with one slice to the jugular with her bedazzled index finger.

With the pace of a snail in the snow, Aurora made her way back to the elliptical machine and began to wipe it down.

Shadley stood there, tapping her foot, her eyes focused on the row of televisions at the front of the gym above the mirrors. A few TVs had various news stations on: one, a Christmas comedy sketch special; another, sports; and the last had a cooking show where the Santa-hat-clad host was teaching some football player how to make something that Aurora could have sworn looked like lard pie but was more likely something festive and fattening like a French-Canadian Tourtière. It was Christmas, after all.

Shadley let out a huff and ran her manicured hand over her bottle-blonde hair, smoothing it back into its long, straight ponytail.

Aurora took her sweet time cleaning the machine, rolling her eyes and making a face of disgust when the woman's hot pink camel toe came into view as she bent over to wipe a few drops of sweat from the footholds.

"Can you speed up?" Shadley asked.

Aurora smiled sweetly. "I could, but I'm not going to. There are eight other machines, and yet you chose this one. There is no sign-up board, so technically, if I wanted to stay on this machine all day, I could. You don't *own* this machine. You don't *own* this gym. You pay your dues just like I do."

Shadley's face burned a bright pink beneath her bronzer, and her dark brown eyes turned fierce. "I could go and complain at the front desk."

Aurora tilted her head. "Okay." Then she hopped back up on to the same elliptical, turned it on again and resumed her workout.

Shadley let out an irritated growl. "You're a bitch."

Aurora shrugged, turned the music up on her phone and pointed to her earbuds. "What? I can't hear you."

She had to hide her smile for fear the woman in front of her might turn rabid and tear out her carotid artery with her Christmas-painted talons.

Aurora fought and argued all day long. Dealt with people slamming doors in her face and yelling at her on the phone more than she cared to count. Usually, by the end of the day, she had no more fight left in her, so she just rolled over and gave in, whether it be a person at the gym like Shadley or someone butting in line at the grocery store. She wasn't going to pick that hill to die on. She had bigger battles to fight, bigger fish to fry.

But not tonight. Something about the way Shadley was looking at her, speaking to her made Aurora see red. She wasn't the weakling of the pack. She wasn't a wounded gazelle on the savannah, the first to be picked off when the hyenas came scrounging. She would be one of the first to get away, one of the fastest in the herd.

Shadley was still flapping her lips, but Aurora couldn't hear her. The filthy rap in her ear was a welcome change from the shrill voice of Camel Toe Susan in front of her.

Aurora shook her head once again and pointed to her earbud. "Still can't hear you. Sorry."

Laser beams nearly shot out of the woman's eyes. Aurora dipped her head down to hide her smile. Stomping her foot, Shadley growled again, then turned and marched away.

Aurora snickered and turned away from where the other woman had retreated to, only to find HIM of all people watching her.

Her smile dropped instantly.

His didn't.

His grew bigger.

Her lips twitched as she debated whether to smile back. Now she just looked like she was having muscle spasms in her face.

His dark red eyebrow drew up on his freckled forehead, and he smiled even wider before shaking his head and glancing toward the front desk where, lo and behold, Shadley was making a complaint.

Ah, crap.

Aurora's gaze slipped from the flushed-face guy behind the desk and a pointing Shadley back to Zak. He was shaking his head again and rolling his eyes. He seemed to find all of this hilarious.

Was he not with Shadley?

Had he turned her down?

The person at the front desk who was handling Shadley's tirade glanced at Zak. Zak rolled his eyes again, shook his head and shrugged.

What was that about?

The employee behind the desk shook his head at Shadley, shrugged and made an apologetic face.

Shadley's head nearly exploded. She stormed off toward the changing room, steam retreating from her ears and possibly even her camel toe, the woman was that mad.

Aurora snickered again. Served the bitch right.

Ah, but where's your Christmas spirit?

Fuck Christmas spirit. Aurora had had a rough day at work, and all she wanted to do was jump on the elliptical at the gym, zone out and stare at Zak for ninety minutes. Was that too much to ask for? That was all she wanted for Christmas.

That was all she was probably going to get for Christmas.

She didn't have enough money to fly home to New Hampshire for the holidays, and her parents were struggling to make ends meet after her dad's heart attack this past spring and his now sudden retirement. She'd told them several times over the last few months that she didn't want them to waste their money and send her anything. She didn't need anything.

But of course, they hadn't listened, and a parcel had arrived in the mail not two days ago.

She didn't have a tree to put it under, so she bought a fake wreath at the dollar store and hung it on her wall, setting the parcel beneath it.

Merry Christmas!

So, yeah. Watching Zak bend and pick things up, flexing that ass of his, was her Christmas present to herself. And it was the only gift she was getting anybody this year, because things were tight—much like Zak's ass—but not nearly as nice.

Once again, in her own head, she'd zoned out completely.

Zak had gone back to his workout, and Aurora spaced out on the elliptical, reading the closed captioning on the cooking channel show and listening to the dirty, dirty rap music in her ear.

For some reason, she loved to listen rap music when she got her sweat on. And the dirtier the better. Maybe it was because the words helped fuel her fantasies about Zak, that he was doing to her what the lyrics of the song described.

Oh, if only.

It was Thursday night. She would head in to work for two more days—because Saturdays off were for bankers and firm partners, not first-year associates, aka mere peons—then have a much-deserved two days off, Christmas Eve and Christmas Day, only to burn the candle at both ends again come December 26.

Two more days of work.

Those days off could not come fast enough. Mind you, she was only getting those days off because the firm itself was closed, not because she dared to take any vacation days, no way. She only hoped that Santa was kind to her and she didn't get a call from one of the partners with an emergency project that she had to do at home. She planned to spend those two days off in her bed with her vibrator and thoughts of Zak doing squats in her mind.

She was six months into her first-year associate position at her law firm, and already she was feeling burned out.

How did lawyers do it?

How did they work eighty-plus hours a week?

Their salaries are better than yours, so that cushions the blow of having no life. That's how.

Right. Money.

A lot of her colleagues would also respond with the answer *alcohol.* Too bad Aurora couldn't afford a bottle of wine from Trader Joe's to save her life at the moment. No, any spare change she had went straight to her parents—or her father's medical bills, to be more precise. Once she paid her rent, her utilities, her student loan payment and her food, she deposited the rest into her parents' bank account and hoped to God they had enough saved up that month to get her dad the heart medication he needed.

Life should not be lived with your fingers constantly crossed.

What was wrong with this world that lifesaving drugs were more expensive than a mortgage?

A tap on her shoulder had her bracing for another show-down with Shadley, only it wasn't Shadley at all. It was the guy from the front desk. "Just so you know, we close in about fifteen minutes."

Her eyes flew up to the clock. Holy crap, was it already nine forty-five?

She'd been pedaling the machine for another forty-five minutes and hadn't even clued in.

She really was exhausted.

No, you're burned the fuck out. You need sleep and lots of it.

Blinking, she nodded, yawned and slowed down her machine. "Right, thanks. I knew that."

He smiled and then took off to inform the next person.

She hopped down off the elliptical and scanned the gym for Zak. He was nowhere to be found.

Probably showering.

Oh God, Zak in the shower. *Yes, please.*

She needed a shower to cool off after that image.

Only she'd never waste the free hot water on a cold shower. Even if she lived on the surface of the sun.

Free hot water was a gift.

Nothing like free hot water. Well, it wasn't free. She'd paid a hefty lifetime membership for that hot water, so she was going to use it. Might as well save her own hot water bill at home.

Anywhere she could scrimp and save, she would.

She sprayed down her machine once again, wiping it clean of her sweat, then she headed to the changing room.

By the grace of God, Shadley was not in there. She must have left when Aurora was staring at Zak's butt. Which time?

She peeled out of her clothes, wrapped a towel around her and headed to the shower, ready to shut her eyes and let the water and soap wash away the disaster of a day—the disaster of her life.

2

AURORA WAS a prune by the time she shut off the water in the shower and wrapped the towel around herself, only to emerge into a dark changing room.

Shit.

The gym was closed.

She'd gotten so carried away shaving and washing, fantasizing and daydreaming, that she let time get away from her.

Was she locked in?

How had the front desk guy not heard her in the shower?

Hastily, she dressed, not even bothering to dry her hair with more than a quick rub from the towel, then she was running—well, more like scrambling—toward the front door.

No. No. No. No. No. No.

She exhaled when her hand landed on the handle and it budged. The frigid wind from outside hit her flushed face, making it sting.

The snow was now coming down in what appeared to be big white cotton balls, and the parking lot was no longer a parking lot but various mounds where cars were, and holes where cars had been.

Her car was the former.

She was going to have to not only dig to find her car but also dig herself out.

And she didn't have a shovel to her name.

Now I bet you're wishing you didn't go to a gym so far from home.

Her gloves were in her car too. She'd have to freeze her hands in order to even get to them.

Tears threatened, and her throat began to clog up.

What an absolute mess.

Was this karma for how she'd treated Shadley earlier?

The fates handing her her just desserts because she'd stood up for herself?

It was already so late, so cold, and now she wouldn't be home for ages—if she ever got home.

She reached into her gym bag and grabbed her pair of sweaty workout pants, wrapped them around her right hand and began to clear the snow from the top of her car. She would be here forever. Probably freeze to death before she got it all cleared.

Should she call a cab?

Were cabs even running in the blizzard?

If so, they were all probably occupied, helping other stranded civilians get home for the night.

Besides, she couldn't afford a cab to take her home.

Why? Because she lived across town.

Oh, what an absolute disaster. And all because of her libido. Because of a sexy man who had turned her brain to mush the moment she walked into the gym and saw his arms. She'd made the dumbest, most rash decision in her life, and now she was paying dearly for it.

Son of a ...

She could barely feel her nose, let alone her fingers, when the rumbling, thunderous sound of a truck emerging from the reserved parking garage below interrupted the eerie quiet of the snowy night.

She paused her efforts and shielded her eyes from the blinding headlights.

The truck was big and powerful. The antithesis to her antiquated little Chevy Sprint with more miles on it than the speedometer had available—or at least it was close.

With nary a snowflake on it, a sleek gunmetal-gray beast with a shiny chrome bumper and wheels slowed down next to her. The passenger window slid down. "Need a hand?"

Aurora squinted through the wind and snow to see Zak of all people, with a black knit cap covering his red hair. But those blue eyes were unmistakable.

She nodded. "I'm buried. Can't even get at my gloves."

He turned off his truck, opened the driver-side door and hopped out. Before he made his way to her, he reached into the truck bed in the back of his Chevy and pulled out a shovel.

A Boy Scout!

Always prepared.

"I'll have you out in a jiff," he said, flashing her a big grin. Snowflakes began to gather on the short, dark red hair that covered his jaw and upper lip. She'd always had a weakness for a man with facial hair.

Licking her lips and blinking away the snowflakes, she stepped aside when he approached her. In her scramble to the front door, she'd caught a glimpse of the clock on the wall, and it said it was 10:05.

"Lost track of time, did ya?" he asked, beginning to shovel behind her back tires.

She swallowed and jammed her freezing hands into her coat pockets. "Something like that."

It was a pity he was so bundled up in black sweat pants

and a forest-green winter coat. She would have loved to watch his muscles pop out as he shoveled.

"Sorry for what Shadley put you through earlier. Stu at the front desk took care of it though, didn't let her railroad you into giving up your machine." He moved over to the other tire and started digging behind it.

Her brows dipped into a hard V in confusion. "It wasn't your fault or in your control at all. You don't have to apologize."

"Looked like you handled yourself just fine anyway. I like when a woman isn't afraid to stand up for herself." The man wasn't out of breath at all. If she was doing the digging, she'd already have sweat beneath her boobs and be needing to take a break.

"I don't take kindly to bullies," she said, hating that she had to almost holler over the wild wind gusts that kept pelting her in the face.

He stopped what he was doing and straightened up, his blue eyes fierce beneath the orange glow of the street lamp. "Neither do I."

Well, that was strange.

He finished with the back tire, then moved on to the front tires.

In no time, her car was free, and he had shoveled her out a path and cleared the rest of the snow from the roof.

"Go start 'er up," he said, tossing the shovel back into the bed of his truck. "I'll wait until I see you're safely on the road before I leave. Hope you don't live too far. Those roads look nasty." He kicked his front tire. "Need winter tires like me. Picked these puppies up in October. Splurged for the studded ones too, as I like to head up to the ski slope from time to time and board."

Oh, to have the kind of wealth so that one could indulge in a weekend away at the mountain in a chalet.

What did Zak do for work? He was probably some high-powered something or other. Or maybe a stuntman in the movies. He certainly had the build for it.

"Thank you," she said, slipping the key into the lock and opening the door. Then she put the key in the ignition, turned it on and set the heater to *blast* mode.

She turned back to face him, expecting him to still be standing by his truck, but he wasn't. He was standing right behind her.

Oxygen fled her lungs.

He thrust his hand out. "I'm Zak. I feel like I should know your name, but right now it's escaping me."

Why should he know her name? He said some really weird stuff.

She took his hand. It was warm—how was it warm? He'd just shoveled in the snow. But it was— it was strong. It was big. It was perfect.

He cocked a brow. "Going to tell me your name or make me guess ... Ariel?"

Ariel?

His smile warmed her insides. "You know, from *The Little Mermaid*? She can't speak, so Prince Eric guesses her name until Sebastian the crab takes pity on him and whispers it."

Who the heck was this guy? Now he was talking about a children's movie. Did he have kids?

"Aurora. My name's Aurora."

"Aurora. Like *Sleeping Beauty*. I like that. It suits you."

Sleeping Beauty?

They were still holding hands. She never wanted him to let go. Never wanted him to leave.

"Well, Aurora, it was nice to finally meet you. Been keeping my eye on you at the gym. You've had some real improvements in your posture and what you're lifting." He released her hand and grabbed her bicep, giving it a playful squeeze. "It's showing too."

Her stomach did a massive flip-flop, and her pussy clenched.

She moved her eyes down his torso to his feet, which were in bright orange running shoes. "Thanks."

He released her arm and rocked back on his heels, shoving his hands into the pockets of his coat. "Better let this old girl warm up a bit before you head out."

She nodded and pulled her gloves on over her frozen and cramping fingers, though she would have much rather held his hand longer to warm her up. She rubbed her palms together to get the circulation flowing again when a noise beneath the hood of her car made her jump.

He scrunched up his face in confusion and took a step back. "Uh-oh. That doesn't sound good."

A clunk, a sputter and finally a loud squeal and then nothing.

Her car had died.

In the middle of the snowstorm of the century, at night, in front of the man of her dreams, her lemon of a car just died.

Now all she had to wait for was the earth to open up and swallow her whole.

"Ah, crap," he murmured, wandering over to the hood. "Pop it up. Let's take a look."

She did as she was told.

He bent over the engine. "You're leaking oil. Might be a blown head gasket or something. I'm not going to be able to fix this, at least not tonight in this mess. You're going to need to get home and then wait to call a tow truck in the morning."

A tow truck?

She could barely afford the gas she needed to get to and from work, let alone a tow truck.

He slammed the hood. "I'll give you a ride home. Hop in. How far do you live?"

Chewing on her bottom lip, she lifted her gaze to his slowly. "Greenwood," she said sheepishly, waiting for his eyebrows to fly clear off his head.

Which they did. "Greenwood! What the heck are you doing at a gym all the way in Rainier Vista?"

Because of you.

"I work nearby," she lied.

His eyebrows dropped down to their normal place. "Oh, okay. What do you do?"

"I'm a lawyer."

Why didn't she tell him that she was a first-year associate? Yes, she was a lawyer, but she was a mere peon. A minion. A subordinate to the overlord partners, who gave her every shit case they could. Should she elaborate?

"Oh cool. A couple buddies of mine are lawyers. Impressive. Big corner office kind of thing? Lots of first-year associates to do your grunt work?" He chuckled and shook his head.

She avoided his gaze. "Something like that."

A shiver raced through her as another strong gust of wind plastered her wet hair to her face and neck, but the look he was giving her warmed her from the inside out. He was impressed with her. Thought she was this high-powered attorney at probably some top-tier Seattle law firm. Only half of that was true.

It was top-tier, one of the top law firms in the city, only she was the complete opposite to *high-powered*. She had no power. Could she have a negative charge of power in this case? Because if she could—she did. She was the electron of the lawyer world.

He pursed his lips. "You're freezing. Let's get going. Grab your bag and whatever else you need and hop in. I've got heated seats. I'll crank 'em to the max, warm you up in no time." He didn't wait for her to answer or agree. Rather he simply opened up the back of her car, grabbed her gym bag and headed to his truck. "Come on, Rory, shake a leg. I still haven't eaten dinner. I'm starving."

Rory.

She hadn't been called that nickname in years.

Pinching her wrist three or four times to make sure she wasn't dreaming, she grabbed her work bag, her scarf, winter boots and knit cap, locked her car and trudged over to Zak's enormous truck. He'd started it up again, and the manly purr of it made her nipples peak. She wasn't wearing a bra, because why? She was supposed to just be heading home, and she was all bundled up. Now she really wished she'd worn one. The weight of her breasts was evident as her arousal from Zak's attention and sheer proximity continued to grow.

"You need help up?" he asked, appearing behind her again as she stared at the closed door to the passenger side. "It is a bit of a climb, and you're a bitty thing." He paused. "I didn't mean that as an insult. I just meant you're on the shorter side. My daughter struggles to get in too."

Daughter?

Without waiting for her to reply, because she was in utter shock at the revelation that he had a child, he opened the door and grabbed all her stuff, stowing it behind her seat. Then he offered her his hand and helped her climb up into the big, powerful truck. "There you go. Buckle up. The roads haven't been plowed, so it might be a bumpy ride."

Was he taking her all the way to Greenwood?

Where did he live?

He was in his seat and putting the truck in gear moments later. "Might take us a while to get you to Greenwood. That's in the complete opposite direction as me."

He pulled out onto the road, where, sure enough, it didn't look like a plow had been by once. He paused at a red light. There were very few vehicles on the road, but those that were on the road were struggling.

He shook his head. "We live in the Pacific Northwest. We get snow. People really need to be more responsible and buy the proper tires for their vehicles. Especially when they have children in their cars."

Children. Right.

She didn't have proper tires on her car. They were practically bald. She had the same summer tires she'd bought the car with and hadn't come up with money to buy new ones. She knew she was running them on borrowed time, but the bank didn't really care about any of that. They just wanted her student loan payment on time, to hell if she died in a fiery car wreck on the side of the road because she couldn't afford decent tires.

"Probably a good thing you didn't drive anyway," he stated, rumbling through the intersection after the light turned green. "Those definitely didn't look like winter tires."

She shook her head. "They're not."

"Should get some."

He reached forward and fiddled with the dash, turning on the radio. The news erupted into the sudden awkward silence. "*Multi-car pile-up on the 99. People are encouraged not to go out unless absolutely necessary. I-5 is backed up after an empty Greyhound bus slid into the median, halting traffic in both directions.*"

"Jesus," he muttered. "It's pretty, but snow is fucking deadly."

"It is." The ball of worry in her stomach twisted like a fist trying to bury itself into her ribcage. Would he decide she lived too far away and pull over, drop her off on the side of the road and wish her all the best in her journey home?

His lips flattened, and he pulled over as best he could, turning to face her. "I only live like ten minutes away. I'm not trying to be some creepy weirdo, but I would honestly prefer to just head home. I have a house with lots of spare bedrooms. You're welcome to one. I can drive you home in the morning once the plows come through, but I'd really rather not be stuck on the road for the next several hours, because that's what it's going to take to get you home and then get myself home. With both highways closed, I'll be forced to do back roads, and we know those are the last to get plowed."

Spend the night in Zak's house?

She reached over and pinched her wrist again.

His kissable lips twisted. "So? What do you say? I'm not the world's best cook, but I don't burn anything anymore. The house is clean, warm."

Yes, please!

But she tempered her enthusiasm because she didn't want him to think she was some obsessed stalker freak. She lifted one shoulder. "Sure, thank you. I mean if it's not too much trouble."

He grinned, threw the truck back into gear and pulled out onto the road once again. "Not too much trouble at all. I'll be sure to have you home for Christmas, I promise."

She shrugged again. "Home, away, doesn't really matter. I have no plans for Christmas."

He nearly drove off the road. "No plans for Christmas?"

"Nope. None. My parents are back east."

"Any siblings?"

A red-hot poker of grief stabbed her heart at the mention of siblings.

"My brother, uh ... he's no longer with us."

"I'm sorry."

She cleared her throat. "Thanks."

At the mention of her dead brother, the atmosphere in the truck shifted, and she didn't like it. A weird fog hung between them now, a distance and disconnect that hadn't been there a moment ago.

"Anyway, um, all my family is on the other side of the country, and besides, even if they were closer, I'm too busy with work to go home or take any time off." *Can't afford it either.*

Zak's grip on the steering wheel tightened as he took a tight corner. "What were you going to do then? Spend Christmas with friends?"

She snorted and glanced out the window at the falling flakes. "What friends?"

What friends indeed? She hadn't had any time to make friends since she started work. All her law school friends had moved to various law firms across the country, and her co-workers were just as slammed with work as she was. They muttered *hellos* and *goodbyes* in the break room, but they were too deep in first-year associate zombie mode to socialize.

She worked eighty- to ninety-hour weeks and spent any free time she had at the gym gawking at Zak or poring over files at home. She was determined to make junior partner by the time she was thirty-five, so that only left her with five years to prove herself to her firm. She needed to eat, breathe and sleep the law if she had any hope of getting ahead, paying off her student loan debts and taking care of her parents.

"You don't have any friends?" His tone wasn't so much accusatory or judgmental as it was simply full of surprise.

She bit her lip. "Not really."

"There isn't anybody in the entire city who was willing to welcome you into their home on Christmas?"

Way to drive that dagger deeper there, buddy.

"Nope," she finally said, hoping her own tone came off as

carefree and unbothered, even though deep down it pained her immensely that she had no one. No village, no sisterhood. Nothing like what she'd had back in law school. Friends she could turn to, rely on, and who she knew always had her back. She shrugged. "I planned to work."

He shook his head and clucked his tongue. "That won't do. I can't have that. Nobody deserves to be alone on Christmas. You'll spend it with me."

What!

"I mean me and my friends. I don't have my kids this Christmas." His mouth tightened as if that was a sore subject. "I'm having friends over for turkey dinner. You'll come too."

Her brain hurt.

Kids. As in plural.

"You have kids?" she asked, needing more information and not caring how she got it or how she sounded.

"Two. Aidan is ten. Tia is eight."

Two kids. Ten and eight. How old did that make him?

"Are you married?"

"Not anymore." Bitterness laced his tone.

"I don't have the greatest track record with relationships either," she muttered.

He gave her the side-eye, his mouth flattening into a thin line. "No?"

She shook her head, hoping he'd leave it at that.

Thankfully, he did.

"She's got them this year," he went on. "She and *Craig* are taking them to Disneyland. It was supposed to be my year, but *Craig* surprised them with tickets. Told the kids before they asked me, so how could I be the dick and say *no?*"

"I'm sorry."

He rolled his eyes, then turned back to face the road. "Thanks. And sorry, I didn't mean to lay that on you. I'm just still pretty pissed off about the whole thing."

"I can imagine."

She was still trying to come to terms with the fact that he was a father.

Did that turn her off?

The more she thought about it, the more it most certainly did not. In fact, the more she thought about it, the more she liked the idea that he was a dad. A sexy single dad. She could just imagine he was probably a super hands-on father too. He just seemed that way.

Maybe she was completely wrong, because she knew absolutely nothing about the man, but she didn't get the deadbeat dad vibe from him. She didn't even get the joint-custody, limited-visitation dad vibe from him. And she knew that vibe well. She worked in family law and saw a lot of parents—mothers and fathers—use their children as bargaining chips and try to weasel out of responsibilities.

"Almost there," he said, turning down another road into another subdivision. A rather fancy subdivision.

"What do you do for work?" she asked. These houses were nice. Not mansion-size, but nice. Big and beautiful, with manicured yards (when they weren't covered in snow), matching address plates on all the homes, and those fancy ornate street lamps instead of the customary city-issued ones like everywhere else. You needed money to live here.

He turned to face her. "I thought you knew."

She shook her head. "How would I know?"

"I own the gym. I own all the Club Z Fitness facilities around town."

Her jaw dropped as they pulled into the driveway of probably the most beautiful house on the block. "Shut the front door."

3

ZAK SNORTED as he pulled into his two-car garage. "No, you shut the front door. You seriously had no clue that I was the owner?"

"Nope. Didn't even know you worked there."

He turned off the truck. "Well, on the days I don't have my kids, I work long hours, then work out in the evenings, which is when you're there, I guess. Do the boss-man stuff during the day. Bounce around to all the locations too. But that one is closest to home, so it's where I work out. When I have the kids, I work out wherever I can when they're in school or in my home gym." He opened his door and slammed it, wandering around to her side to help grab her stuff. She was cute, that was for sure. He'd noticed her a few times at the gym. She seemed really shy, kept to herself. But over the last six months, he had noticed that she'd increased her free weights, and her form on her squats and lunges had improved.

You've more than just noticed her. You've been watching her.

Had he?

Then why didn't he know her name?

He grabbed her stuff from the back and led her around the front of the truck toward the door leading to the house. "Kick your shoes off here," he said, doing the same. "Don't want to track snow in. We'll hang our coats up over the heater too. They'll be dry in no time."

She followed suit. "Makes sense," she murmured. "Thanks again for offering to put me up. I'm sure I could have found a cab home eventually."

He made a dismissive face and continued on through the door into the house. The heat was on, as were the lights. *Ah, modern technology at its finest.* "Nonsense. You'd be waiting for hours for a cab. Cost you a bloody fortune to get home. I have this huge, empty house. I'd be a prick not to offer you a room."

My room ...

Fuck, where did that thought come from?

They made their way into the kitchen. His oven was already preheated, so he just had to pull his meat and veg from the fridge and toss it in.

As he grabbed the casserole dish from the fridge, he was halted by the Christmas picture Tia had drawn him. It was stuck beneath a magnet of Santa Claus holding a San Camanez Island beer. She'd worked so hard on that picture. Sat at the kitchen table for nearly two hours with her head down and colored pencils all spread out. She was quite the little artist too.

"Did one of your kids draw that?" Aurora asked behind him.

He smiled, and his heart tightened in his chest at the thought of his kids, at the thought of spending Christmas without them.

"Yeah, Tia. She loves art." He turned to face her. "Both kids do. They get that from their mother, because I can barely scribble a stick man."

Her bright smile warmed him. "I'm sure they inherited a bunch of other amazing qualities from you."

His own smile was small and tight. But he liked that she was interested in his life, in his kids. As he went about unwrapping the casserole dish, he began to speak. "Two weeks ago, Tia and Aiden helped me set up and decorate the Christmas tree in the living room."

She craned her body around to look into the living room from where she was now perched on the bar stool. "I can sort of see it," she said. "I'll go take a peek in a minute."

He nodded, appreciating her interest. "Then Tia made red and green paper chains that nearly stretch clear around the earth, not just from the kitchen to the living room."

Aurora's laughter filled the kitchen, making the ache in his chest just a touch lighter.

"We also made a popcorn garland for the tree, and I brought out some of their old ornaments that they made and decorated when they were in preschool."

"My mom still has some of mine that I made when I was in preschool. She offered to send them out to me, but I didn't put up a tree, so there wasn't any point."

Zak didn't have a lot in the way of decorations—most of those had gone with Loni—but he wanted to make his house festive for his kids. Wanted to make it feel like a normal *family* Christmas.

He opened up the oven door and slid the casserole dish onto the rack. "A fundraiser at their school for Aiden's band had him peddling real cedar bough wreaths."

"Is that what that smell is?" she asked. He could hear her inhale deeply behind him, then exhale and hum softly. "I thought it was just a very fragrant Christmas tree."

He turned to face her. "It's both. I ended up just cutting Aiden a check. Now I have about five of the things around the house and on every door. House smells like the deep woods."

She shrugged. "I like it. And besides, you did it for your kid. That's what matters, right?"

Holy fuck, she got it.

He nodded vigorously. "Yeah. It's all for my kids."

Everything I do, everything I am, is for them.

And he was supposed to have them this year. He was supposed to be with them.

Fucking Craig.

This was going to be his first Christmas away from them since they were born. It just didn't feel right. It didn't make sense for him not to be with them on Christmas morning.

"This must be tough, being away from them for the holiday," she said quietly.

His chin trembled, and he sniffed, unable to do anything but nod out of fear that if he spoke, he might crumple to the ground and let the devastation take over. He turned away from her. He didn't want her to see him so vulnerable, so weak. Because his kids were his biggest weakness. His Achilles heel. But they were also where he found the greatest amount of strength. Where he found his peace and his purpose.

"We can talk about it more if you like," she offered. "Or we can change the topic. I'll take your cue. But just know, I'm here to listen if you like. I'm a pretty good listener."

Suddenly caught up in a harsh strangle of emotion, he cleared his throat, wrinkled his nose and cracked his neck before turning to face the beautiful woman he'd insisted accompany him home. "Dinner will be in about thirty. I'll show you to your room, then I'm going to jump in the shower."

"You don't shower at the gym?" she asked, slipping off the bar stool and curiously wandering around his open floor plan kitchen and dining room, her eyes wide as she took in his art and décor. He'd totally revamped the entire house when Loni moved out. He needed a fresh start, and that meant new paint, new everything. His vision, not *hers*.

"Sometimes I do," he said. He made sure to set the oven timer so that their dinner didn't burn. "But tonight, I didn't. I had to finish up some paperwork before I left, so I did that in lieu of showering."

She swallowed, the sexy line of her throat gently bobbing. "I see."

While in his truck driving through the snow, she'd piled her sandy-blonde hair up into a messy topknot on her head, revealing several piercings in her ears—all studs or tiny hoops. He could count at least four on each ear.

He already knew she had a fit body, but when she pulled off her hoodie and tucked it under her arm, he was reminded of just *how* fit she was. He could also tell she wasn't wearing a bra beneath her black T-shirt.

She cleared her throat.

Shit! Had he been staring at her chest?

Yep. Yep, he had been. He lifted his gaze to her light brown eyes and smiled his famously flirty grin. Her smile back was small, but it seemed to be genuine.

Phew. No harm, no foul.

He grabbed her duffle bag off the counter and headed in the direction of the stairs. "Rooms are this way."

He didn't bother waiting for her to follow him and took the stairs two at a time. He hadn't smelled it when they were out in the snow and she was all bundled up, but now that she'd taken off her coat, the woman smelled incredible. Spicy and feminine.

He headed down the hallway toward the guest bedroom. Each of the kids had their own rooms, and he had the master suite, but there was still another empty room at the end of the hall. That had been where he slept when things between him and Loni started to go south.

"In here." He opened the door, flicked on the light and plopped her bag down on the bed. She entered behind him moments later.

"Your house is beautiful," she said quietly.

"Thanks."

Her eyes focused on the queen-size bed in the center of the room.

He had a king-size bed in his room. Not that it'd seen much action as of late.

She nibbled on her bottom lip and worried her hands in front of her waist.

What was up?

"Everything okay?" he asked, the sudden urge to rest his hand on her shoulder taking him by surprise and causing him to take a step back toward the door.

She lifted her gentle brown eyes to his, and that's when he noticed the copper flecks within the iris. They were unlike eyes he'd ever seen before. They were beautiful. "This is weird," she said quietly. "I mean ... I don't know you at all, and suddenly I'm in your truck, then your home, then your ... "

Ah, right.

He held his hands up in front of his body and shook them in protest. "This isn't my bed, if that's what you're getting at. My room is across the hall. This is the guest room."

"The guest room ... "

He exhaled in confusion. Fuck, he needed a shower. "Do you want to call or text a friend? Let them know that you're here, where you are? Are you feeling unsafe?"

Christ, how would he feel if he found out Tia did something like this? Got into a vehicle with a man she didn't know, went to his house, agreed to spend the night. Obviously, she wouldn't do this at eight years old, but he wasn't sure he'd be okay with her doing it at any age. How could he not think about how this looked? About how this woman felt? Had he cajoled her? He'd only been trying to help. Get her home safe.

Son of a bitch.

He took a few more steps back until he was completely in the hallway and not in the room with her any longer.

"I am not a bad guy, I swear. I have no plans to ... " Fuck, he couldn't even say the words, let alone think them. He huffed in exhaustion. "Your virtue is safe with me." His lip tilted up on one side before he bowed his head just slightly for good measure. "Ma'am."

Was that a whimper?

His head snapped up from where he'd been staring at the floor. The look she was giving him was anything but unsure, anything but nervous or uneasy. The look she was giving him was pure lioness. Full apex predator.

Now he was just plain confused.

She'd switched on a dime from worried and unsure, to looking like she wanted to skip dinner and go straight to her own version of dessert.

Blinking, he took another step back toward his bedroom door. "I'm going to go shower. You call who you need to call, let them know where you are and that I'll do my damnedest to get you home tomorrow when the roads are cleared. You can decide later if you want to come back for Christmas dinner. Who knows, you might be sick of me by morning and run back to the gym to cancel your membership." He chuckled awkwardly. Then, before her looks could confuse him anymore, he turned around and headed into his room.

AFTER DOING as she was told and texting not only her parents, but her one and only friend-slash-work colleague, Colleen,

Aurora sat on the bed in her temporary bedroom and listened to the shower running.

Zak was in that shower.

Zak was across the hall, only feet away, and he was naked and covered in soapy bubbles and hot water.

Yes, please.

Everything inside her tightened, including her nipples and pussy.

She knew what she'd done was reckless—jumping into the vehicle of a man she hardly knew and agreeing to go back to his house and stay the night—but it was Zak!

She'd never done a one-night stand in her life. Never left a bar with a guy, spent a night tangled up in the sheets as they explored each other's bodies. She'd had all of four boyfriends her entire life. One for two years in high school, one for two years in college, one for two years in law school, and ... Pressley.

And they'd all dumped her. They'd all called it quits with her.

Although none of her ex-boyfriends had been bad guys, they hadn't been bad boys either. They'd been kind, smart, funny, sweet and attractive. On paper, they were perfect. The kind of guy any girl's parents would be happy to see their daughter marry.

Only Aurora had never come close to marriage with any of them.

None of them wanted her for life.

Truth be told, she hadn't wanted any of them for life either.

Perhaps they were too perfect. Too squeaky-clean and her affections had been simulated. She said she loved them because it's what she thought she should say and feel, not how she *truly* felt. They were not what she truly wanted.

Because what she wanted was a bad boy. A buff, tattooed

redhead with scruff and muscles for days who wasn't afraid to get a little *dirty*.

And there was such a man across the hall.

The sound of the water shutting off drew her from her thoughts.

Straining her ears, she waited for a bathroom door to open.

Could she?

What would he do? Reject her? Shoot her down? Toss her ass out into the snow?

She shifted where she sat on the bed so that her view out her bedroom door was directly into his room—because he'd left his door open.

His. Door. Was. Open.

Was that on purpose?

Had he done that as an invitation?

Her nerves ratcheted up to eleven, and the hair along her arms began to tingle. Her stomach did an enormous somersault.

She had to try.

If he dropped her off at her apartment tomorrow and she hadn't at least let him know how she felt about him, she'd never forgive herself.

The bathroom door opened and out he stepped, wearing nothing but a towel.

A.

Fucking.

Towel.

It was slung low on his hips, revealing that Adonis line in an erotic V that pointed at all the goods hidden beneath the white terry cloth. Abs upon abs, muscles rippling and dripping wet, glistening because he hadn't bothered to towel off—thank fucking God. He had more tattoos than what she saw at the gym on his arms. They were across his chest, down his sides and over his belly. The man was covered. The man was perfection.

The lump in her throat tripled in size.

He was perfection.

The perfect bad boy.

And boy oh boy, did she ever want to be bad.

For once in her life, in her perfect, law-abiding, straight-A-student life, she wanted to throw caution to the wind, let her inhibitions scatter in the gusts with the snowflakes and give herself the Christmas gift of a lifetime.

He was the only thing she wanted. The only thing on her list.

The only question was—would he play Santa Claus and let her unwrap her present, or would he turn her down and kick her to the curb with nothing more than a broken heart and a lump of coal in her hand?

4

WHISTLING *JINGLE BELLS*, Zak pulled open the top drawer of his dresser and grabbed a pair of black boxer briefs.

The timer on the oven would probably beep soon. He needed to get down there and check dinner.

His stomach grumbled at the thought of finally getting food.

It was Thursday. Could he break his rule and have a beer?

He normally only drank on the weekends. Stayed clean and healthy during the week and indulged on red meat and alcohol Friday and Saturday.

It was these rules that kept him fit. Kept him healthy. Kept him in line.

He was about to toss his towel onto the floor and pull on his boxers when a knock at the doorjamb gave him pause.

He turned around.

Shit, he hadn't shut his bedroom door.

He wasn't used to having anybody but the kids in his house, and even then, nudity had never really been an issue with them.

She stood there on the threshold of his bedroom, her

nipples making points form at the front of her T-shirt, her chest practically heaving.

Was everything okay?

He was about to ask as much when she moved toward him, her pace full of purpose. She grabbed his face and kissed him.

And it wasn't just a peck on the lips. No, this woman knew how to kiss. She knew how to throw her whole body into it. A low and pleasant hum warmed him from the center outward.

Her soft, slippery little tongue pushed its way into his mouth. Then she started to suck. She started to fucking suck on his tongue. He moaned as his cock stirred beneath the towel, his hands moving to wrap around her back.

This had been so unexpected, and yet he couldn't get over how much he suddenly wanted it—wanted her.

A shrill beeping sound from downstairs made them both still. She was the first to pull away.

Her light brown eyes were glassy, and her cheeks held an adorable pink flush. He dropped his gaze to her plump, wet lips and he swept his thumb over the bottom one back and forth. He stilled when she pressed the tip of her tongue to his thumb, then parted her lips and lunged at it with her teeth, nipping the pad.

He tugged it away, grinning.

Oh, she was a wicked little thing.

Grabbing her around the back of the neck, he crushed his mouth to hers, taking control of the kiss this time, forcing her lips to part for his, to mold to his. She gave over all the power and melted against him, her arms wrapping around his neck and pulling him down to her. He was about to push the hem of her shirt up to explore her lack of a bra when the loud beeping of the oven timer downstairs had them pulling a part once again.

Her ample chest rose and fell rapidly, his did too.

"Hold that thought," he murmured, grabbing hold of his towel and heading downstairs toward the kitchen. "Be right back." Then he took off as fast as his legs could carry him, hoping that his chicken wasn't burning, but even more so that the woman in his bedroom would still be there when he returned.

AURORA'S FACE hurt from how hard she was smiling.

He wanted her.

Zak wanted her.

Oh my God.

She heard him bounding back up the stairs and toyed with the idea of throwing herself provocatively onto the bed.

What would that look like?

She had no time to even consider a position because he was back. In all his naked, tattooed glory.

Like a proud male lion, he stalked toward her, his fist holding his towel in place, but the fact that he was turned on pointed right at her through the terry cloth. His grin was wide and salacious, making every ember of arousal inside her flicker into raging, licking flames. "Now, where were we?" he asked, coming to stand in front of her.

She licked her lips at the thought of tracing her tongue over his abs, over his ink and down to his …

"My, those thoughts are dirty, Rory," he purred, tucking his finger beneath her chin and tilting her eyes up from his towel to his face. "They're written *all* over your face, darlin'."

Her top teeth snagged her bottom lip.

His thumb pulled it free. "I'm not reading into this wrong, am I?" Unease flashed across his face. "You're not … *here* because you think you owe me something, right?"

His thumb slid along her bottom lip, and she flicked her

tongue out to lick it like she had before. Heat flared in his intense blue eyes. "I'm here because it's all I've wanted since I first laid eyes on you over six months ago."

The corner of his mouth quirked up at the same time he pushed his thumb past her lips into her mouth. "Six months, huh? Now I feel like a right fool that it took me this long to notice you."

A slight sting singed her heart. She pushed it away and welcomed his thumb into her mouth, swirling her tongue around it, nipping it with her teeth. Lust burned in his eyes.

"What do you want, Rory?" He removed his thumb, and she had to suppress her whimper.

Her breathing was already erratic, her nipples achingly tight and her panties saturated. All her fantasies were coming to fruition. Could she have him in all the ways she'd imagined these past six months?

His brows rose in query. "Hmm, Aurora, what is it you *want*?"

She was having a hard time keeping her gaze on his face and not letting it roam his perfect torso. It was an even bigger struggle not to reach out and pull the towel free.

Unless ...

She lifted her arm, extended her hand forward and gripped the towel, pulling him closer. Then she tugged harder, until the towel slipped off his body and she was face to face with an image she had only dreamt about. And her dreams had in no way done him any kind of justice. He was spectacular. A bead of pre-cum glistened like a shiny pearl on the plum-hued crown. Her mouth flooded with moisture as she realized she was finally going to get to taste him.

She dropped to her knees, lifted her eyes to his, gripped him by the base of his cock and brought her head forward. "I want *this*," she said, never breaking their eye contact as she slid him into her mouth. He tasted incredible. A flavor she could easily find herself craving. She shut her eyes and went to task, taking him to the back of her throat and then back out to the tip, swirling her tongue around and around, using her hand to help pump.

His hand landed on top of her head, and a sigh above her fueled her fire, causing her to push him deeper down her throat, suppressing her gag reflex as best she could. She cupped his balls with her other hand and massaged them in her palm.

In addition to being ripped as hell, the man took care of himself downstairs as well. His balls were shaved and his pubic hair trimmed short. He really was fucking perfection. And for the night, he was hers.

She released his cock from her mouth and dipped her head, taking a ball into her mouth and rolling it around on her tongue while still using her hand to stroke him.

"Fuck," he breathed, bucking his hips and pushing himself into her palm. "Mouth again," he grunted, cupping her cheek and guiding her head upward again. His thumb landed on her bottom lip again, and he pushed down. "Open up, baby." She lifted her eyes to his once again and did as she was told, opening up her mouth.

His eyes were hooded, his cheeks a sexy shade of dusty rose.

He batted her hand away from his cock and gripped the base with his own hand, guiding it into her open mouth. He released his shaft, grabbed her hand and put it back where it had been. His other hand remained cupping her jaw though, his thumb resting just beneath her lip.

"Love seeing and feeling my cock slide into your mouth, Rory. Fucking love it."

She loved it too. Loved watching his reaction as she took him deep, brought him to the edge.

She blinked up at him, widened her mouth and bottomed out again.

A growl rumbled low in his chest. His grip on her jaw and cheek tightened. "Gonna come soon, babe."

Yes.

She pulled him free and ran her tongue over the tip as if it were a popsicle on the hottest day of the year and she needed to catch all the drips. *Can't waste a drop.* Not when it tasted that good—she'd never met a man whose cum tasted good, let alone delicious—not until Zak. With Zak she'd never waste a drop.

"Fuck, babe," he groaned. His thumb pulled down on her bottom lip. "All the way to the back. Take it all."

Yes.

She slid him back into her mouth, slow. She knew it was torture for him. His grip on her jaw told her he was struggling. The cadence of his hips faltered too. He was close.

"Deeper, baby. Know you can take me deeper. Gonna come."

She did as she was told and pushed him just a little deeper. A tear slipped down her cheek, but she managed to get him down without gagging.

"That's right, Rory. So fucking ... so fucking hot. Good girl." He pumped one, two, three more times, then tossed his head back, fisted her messy bun and let go.

Warm, salty semen squirted down the back of her throat in thick, ropey spurts. She swallowed as fast and as much as she could, taking everything he gave her and wishing he had more.

Her dream, her fantasy was finally becoming a reality, and even if it was just for this one night, she was going to enjoy every single second of Zak.

ONCE HE KNEW his balls were empty, he slowly slipped from Aurora's mouth.

He'd squeezed his eyes shut but figured now was probably a good time to look at her, and, fuck him, the smile that she gave him back. Holy fucking shit.

Never in his life had he met a woman who looked that happy after giving a blow job. Never. Her smile was electric, her eyes bright, her cheeks flushed. She looked so incredibly fuckable, he prayed he had condoms in his nightstand and that they hadn't expired. He also prayed that he'd be able to get it up again soon.

It'd been a while since he'd been with anybody besides his fist in the shower, and that was only to help him sleep.

Where the hell had this woman come from?

And she'd wanted him for six months to boot. Did they even make women like her anymore?

Apparently, they did. He'd just had to weed through a few harpies to find the goddess.

He was still cupping her jaw, something he liked to do when getting head. Control their head, their mouths, their lips. Feel them swallow as he came hard down their throats.

But Aurora hadn't balked at all. She seemed to like him taking the control, seemed to like his hand on her jaw, his thumb on her lip.

He traced that thumb over her bottom lip again before hauling her up to her feet and crushing his mouth against hers.

She welcomed him, opened for him, tangoed her tongue with his.

His hands fell to the hem of her T-shirt, and he made quick work of pulling it over her head, only breaking their kiss for a moment. But the moment was long enough to see she had incredible tits. Big tits. Like more than a handful.

The perfect size tits for sliding his dick between so he could titty-fuck her into next Tuesday.

And those raspberry nipples and dusky puckered areolas ... He pulled his mouth from her lips once again and dipped his head, taking a nipple into his mouth, sucking hard until he felt the skin around it grow taut in arousal.

A moan in the depths of her throat had him using his other hand to push down the waist of her pants, past—oh fuck, she was hairless—until he found slick, silky folds. Her clit was already swollen, and her panties damp. Oh, fuck yeah.

Gently, he guided her back to the bed, taking her pants and panties down with him.

She watched him with eyelids at half-mast and her lip between her teeth. He leaned forward and tugged her lip out. "That's my lip, got it?"

She nodded.

"I want to hear you say it."

"Your lip."

"That's right. Only I get to bite it."

"Only you get to bite it."

"Good girl." He smiled, his eyes climbing along her body, appreciating every inch, every freckle. She was fit but still soft. He liked that.

Healthy curves, womanly curves, but she still took care of herself.

"Touch yourself," he ordered, taking her hand from the bed and placing it between her legs. "Show me what you like."

Her eyes grew wide and avid as she nodded again, spread her pussy lips and began to flick her bean.

The inner lips of her pussy were a gorgeous, glistening pink, and it took everything inside him not to sink onto his belly and bury his face up to his ears in her cleft, let all her juices cover his face, coat his tongue and slide down his throat.

His cock jerked, and his balls tightened.

He really needed to check the condom box, make sure there were a few in there that still had some life to them. But he couldn't peel his eyes from the beauty on his bed who currently had her eyes closed, her lip back between her teeth and her fingers going around and around on her clit.

It was an absolutely magnificent sight to behold.

"You want some help?" he asked, needing to taste her, to feel her come around his fingers and across his lips.

Her eyes fluttered open, and she nodded. "Yes, please."

Please.

Such a good girl.

Grinning, he slid down onto his belly and shouldered her knees apart. He didn't want her to stop her efforts on her clit. No, he wanted them to work together. Get her there together. They had the rest of night for him to take her on his own, show her just what his tongue was capable of.

He explored her slippery slit with two fingers, pushing them inside her just enough but then pulling them out and meandering around her folds, the nub of her clit and her perineum.

Was she into ass play?

Was tonight too soon to ask?

Was tonight all they had?

He hadn't been with anybody in a while, and now that he'd broken his dry spell—and with a woman as enigmatic as Aurora—he wanted to go crazy.

She writhed on the bed beneath his fingers and hers, her head thrashing from side to side. He placed his mouth over her just as a warm gush of liquid spilled across his tongue. He lapped it up. Drank her sweetness down, then slipped his tongue into her tight channel and demanded she give him more.

She pressed her cleft against his face, her fingers picking up speed as she continued to squirm. Her hips leapt off the mattress, and his nose knocked her fingers. He removed his tongue from her and replaced it with his fingers once again, enjoying the way she squeezed her muscles around him, drawing him in, encouraging him to go deeper. His tongue lazily laved at her dripping pussy lips, making its way north. He sucked and licked on her fingers as they worked her clit, pushing his tongue between her fingers to flick her clit, tasting her flavor on her digits.

A moan from above was all the response he needed to know that she liked what he was doing.

He raked his chin up between her legs, letting the scruff of his close-shaved beard tickle her sensitive labia. He pushed her fingers away from her clit and worked his chin over it, back and forth, then around and around.

"Oh God!" She pushed her mound harder against his face. "Do that again."

He complied, continuing to plunge his fingers in and out of her while raking his beard across her slippery slit.

"Fuck, yes."

Fuck, yes was right.

Her hip jerks grew erratic, and more honey spilled across his fingers. She was close.

He removed his chin and sucked hard on her clit.

Her back arched, her hips shot off the bed higher than ever, and then she collapsed to the mattress, chest heaving, fingers bunched in the duvet, pussy rippling and pulsing around him.

Once her tremors subsided, he slid off the bed and made his way to the bathroom. He quickly washed his face, not that he really cared whether or not her juices coated him for the rest of the night, but some women cared.

When he returned to the bedroom, she had pulled her T-shirt, underwear and pants back on and was sitting flush-faced and gorgeous on the edge of the bed. He grabbed his boxer briefs off the floor and tugged them on, then pulled on a pair of pajama pants and a Henley.

He was already sporting another stiffy and was surprised to find her dressed.

She glanced up at him with a look that caused all kinds of weird emotions to bubble up inside him.

He sat down next to her on the bed. "You okay?"

She nodded. "More than okay."

Well, that was good.

Her stomach growled, then his growled in response.

He linked his fingers with hers. "Come on. Let's go have something to eat, and we can get to know each other." He tugged her up off the bed with him. "I must say, this is shaping up to be one hell of a snowy adventure," he said with a chuckle as he kept his hand clasped with hers and went ahead of her down the stairs. "Never saw that coming."

"You should see what we do in my dreams," she murmured behind him.

Zak missed a step, and before he knew it, he had let go of her hand and was falling down the stairs.

He landed at the bottom on his ass only to see her standing where he'd left her, her eyes wide and mouth open in shock. "You okay?"

He blinked up at her and rubbed the sore spot on his ass. "Just swept off my feet is all."

5

"I DON'T NORMALLY DRINK during the week," Zak said, the cords in his neck standing out in a sexy way as he heaved on the cork, opening up a bottle of wine. He poured them each a glass and slid hers across the quartz countertop toward her. "But I think I'm willing to make an exception."

She picked up her wineglass and held it to her nose. It was a deep, dark red, and it smelled incredible. Several tiers up from the supermarket boxed wine or the Trader Joe's buck-fifty special she bought herself from time to time. Not that she drank much, because booze was a luxury she just couldn't afford. Not when there was heat and Wi-Fi she needed to pay for first. Electricity was an important one too.

He lifted his glass up. "To ... "

Stalkers finally getting what they want?

Dreams becoming reality?

Christmas miracles?

Mother Nature finally throwing me a bone?

"To snowflakes and shoddy engines," he finally said, a big, sexy grin slowly sliding across his talented lips.

A smile of her own broke out on her heated face. "To snowflakes and shoddy engines."

He clinked his wineglass against hers, then they both took a sip, their eyes locking over the rims of their glasses.

"I've never liked snow so much in my life," she said after she swallowed down the incredible wine. "Or been apprecia-tive of crappy cars. Things are finally looking up."

He pulled the casserole dish from the oven after donning oven mitts and then began to dish up their meal. It smelled incredible.

A man who could cook?

She hadn't met one of those in a long time.

"You need a new car. Surely, the law firm you work for pays you well enough that you can afford some new wheels. Even new tires, if you can't afford an entire new vehicle."

Not on a first-year associate's salary they don't.

"Yeah, one day I'll come up with the cash to replace it," she said blandly. "Student loans really take a chunk out of the paycheck, though."

He lifted one well-defined shoulder. "I get it. My brother was up to his eyeballs in those too for the longest time. At least get some winter tires when you can afford it."

She glanced up at him, her jaw tight, ready to fight, but what looked back at her instantly eased her out of defense mode. He didn't look at her with any kind of pity, just under-standing.

"Had a clunker myself for a while. *As long as it runs*, I used to say. But then I had kids, and I couldn't bring myself to install a car seat into that death trap, so I sold it to a scrap yard, charmed the ass off the lady at the bank for a loan and bought my first *safe* vehicle."

She made a noise in her throat, her stomach rumbling at the same time.

He placed a plate in front of her. Rich aromas—basil and

garlic, parmesan and roasted veggies—filled her nostrils. Moisture flooded her mouth.

Zak reached into a drawer, pulled out cutlery, grabbed a napkin from another drawer and folded it. Then he placed the knife and fork on the little triangle and slid it across the counter to her, settling it next to her plate.

"Such a gentleman," she said, climbing onto the bar stool.

He grabbed the other full plate and wandered around behind her. "Not in the bedroom I'm not," he purred, his breath tickling the nape of her neck as he leaned in next to her ear. The warmth from his body at her back made every muscle inside her tighten and every hair on her arms tingle.

But she needed to play it cool. She needed to calm down and cool off. She took another sip of her wine and smiled at him over the rim of her glass. "I noticed."

His grin was huge and sinful. "So," he started, diving into what appeared to be a delicious-looking chicken breast and roasted veggies in an aromatic pesto sauce, "tell me about yourself."

Aurora set her wineglass down and lifted her shoulder in a shrug. "Not much to tell, really. I work *all* the time. I'm from New Hampshire. Went to law school here in Washington. My goldfish just died, and I'm pretty sure I killed my cactus."

He cut into his chicken, that sexy smile still on his face. "Ah, so you're a murderer?"

"More like negligent pet and plant owner. But yes, I suppose you could say my demanding work life inevitably caused me to kill the only pet I've ever had and a plant that is supposed to be resilient to drought."

He grabbed her hand and brought it to his mouth, pressing a soft kiss to her knuckles. "That's because you're this super-sexy high-powered attorney, right? Saving the world one lawsuit at a time? Putting away the bad guys. Taking down the corporate demons in their ivory towers." His eyebrows bobbed salaciously as he planted another kiss to her knuckles before releasing her hand. Desire rolled through her in big, lazy waves, enveloping every cell in her body until they all burned hot for the man whose big, muscular thigh was currently touching hers.

"Something like that," she murmured. "Too busy burning the midnight oil to care for a damn cactus."

"You're a fourth-year associate, you said?"

"I'm an associate, yeah."

Oh, fuck, why couldn't she just tell him the truth? That she was like tenth or twelfth pick in the draft. That she'd started off law school strong but petered out midway, eventually scraping by, by the skin of her teeth, and just barely passing the bar.

Not that she didn't have good reason for being distracted during school. Hell, she was more than just distracted. She was grieving. She was furious. She was broken.

Her parents tried to convince her to take a leave of absence from school or transfer to a law school closer to home, but she needed the space. She needed the distance. If she'd stayed in New Hampshire, she would be forced to drive past the lake daily, constantly reminded of what she lost—of *who* she lost.

So she packed her bags, put her head down and flew back to Washington after the funeral, resuming her third and final year of law school, only to barely make it through because she just couldn't get her head in the game.

The only reason she'd been hired at Wallace, Dixon and Travers in the first place was because Dina Steele, a senior partner, had taken pity on her after Aurora had broken down in her interview and told the woman her entire story. Dina was a no-nonsense woman but also a fair woman and had offered Aurora the job with the caveat that Aurora join a gym and start seeing a counselor to work through her issues.

Hence, why she started at Club Z.

She saw her counselor once a month, because that was all her benefits allowed. Once she was with the company for a year, she could afford a better medical plan and hopefully start seeing her therapist a bit more often.

She closed her eyes and summoned a deep breath, holding it in, then looked blindly skyward.

Yeah, Dina Steele had saved Aurora's ass. She'd saved her law career. She'd saved her life.

May God rest her soul.

The poor woman had been killed in a mall mass shooting in August, and the whole law firm was still trying to make sense of it all. Make sense of their loss—because losing Dina had been like losing a limb, losing a chunk of their heart, for all of them. She had run the firm with an iron first encased in marshmallow. She was tough, but she was kind, and everyone at the firm loved her.

And now her mentor, her savior, the person she went to for all her work—and life—problems, was gone. Taken too soon by such a senseless and malicious act of hate.

Her heart stuttered, and then there was this falling, spinning-down feeling. She clutched the edge of the counter with both hands and blinked back the harsh sting of tears.

God, she missed Dina. Life had ceased to make sense after she'd walked into work on that Monday after the shooting, only to find every one of her co-workers bawling their eyes out.

A throat clearing next to her drew her out of her thoughts. Her shoulder was nudged. "Where'd you go just now?" Zak's voice was like pure melted chocolate. Deep and thick and with just the smallest hint of a twang. A finger landed under her chin, and he turned her face to his. "Everything okay? You're not having second thoughts about upstairs, are you?" With his other hand, he reached over and ran his finger beneath her eye, clearing away the tear before it even had a chance to fall. "Hmm?"

His big, warm palm cupped her cheek. She leaned into his gentle embrace and closed her eyes. She was tired. Tired of the day, of the week, of the month, of the year. Tired of never getting ahead, tired of constantly feeling like she was treading water with a weight belt on. Tired of losing people she loved.

"I'm tired," she finally breathed, her eyes still shut, her breathing now ragged and her body growing hot. "Even when I'm not at work, my brain can't seem to leave the job. I can't remember the last time it really, truly shut down."

His thumb caressed her cheek, sending warm coils of need spiraling through her. "I can see that. We'll eat and then go to bed." He released her face, and they both turned back to their meals. "Up to you which bed you'd like to sleep in."

She glanced at him sideways, a small smile curling up her mouth as she picked up her fork and knife and dug into her meal. "Your bed seemed pretty comfy. Is that a king?"

His nose wrinkled as he dove into his own chicken and vegetables. "California king, baby, and it's hella comfy. Great for sleeping ... fantastic for other things as well."

She took a bite of broccoli and began to chew, loving how his smile and joking tone eased the ache in her heart and made her want to laugh. She needed more laughter in her life, needed more happiness, more nights like this spent with a good man drinking wine and eating dinner as they enjoyed each other's company.

"Zak?" His name felt smooth against her tongue, slightly cool. She licked her lips, as if savoring its sweetness. He definitely suited his name. Strong, powerful and sexy.

He put his fork down and turned to face her, giving her his full and undivided attention. "Hmm?"

She swallowed. "Thank you for rescuing me tonight." She

felt the heat of a blush warm her cheeks, and she dipped her eyes down to his now covered chest. "And for the other thing, too."

Once again, he lifted her chin with his knuckle. His dark blue eyes burned with an intensity that both excited and scared her, as if he already saw everything that she was ... and everything that she wasn't. "No need to thank me, darlin'. Got to keep the customers happy."

The customers. Right.

A small piece of her heart chipped away from his words.

She wasn't sure it was possible, but his eyes darkened even more, and before she knew it, she found herself hauled off her stool, his plate pushed to the side and her butt firmly planted on the countertop. He wedged her knees apart and pushed his body into the V of her legs, his arms on either side of her thighs. "That was a joke, you know."

Her heart pounded hard in her chest as his need for her hit her in heated waves. His fingers bunched in the fabric of her pants, and he pulled her closer to him.

"I feel like a complete ass for not having noticed you sooner. I mean, I knew who you were, have watched your progress, but I don't date or sleep with members. Ever."

Ever.

She hadn't even been aware that she'd been biting her lip until his thumb landed on her bottom lip and gently tugged it free of her teeth.

"My lip, remember?"

Swallowing again, she nodded.

"I haven't been with a woman in a while. A long while. Kind of swore off them until my head cleared from the divorce. It was a rough one. I haven't even been looking to date." He ran the pad of his thumb over her lip, pushing it inside just a touch, then drawing it back out. "Maybe that's why I didn't notice you, because I wasn't looking." He removed his thumb, and she had to push down her whimper. The flash of lust behind his eyes said she hadn't done a good enough job suppressing it though. He dipped his finger into his wineglass, then brought it back to her mouth, rubbing it along her lips before pushing it into her mouth. "Suck."

She did as she was told, loving the eroticism of his demand and the way the fire burned in the deep blue of his eyes as she swirled her tongue around his digit, savoring the excellent vintage and Zak.

"I may not have noticed you before," he began, regret in his tenor, "but I sure as hell notice you now. Stay the night in my bed. Stay the next few nights in my bed. Call in sick to work tomorrow and spend the day in bed with me. Let me make up for being a fool and not noticing you until now."

Not taking her eyes from his, she pinched her wrist, just to make sure she wasn't passed out in a snowbank back in the gym parking lot or in the bed upstairs. Or even worse, back at her cold, tiny, lonely studio apartment with her dead cactus and dollar-store Christmas wreath.

He pushed himself out of his stool and stood up, towering over her even though she sat on the kitchen island.

Damn, he was tall.

"Stay." He pulled his finger from between her lips, cupped her face in both hands and slanted his mouth over hers, bringing their mouths within the same breathing space ... and kissed her. His tongue pushed its way inside, demanding she open for him; she met it and gave it teasing laps with her own. He took that as a challenge and assumed control over not only her mouth, but her body, her muscles and every one of her senses. All she could see, all she could smell, all she could taste, touch and hear was Zak.

Zak.

She sank into his body instantly, the hard planes of his muscles enfolding her. She wrapped her arms around his neck and pulled him down to her, feeling his arousal knock against her inner thigh as he drew her up off the counter and onto his waist.

He took the stairs two at a time, she was pretty sure, collapsing them both onto his bed and stripping her naked with a speed that frightened her in the absolute best possible way.

She'd never been wanted with such ferocity before. Never been craved or desired the way she could tell Zak craved her.

He opened up his nightstand drawer and pulled out a condom, tearing the packet open and sheathing himself in seconds.

She cupped her breasts and pulled at her already diamond-hard nipples, needing more to ease the ache she felt deep in her belly.

"Stay," he demanded again. It had never been a question.

She reached for him, and he lowered himself to her, sinking into her body and stretching her, filling her, fulfilling her fantasies but only a million times better than she ever could have imagined.

"I'll stay," she whispered, tracing her tongue over one of the tattoos on his shoulder. "I'll stay."

His smile made everything inside her tighten and heat up. So this was what it felt like to finally have your fantasy come to life. To finally have the man of your dreams ask you to stay the night, the weekend with him.

Would he ask her to stay for forever?

He dipped his head and latched on to a nipple at the same time his hips began to move—and boy, did they know how to move. All that working out had not compromised his flexibility one iota. The man was like a contortionist.

The closer he brought her to the edge, the closer Aurora felt herself on the verge of tears. Tears of joy, tears of disbelief, tears of pleasure. Tears of fear.

Because true to form, she wasn't able to just enjoy the moment. She was caught up with the thoughts in her head. Plagued by them. Worrying that even though he asked her to stay, he might one day ask her to leave. That she wasn't enough for him. She was just a douse of rain after a drought. Anybody in their right mind would reach for the skies with their mouths open when the clouds finally turned dark and began to pour. Quenching their thirst, easing their parched tongue. It only made sense that he would take what she offered him. And then he would grow tired of her, and she would be asked to leave.

They all eventually ended things with her. She was always the dumpee, never the dumper.

Even with the most recent boyfriend.

However, none of those past lovers could hold a candle to Zak. None of them had piqued her interest or made her fantasize about a future the way she did about Zak. And now that she'd finally had a taste of him, discovered how great he was—she knew that when he finally asked her to leave, it would probably destroy her.

6

ZAK TOOK the steps one at a time, careful not to drop the tray of plates and wineglasses that he carried. After their impromptu second round—and third round—he'd ducked back downstairs and reheated their dinner, deciding that dinner in bed with the incredible woman who'd just emptied his balls down her throat for the second time that night was WAY better than sitting in the kitchen with clothes on.

He should crank the heat tomorrow and make it a no-clothing day. That way he could take her in every room of the house as often as Mother Nature would let him. So far, Mother Nature—or in this case Father Ballsack—hadn't let him down, though he was also no longer a spring chicken and couldn't get it up a dozen times a day like he used to. If he needed an hour or two to recharge, he always had his tongue and fingers to keep Aurora happy.

On the steps of the landing, he paused and glanced at his shoulder. The ache from her bite as she came still stung a touch, and her teeth marks over his tattoo were plain as day.

He liked a little teeth. He liked it a little rough.

Did she?

He had nipple clamps, a blindfold and handcuffs some-where in the back of his closet, would they get to a point in their relationship where he could bring them out?

Rounding the corner into his bedroom, he had to keep himself from dropping the tray. Aurora—Rory— was on his bed, naked, wearing glasses and reading a book. Her sandy-blonde hair tumbled wildly down her shoulders, and her light brown eyes scanned the pages with pinched brows of concentration.

Had he ever seen anything sexier in his entire life?

Nope, he fucking hadn't.

"I was thinking to myself maybe we should make tomorrow a clothing-optional day," he said, kneeling on the bed and resting the tray between them. Then he stood back up, shucked his pants and slipped naked beneath the covers. "But now, I'm thinking we need to not only make it clothing-optional but that you also *have* to wear those sexy-as-fuck black glasses all day."

She finished reading the page she was on, closed the novel and then turned to face him, a big smile on her face. She hummed. "Sorry, I always keep a book in my gym bag, but I haven't read it in ages, figured I had time to start from the beginning this weekend." She removed her glasses and folded them closed, placing them on the nightstand. "I only wear these for reading, so just close up."

He handed her a wineglass. "Don't plan on getting too far away from me there, darlin'. Plan on staying pretty close."

Her cheeks pinked up a nice deep shade. "Where are you from? I detect a hint of an accent." She took a sip of her wine. "A super-sexy accent."

He sipped his own wine and grinned. "South Carolina."

His brother Adam didn't really have any twang left, though he'd been living on the west coast longer than Zak, and he'd made a point of losing it. Zak, on the other hand, didn't mind the drawl, and women seemed to eat that shit up, so he often played it up when the fairer sex was around. *Darlin' this and darlin' that.* Made flirting easy, not that it'd been a challenge for him—not since puberty hit, that is.

She thanked him when he handed her her plate of barely touched chicken and vegetables. "You still have family there in the South? Parents? Siblings?"

Zak set his wineglass down on his nightstand. "My grandparents still live there. Parents died thirty-one years ago when I was four. My brother lives here."

"I'm so sorry about your parents."

He nodded, scratched the back of his neck, then picked up his utensils with one hand and hooked a thumb over his shoulder with the other, pointing to the tattoos on his shoulder blades and turning so she could see them. "Thanks. Those are their birth flowers. January for my mom on the right, August for my dad on the left. It's like they've got my back."

She placed her plate on the nightstand and pushed up to her knees, tracing the tattoos lightly with her fingers. "They're beautiful. All your tattoos are." She ran her fingers over the footprints that ran down his arm. "I'm guessing these are your kids?"

He nodded.

"All your ink is gorgeous."

He grunted and thanked her. "You should eat. Get your strength back."

Her mouth wiggled in a little smile as she sat back down against the headboard and grabbed her plate. "How did your parents pass, if I might ask?"

He swallowed hard but nodded. "It was a car accident. Dad was on his way home from night school. Car broke down. He called my mom to go and pick him up. She left

Adam and me with the neighbors, and they were hit by an off-duty sheriff drunk off his ass."

She drew in a sharp breath. "I'm so sorry."

"Yeah, it was pretty awful. My parents were really young too. Had my brother Adam when they were still teenagers. My dad's parents didn't approve of my mom, so they cut them out of their lives. We were raised by my mom's parents."

"And they're still alive?"

He nodded, forcing a tight smile. "And kicking."

"Is your brother coming over for Christmas dinner or something? Does he have a family?" She set her fork down and took another sip of her wine.

"He does have a family. Has a daughter, Mira, and a new girlfriend, Violet, and she's pregnant. They're all in Hawaii for Christmas with Adam's ex-wife, Paige, and her new boyfriend, Mitch, and his daughter, Jayda."

Her eyes went wide, and her adorable button nose wrinkled in confusion. Even perplexed, she was drop-dead gorgeous. His cock jerked beneath the covers and knocked the bottom of his plate.

Chuckling, he reached over and wiped a droplet of wine from the corner of her mouth with his thumb. "I've seen that look before. But wait, here's the kicker, just to baffle you even further—Mitch is Violet's brother." He slapped his thigh and tossed his head back with another laugh.

Aurora blinked again. "Wait—your brother's ex-wife is dating his current girlfriend's brother? And they're all okay with each other?"

He sipped his wine, nodding. "They're more than okay with it. Paige and Violet are great friends now, as are Mitch and Adam. They all share the girls, go on family trips together, have dinners with each other. Jayda and Mira are as close as two sisters can get. It's a win-win for all of them."

She shook her head and took another, longer, bigger sip

of her wine. "Never heard of a split that amicable in all the cases that have crossed my desk in the past while," she said simply. "A rarity for sure."

Zak made a noise in his throat, picked up his fork and knife again and continued eating. "Mine certainly wasn't a bed of roses. Still isn't. Probably never will be."

He let his gaze slide her way only to find her staring directly at him, her eyes boring into his soul. "I'm sorry," she said softly. "I've seen a lot of ugly divorces, and I know that it's not fun for either side. I hope that you at least got what you wanted with your children?"

With a stiff smile, he grunted, nodded once and continued eating. "I did. Had one hell of a good lawyer. She tried to take them from me, render me down to nothing more than an every-other-weekend dad who paid a butt-load in child support and alimony. She lied about who I was, the type of father and husband that I was. She claimed I was an alcoholic." He cleared his throat for the umpteenth time, spotted his nearly empty wineglass on the nightstand, reached for it but didn't drink a drop.

A cool, delicate hand landed on his heated shoulder. "I hardly know you," she whispered, "but I can already tell you're none of the things she claimed you to be. I have a sixth sense about people, and I don't get any of those vibes from you."

Zak clenched his jaw tight until a dull but not altogether unwelcome throb pulsed just below his ears. He continued to stare at the wineglass. If he squeezed the stem any tighter, it would probably snap.

She tugged on the glass to remove it from his grip, and he slowly released it, his knuckles aching from how hard he'd been holding it.

"I've *only* ever drunk alcohol on the weekends," he said, more to himself than anybody else. "I've always maintained control over my life, over my body and what I put into it. That's how I've stayed so healthy, how I overcame ... " He licked his lips, then turned to her. Her eyes were wide, inviting, welcoming him to share with her. "I was a sick kid," he started. "Really sick. Every allergy on the planet, diet and otherwise. Hay fever, eczema, nosebleeds—I had it all. I was in and out of the hospital for years with one ailment or another. My grandma had a tough time getting enough food into me so that I didn't look like a skeleton. I was anemic, had thyroid issues, insomnia ... " He scrubbed his hands over his face. "I wet the fucking bed until I was nine."

He lifted his head from where he'd been staring at his lap, waiting for the flash of judgment to flit through her gaze, but it didn't. Not at all. She set his wineglass down on her nightstand and reached for his hands, linking them through hers, encouraging him to continue.

"I was this weak little fucker. Forty pounds soaking wet when I was eleven. I was short too. Constantly bullied. Adam defended me as best he could, but if there was anything our grandparents instilled in us, it was not to fight. No scrapping."

"Sometimes a good punch to the face does a world of good for a bully though. A taste of their own medicine." She ran her thumb over the back of his hand and lifted her eyes back up to his, a small, reassuring smile coasting across her lips.

He breathed out a laugh. "I couldn't have said it better myself, actually."

"Then what happened?"

He exhaled deeply, moving his gaze to blink up at the ceiling for a few silent moments and leaning his head against the headboard. "By grace and by God, puberty hit. And it hit me like a tsunami. Only instead of devastating everything in its path and fucking me up even more than I already was, it was more like when Spiderman got bit by the radioactive spider. Puberty kicked ninety-nine percent of my allergies to the curb, my thyroid levels evened out, and I started sleeping better. I also shot up like eight inches in one summer, gained nearly a hundred pounds in like six months, too. And I just kept growing. Went from a size seven shoe to a size thirteen in less than a year. Was over six feet tall by the time I was fourteen. Started working out every day at the gym for two hours. Made friends with some of the bodybuilders there, and they took me under their wings, showed me how to train, how to bulk up. Nobody recognized me when I entered my freshman year at a new school. It was like a rebirth. A second chance at life."

"The phoenix rising from the ashes, burned but never broken. Your wings might have been singed, but your spirit was strong and determined."

Zak's bottom lip dropped open. "Again, I couldn't have said it better myself." He tilted his body a bit and untwined their hands so he could point to the tattoo on his side running from beneath his armpit nearly down to his hipbone. "That's exactly how I felt. Like a phoenix."

Her smile was demure and almost bashful as she traced her cool fingers over the red and orange tattoo of a phoenix he'd gotten when he was eighteen. It embodied who he was. Burned, but not broken. Weakened but not vanquished.

Only now, he was stronger than ever. In control and determined to keep it that way.

"It's beautiful," she whispered. "I take it you dealt with your bullies, then?"

"I did. But not how you would think. I didn't go looking to beat them up. Didn't even swing the first punch or the last. But I hit them all where it hurt the most—their pride. I stole their top spots on all the major sports teams, stole their girlfriends, stole their limelight, their popularity. Almost overnight, I became this school sensation—a freshman who looked like a senior, dating senior girls, all that. I was awkward and bumbling at first, but the guys at the gym helped me overcome that, and by my sophomore year, I was playing for the senior varsity football team, varsity wrestling team. I didn't have to land one blow to anybody's gut or temple to cripple them."

The sexy line of her throat bobbed on a hard swallow. "Wow."

Why did he get the feeling she wasn't as impressed as most women would be?

She lifted her gaze to his. "And what did you do with that new fame besides steal girlfriends, throw around a ball and party every weekend?"

Ouch!

"I didn't party every weekend," he said, shaking his head. She was forming the wrong idea about him. He needed to put a stop to it. "My parents were killed by a drunk driver, don't forget. My grandparents drilled the dangers of alcohol and drunk driving into Adam and I from day one. I didn't drink until college when I lived on campus and home was just a stumble away."

Her eyes dropped down to her lap and her chest deflated on a slow exhale. "I'm sorry."

He needed to continue. She needed the whole story, she needed to *know* him. "I was nominated student body president, and I was captain of the debate team. I took the football team to nationals—and we won. I was awarded a wrestling scholarship to USC. I led the fundraiser for the twenty-four-hour cancer walk around the track."

Suddenly, he felt like her approval of him was all that mattered in the world, that she needed to know he didn't abuse his power or prestige in school, that his grandparents kept him on the right track and insisted he continue to do well.

He shook his head. "That's not what we're talking about right now, though." He tugged on her fingers and laced his with hers again. "I need you to know that I've never abused anything in my entire life. Power. Women. Drugs. Alcohol. None of it."

Okay, well maybe not none of it. Not if you counted that summer after his first wet dream where he spanked the monkey like five times a day for two whole months. That was a lot of self-abuse—and lotion.

His grandfather joked that they should have bought stock in Lubriderm.

"I told you that only drink on the weekends." He tilted his head toward their wineglasses on her nightstand. "And I mean that. This is a one-off for me, I swear it. Loni claimed that I was a raging alcoholic, that I took performance-enhancing drugs and did doping. That I had 'roid rage." He cupped his balls over the duvet. "Does this look like the sac of a fucking steroid user?" Her lips twitched as if she were trying to hide a smile, but instead she simply shook her head. "I've never touched that fucking poison in my life. Everything that I am, that I have, I have worked my fucking ass off for. I eat healthy, I work out and fucking meditate, and that's all to keep me being the best person I can be. To be the best person I can be for my kids. Because I know that I was granted a big fucking gift when puberty hit and I sprouted and grew and was finally healthy. And I'm not about to abuse that gift. I just thank God every day that neither of my kids developed any of my childhood ailments. They're both healthy as horses."

Emotion hung heavy at the back of his throat, and he made to clear it but coughed instead. He stared at their knotted hands. She hadn't said much, simply let him vent, let him dump all his pain and past on her—and yet she didn't seem to mind.

Unless she did mind and was getting ready to make a quick exit.

Had he said too much?

Adam always chastised Zak for being a bit of an over-sharer, saying that he came on strong and if the person wasn't into that kind of personality, they were immediately turned off. Was Aurora turned off? Had he gone too far? Had he overshared?

"I'm going to go get you some water," she said quietly, disentangling their fingers and sliding her lithe frame from the bed. She pulled his T-shirt on over her head and then gently padded across the bedroom toward the door. "We can talk more when I get back if you want to."

Then she was gone. Leaving him staring at the doorway to the dark hallway where the most incredible woman had just left, wondering if he'd scared her away or if she'd be interested in staying with him until the new year ... and maybe longer.

7

AURORA FLICKED on the light in the kitchen and went in search of a couple of drinking glasses, her mind reeling after all that she'd just heard. She needed to be careful not to pity Zak though. Nobody wanted anybody else's pity—she knew that firsthand. But she did feel sorry for him—at least the younger him—and the older him when it came to his ex at least. She sounded like a real piece of work. Lying before the judge, accusing Zak of heinous actions, all to stick it to him even further than she already had.

She thought back to the last divorce case she'd worked on and shuddered. It'd been an ugly one too. Only in this case, the husband had cheated—with his wife's ex step-mother, no less—and both he and his new mistress were dragging Aurora's client through the mud.

It was enough to swear her off marriage and children for good—had she not had the best marriage in the world as an example of how to do it right. Her parents were more in love now than they ever were. The way her mother cared for her father after his heart attack kept that one ember of hope alive and still burning inside Aurora, that maybe she could also make the whole till-death-do-us-part thing work. She just needed to find the right man.

After opening up a few cupboards and coming up empty for glasses, she finally found them and went to the fridge, where he had one of those fancy water dispensers built into the front of the door.

And here she was drinking tap water at home.

Their lives were so different.

Too different?

She finished filling up their glasses, then turned to leave when a dark shadow at the foot of the stairs made her halt and nearly drop the water.

Slowly, almost cautiously he approached her.

She set the glasses down on the island and walked toward him.

"I thought maybe I'd scared you off and you decided to take your chances with the snow," he said quietly, stopping directly in front of her but not close enough to touch. That didn't mean she didn't have to keep herself from swaying where she stood from the heat and strength radiating off him in powerful currents.

She lifted her eyes from his abs up to his face before reaching out and placing her fingers over his perfect stomach. "I'd have to be wearing a bit more than what I am to brave that blizzard," she teased, pushing up to her tiptoes and nipping his chin with her teeth. "I'm not scared of what you told me, not in the least, if that's what you're worried about."

He was in his boxer briefs now, but there was no mistaking his need for her as he pressed his hips against her belly and guided them over to the couch.

He plopped down first and helped her straddle him. She was in nothing but his shirt, and when the crown of his cock through his boxers brushed her clit, she trembled in his hands and ground herself down farther, rocking against him at the same time her lashes fluttered closed.

"Thank you for sharing all of that with me," she said, playing with the hair at the nape of his neck, twirling it around her fingers. "I know that was probably hard for you. But it means a lot. Especially since we hardly know each other but that you trust me enough to let me in like that." She leaned forward and brushed her lips against his. "Unless you want me to leave, I'm not going anywhere."

He growled against her mouth. "I don't want you to leave. I've only started to get to know you." His hands worked their way beneath the shirt and pulled it free over her head. "And something tells me there are a lot of unexplored layers to you."

Oh, if only he knew.

But that was the point, right? She didn't want him to know —not yet, anyway. Her layers were not altogether charming, nor did they paint her in an overly favorable light. Zack needed to see a different side of her, the untragic layers, before she showed him the tragic ones. Otherwise, he'd run for the hills and never look back.

He dipped his head and drew a nipple into his mouth. "And I plan to uncover every single one of them before the weekend is through."

Focus on the now. Focus on Zak.

She tilted her head skyward and pressed her breast against his mouth, loving the way he teased and tormented her, bringing her so close to that sweet edge of bliss, only to bite her and tug her back down the mountain.

"Condoms are upstairs." The disappointment was palpable in this voice.

Right!

Crap!

Twisting her lips, she swirled her hips around him. "I'm clean, and I have an IUD, if that helps."

The thought of Zak inside her with nothing between them made her nearly come on the spot—that and the fact that he was tugging so hard on her nipples, she felt it in her toes.

"I'm clean too, but Violet got pregnant with an IUD in, so ... "

Her eyes went wide, and she stopped her gyrating and stared down at him. "Seriously?"

He nodded. "Yep. Nothing is a hundred percent, darlin'."

Jesus.

He removed his mouth from her chest. His lips turned up into a wily grin. "Doesn't mean I can't take care of you down here." He helped her off his lap, sitting her on the cool, brown leather of his couch, then he swung his body over and reclined down. "Come sit on my face, darlin'. Let me drink you down."

Let me drink you down.

Had she ever heard anything hotter in her entire life?

No, she damn well hadn't.

ZAK'S MOUTH split into a big smile as he glanced down at Aurora. They stood in his bathroom side by side in front of the mirror, brushing their teeth. He'd found a brand-new spare toothbrush in his medicine cabinet and gave it to her, as she didn't have one in her gym bag. He'd also lent her one of his white tank tops and a pair of his boxers to sleep in—at her request. He slept in the buff, but to each their own.

He leaned over and spat into the sink. "You look good in my clothes," he said, rinsing out his mouth. "Look even better out of them, though. I can't convince you to sleep naked with me?" He stepped aside so she could spit and rinse as well.

"I've never been one to sleep naked," she said simply, spitting water into the sink. "Can't do it. I'm always worried there'll be a fire or an earthquake or a break-in and I'll be forced to run outside in my birthday suit. To me, clothes just make sense unless you're in the shower ... "

"Or doing *other* things," he said, bobbing his eyebrows up and down playfully as he reached into a drawer beneath the sink and pulled out a box of floss.

She rolled her eyes. "Yes, or *other* things."

"Need some?" he asked, offering her the floss. She nodded and thanked him. Then they both stood there once again, quiet, staring straight ahead into the mirror as they flossed their teeth.

Why did he get so much joy out of that moment? Why did it make him practically giddy?

Yes, giddy.

What a terrible word, but nevertheless, he felt something akin to that ridiculous word.

Maybe it was because he wanted that domestic bliss back. He wanted the routine, the blissful monotony and comfort that came with having a person in your life—someone who appreciated you for who you were, accepted your faults and celebrated your strengths.

He wanted a partner.

He hated the dating scene with a passion, had never really liked it to begin with. Maybe that was why he'd only had a handful of girlfriends over the years. And then Loni came along. She was gorgeous. He'd just lost his wrestling scholarship from an injury and was quitting college. She gave him hope for a future.

Then she told him she was on the pill—when she wasn't

—and then she gave him Aiden when he was all but twenty-four years old.

He'd had domestic bliss with Loni for a few years. The quiet family life with the two-point-five kids, small house in the suburbs in a good school district. And then it all went to hell.

"You're thinking awfully hard over there," she said, breaking his train of thought and bringing him back to the moment. She'd tossed her floss and was now fixing her hair up into another messy bun on the crown of her head.

He'd been flossing the same spot for a while now, and his gums were sore.

"You okay?" she asked.

Zak started flossing a new spot. "Yeah, sorry. I guess I'm more tired than I thought."

She glanced at the watch and fitness tracker on her wrist. "Well, no wonder. It's nearly three in the morning. Jeez, I'm really sorry."

He dropped his floss into the garbage and turned to her, grabbed her around the waist, tossed her over his shoulder and loped into the bedroom, only stopping to shut off the bathroom light in the process.

Aurora squealed when her belly landed on his shoulder and then squealed again when he tossed her onto the mattress. He climbed onto the bed with her and pulled the covers up over both of them before he leaned over and turned off the lamp on his nightstand. Then he reached for her, turned her over onto her side and tucked himself in tight behind her, until her butt was nestled right against his cock, his chest to her back.

"Now, we sleep," he said, planting a kiss just behind her ear.

"But what about you?" she asked, the sound of disappointment in her voice making his balls cinch up and his cock stir.

He chuckled and kissed her again, his hand cupping her breast and fingers pulling on a tight nipple through the fabric of the tank top she wore. "I appreciate your dedication, but I can wait. If you stay the weekend, I assure you I'll even the score."

He buried his nose in her hair and inhaled her spicy, feminine scent.

"What's that in your hair?" he asked, unable to temper his curiosity. "It smells amazing."

She turned her head and then gently spun in his arms until she was facing him. "It's ginger. I use this locally made hemp and ginger shampoo. It's really great. Found it at a craft market last month."

He leaned in and put his nose next to her temple, inhaling a deep breath once again. "I like it. It's so you."

Although it was now dark in the room, they were close enough he could make out most of the features on her face. He loved the way her lips tilted up on one side in an almost skeptical smile.

"Yeah?" she asked.

He nodded. "Yeah. Spicy but also sweet." He ran his hand down over her hips and the curve of her ass. "I love your body. It's strong and feminine, fit and fierce, but not rail-thin. Curves in all the right places." He gripped her butt cheek and tugged her hard against his body once again, his cock now like an iron bar between them. "Curves I can hold on to." He wedged her legs apart with his knee until she was riding his thigh. "Curves I can run my tongue over. Curves I can kiss."

The kittenish noise deep in her throat made his blood pump hot and heavy in his veins.

"Curves I can sink into and hammer into the mattress without the fear of snapping you in two."

"Yes." Her words were more like a whisper on a harsh wind, barely audible, but just enough for him to hear.

He brought his hand up and pushed beneath the waistband of the boxers she wore and moved his fingers around to the front, cupping her mound and pressing his thumb against her clit.

"What about sleep?" she asked, her hand between them finding his length and beginning to stroke him.

Gently, he rolled her to her back, then he reached into his nightstand, pulled out a condom and had it on in a flash.

"We're going to be exhausted in the morning." She chuckled, opening her legs for him and letting her arms drift up around his back.

He settled down between her warm, welcoming thighs. "I'll sleep when I'm dead," he said, sinking into her wet heat. "But while I'm awake, I'm going to fuck you until we both pass out. Sound good?"

Her breath hitched when he made sure his pelvic bone hit her clit. "Sounds perfect."

8

AURORA blinked open her eyes and tried to shift where she laid on her side, but she couldn't. Warm—no, more like hot—bars of titanium wrapped around her chest and waist, pinning her back to a rumbling furnace behind her. A furnace with an even harder bar of titanium, which was currently prodding her in the backside.

Obviously, this was some crazy *Inception*-style dream within a dream she was having. This couldn't be real. She waited for her brain to wake up, revealing her asleep in her crappy apartment, her dead cactus glaring at her—but nothing. This was no dream.

Well, it was a dream—a dream come true.

She was in Zak's house. She was in Zak's bed. She was in Zak's arms. And for a large portion of last night, Zak had been inside *her*.

A giggle bubbled up in her throat as an enormous smile spread across her mouth.

Maybe wishes do come true.

After all, it *had* been what she'd wished for the last time she saw a shooting star. Because there most certainly hadn't been a birthday cake or a candle to blow out for her birthday last week. Nope.

Her parents had sent her a card with a twenty-dollar bill in it—which she'd promptly re-deposited into their bank account—and they'd talked with her on the phone. That had been the extent of her thirtieth birthday. No drinks or dinner with friends. No breakfast in bed with her boyfriend—what boyfriend? He was long gone by the time her birthday came around. Had he dumped her so he wouldn't have to celebrate it with her? She wouldn't put it past him. All her boyfriends dumped her eventually. Some picked arbitrary dates, while others, like her college boyfriend, picked the day before Valentine's Day. Maybe Pressley had been thinking the same thing. Kick her to the curb before her birthday or Christmas so he didn't have to get her anything.

Nobody at work had even known it was her birthday— not that she'd advertised it. Some people brought in cupcakes or donuts on their birthday to share the love and celebration, but for some reason that just felt weird. As if she were trying to draw attention to herself, being like, "Hey, it's my birthday. Here are some cupcakes. Now who wants to go out for drinks tonight with a person you hardly know?"

Nope. Not her.

It had been a clear night on her birthday though, which was unusual this time of year in Seattle, and when she was leaving the office at ten thirty, bagged from the day and ready to say goodbye to another birthday gone by, a bright star shot across the night sky right in front of her. It had been her birthday candle. The universe letting her know that even at the age of thirty, she still deserved to make a wish on her birthday.

And her wish had been granted.

Zak noticed her.

She snorted a laugh.

He did a hell of a lot more than notice you last night.

Anticipation and desire pirouetted through her at the thought of all that they'd done last night and the fact that he wanted to do it all again today.

She'd probably be walking bowlegged by the time their little blizzard tryst was ended by the snowplow.

Oh well, it was worth it.

He shifted behind her and pulled her tighter against him, her back becoming a sweaty mess from his blazing hot chest and the way his limbs and body completely enveloped hers.

But the need to pee overcame her, and she gently, quietly pried his arms off her and slipped from the bed, carefully tiptoeing over to the bathroom and silently sliding the pocket door shut.

She hobbled—yes, hobbled—to the toilet, because as she'd thought, the man had done a real number on her, and a pleasant throb tingled in her joints and throughout her lady parts. Muscles that she hadn't used in far too long had been put to the test and were now in recovery mode.

Too bad Zak wasn't going to give them much time to recuperate

Nope.

She smiled again and this time let the giggle come out as she paused next to the window on the way to the toilet.

Zak's bedroom had blackout blinds that were drawn, but the bathroom didn't, and the dim light of the morning illuminated the small space enough that she really didn't need to turn on the light. Before she sat down on the toilet, she peered out the window.

Her heart did a little gallop in her chest.

It was a total whiteout.

The blizzard of the decade. Of the century.

Like a beautiful blanket of cushiony soft cotton, the snow piled up over the streets and houses. And it continued to fall in big, fluffy flakes, landing silently on top of the mounds, only to get lost among the other billions of uniquely shaped crystals.

She glanced at her watch. It was nine in the morning.

She'd already decided to call in to work. Well, *Zak* had decided that for her, and who was she to refuse such a man, who promised to make her come more and harder than she'd ever come before?

She'd be an idiot not to give in to his request. His order. His demand.

A tremor of lust shook her at the memory of his demands from last night.

He'd demanded so much from her—demanded more orgasms than she had in her to give. And yet he was also the most generous lover she'd ever had.

She finished in the bathroom, washed her hands, brushed her teeth again and washed her lady parts before sliding the door open only to come face to face with a tattooed God wearing nothing but a smile.

"Come back to bed." His voice was deep, thick and hoarse from lack of use. "But ditch the clothes."

Aurora's top teeth slid over her bottom lip as her mouth drew up into a smile and she approached the end of the bed. She lifted his tank top over her head, then shimmied out of the boxers.

He pushed the covers down to reveal the titanium rod from earlier. It looked harder than ever. He gripped it in his fist and gave it a couple of super-sexy tugs. "Let's even the score, shall we, darlin'?" His eyebrows jiggled. "Bring that sexy little mouth of yours over here."

He didn't have to ask her twice—not that he'd asked —nope.

He'd ordered her.

He'd demanded.

And he was totally playing up the Southern charm now. He was all *darlin' this* and *darlin' that*. She bet once he was clothed and out in public, that twang barely popped out. Maybe when he was drinking, but he probably kept it in check most of the time.

But she liked it. She liked his pet names for her.

She was his *darlin'*. She was his *Rory*.

She made to climb onto the bed, attempting to do her best lioness prowl.

"That's right, Rory, just like that, baby." His voice was a deep purr that made her lady parts tingle and her nipples pebble.

She grabbed his shaft and was about to angle him into her mouth when her phone on the nightstand began to vibrate and ping.

Her heart fell.

Work.

"Ignore it," Zak ordered. "They can leave a message."

Unease climbed up her spine.

If it was work, it could be important.

Zak stroked his length. "I thought I told you to call in to work today."

She walked around to her side of the bed and grabbed her phone from the charger. "I did email my boss. But that doesn't mean that I can't still be available for a project. I *do* have my laptop here. I could still work. And they know that."

She brought up her messages only to find a text message.

From Pressley.

Why the fuck was he texting her?

Merry Christmas. I went by your place. Where are you?

What the hell?

Heat climbed up through her abdomen and into her chest and then finally her face. She clenched her jaw and slammed her phone down on the nightstand.

"Everything okay?" Zak asked, turning over onto his side, propping his head in his hand and resting on his elbow. "Big boss man or woman being a demanding jerk?"

She glanced up at Zak from where she still was staring at her phone. He was giving her a curious look.

"Everything's just peachy," she said through gritted teeth.

Why did Pressley have to bother her over Christmas?

Why did he have to bother her at all?

Zak's mouth flattened into a thin line, then he tossed the covers off his legs completely, swung his legs over the side of the bed and was around to her side in seconds. "Get dressed."

He pulled a fresh pair of boxer briefs out of the dresser beside her and pulled them on. She did as she was ordered and pulled his boxers and tank top back on her body.

"Let's go have some breakfast. You're obviously hungry for more than just cock, so how about I feed you before I *feed* you." His lip tilted up as he gazed down at her, his eyes dancing with amusement. He reached for her hand.

Aurora couldn't stop herself from smiling. This man just had a way of pulling all the best parts of her to the surface. She laughed. "You certainly have a way with words."

He tugged her toward the stairs with him, his hand warm and sure in hers. "It's one of my *many* redeeming qualities."

His wrist flicked, and she was suddenly propelled forward and ahead of him. He slapped her ass. She squealed and jumped, released his hand and took off running down the stairs. "Great with words and eating pussy. I'm a savant at both."

Then he chased her down the stairs, making her giggle and squeal and forget the text message from Pressley in the blink of an eye, giving her the hope and happiness that she so sorely needed.

AURORA SAT at Zak's kitchen bar, patiently waiting for her coffee. The look in her eyes was introspective. As much as Zak tried to get her to forget whatever that text message had said to put her in such a foul mood, she still seemed off.

Whoever had texted her had cost Zak a blow job and whatever else he and Aurora could have gotten up to in bed. He needed to get her happy again. He needed to see that sparkle in her eye, the sultry smile on her face that he was coming to love.

He poured them both a mug of coffee, watching her out of the corner of his eye.

"Are you cold?" he asked, sliding a steaming mug with just a splash of cream across the island to her. "Your nipples look like they could cut diamonds."

She picked up the mug carefully, and cradled it in both palms, blowing on it. "I'm a little chilly," she admitted. "This time of year, I'm usually in more than shorts and a tank top. It's full flannel pj's for this girl."

Zak grinned at her, his eyes roaming across the delicate line of her collarbone and neck. "I'll turn up the heat," he said, wandering over to the wall where the thermostat was and hitting the button a few times until a pleasant seventy-five blinked twice at him. "Seventy-five sound good?"

She nodded. "Should be perfect."

He made his way back over to the island, planted both palms on the countertop. "What can I make ya? You name it, I'll make it." He wanted her to feel at home in his house. He wanted her to feel comfortable.

He hadn't dated a soul since his split with Loni. Hadn't slept with anyone either. Not that they'd been sleeping together in their marriage for quite some time—things hadn't been good between them for a while.

Which resulted in the longest dry spell of his life. Twenty-six months.

But now that he'd quenched his thirst, he was greedy to make up for lost time. And there wasn't a woman he'd rather do that with than Aurora. He didn't just want the weekend or as long as they were trapped inside, he wanted more. He wanted to explore the connection between them and see if it wasn't just lust and snowflakes that made him feel like a new man when he was with her.

"Fridge is stocked," he went on, after she still hadn't said anything. "I normally just have a greens smoothie and a couple of hardboiled eggs—whites only—in the morning. But I kind of go a bit rogue on the weekends. Particularly when the kids are here. We usually have blueberry waffles on Sundays."

He felt the need to keep talking. Her silence was throwing him for a loop.

He'd put an apron over his bare torso—oil burns were no joke.

She tilted her head to the side and studied him, a small, almost coy smile lifting up one side of her mouth.

What on Earth was she thinking about?

Slowly, her eyes ran the length of him, from his navel to his face and then back down, lingering on the spot between his legs. Her little pink tongue darted out and ran along the seam of her lips, her eyes growing a darker brown by the second.

Oh, this woman was an insatiable little beast. She had her kitten motor—or should he say her lioness motor—on purr mode. Next thing he expected was for her to lick the back of her hand and preen herself with the intense way she was watching him. Devouring him with her eyes. It was the same look she'd given him earlier before taking him in her hot little mouth.

He chuckled, shaking his head. "Ah, so *that's* what you're hungry for." He wandered around the island to stand in front of her, his cock already rising to the occasion once again. "You're insatiable, woman," he murmured, pushing her knees apart and letting his hands drift down to her hips.

She still hadn't spoken.

"Are you even hungry for food?"

Her eyebrows lifted a fraction of an inch.

This sudden silence of hers was both frustrating and exciting. She gave away so much with her body language, and her eyes were incredibly expressive.

She hadn't gripped him by the cock yet, so he didn't know what her plans were.

"We should really eat some food, darlin', keep our energy up. I won't be able to keep satisfying you if I don't feed the troops."

She batted long, dark lashes at him, her hands finally leaving her sides and settling on his shoulders. She pushed down gently.

His eyes flared wide when he caught her wavelength.

Her top teeth sawed over her bottom lip. She pushed down on his shoulders harder until he sank to his knees. She pulled the pair of boxers she wore to the side so he was face to face with her glistening pink pussy.

"Eat," she demanded. "Then I'll tell you what I want for breakfast." Her hand landed on the top of his head, and she tugged on his hair until his face was buried between her thighs, his face covered in her juices, her scent surrounding him.

She held on tight to his hair.

He went to work.

And as he swirled his tongue around her clit, he couldn't stop the thoughts that raced through his mind. He had to figure out a way to keep Aurora, keep this woman in his life, in his house, in his bed. Because Santa only delivered a woman like this once in a lifetime.

AURORA PADDED BAREFOOT across the wood floor of Zak's home after zipping upstairs to the bathroom to wash herself. She giggled inwardly at what she'd just done.

Fulfilled another one of her fantasies, that's what.

Right down to demanding he eat.

She'd never been so bold or brazen in all her life. But as she sat there in his kitchen atop his bar stool and the thoughts broke in, there was only way to get them back out. She needed to take them from being just thoughts, just fantasies, to a full-fledged reality.

And thank God Zak had been so willing.

She slipped back onto the bar stool and watched the exquisite globes of his ass bunch, shake and flex as he purposefully moved around the kitchen. She'd requested fried eggs on toast with bacon. He'd countered with poached eggs on nine-grain toast with turkey bacon. She'd agreed.

What kind of a lawyer was she if she couldn't negotiate?

Plus, to have someone else cooking for her was a major bonus and not something she'd argue too heavily about. Besides, his alterations were healthier.

He cut open the package of turkey bacon, smiling at her boyishly when he lifted his eyes back up to hers. "I must say, I am loving you being here," he said. "You can go all boss-lady on me anytime. It was fucking hot."

Her grin hurt her face.

She normally never took control in the bedroom, and she quite liked how demanding Zak was, but something about seeing the unease in his eyes, his eagerness to please her and willingness to drop to his knees and acquiesce to her demands made neurons fire inside her like never before.

Besides, she needed to get the thoughts of Pressley out of her head, exorcise him from her mind—and what better way than with a mind-blowing orgasm from the god currently making her breakfast?

"How's your coffee?" he asked, grabbing the carafe from beneath the coffeemaker and holding it up. "More?"

She nodded and slid her mug across the island. "Please. You make a mean up of Joe."

He filled her up, then grabbed the milk carton from the fridge and added a splash to her mug. "Years of practice. Also, years of buying garbage no-name brand coffee—that shit shouldn't even be called *coffee*—it should be called caffeinated swill. Swamp water with a pick-me-up." He made a grossed-out face. "Blech!"

"Where is this from?" she asked, reaching for her mug and holding it up toward her nose again, letting the steam and intoxicating aroma fill her senses.

"It's Lunar Legacy brand coffee. They're Arabica beans, obviously, but from Costa Rica. I like medium roast, low acidity. Ethically sourced, fair trade, of course. Costs a bit of a fortune for a month's worth, but seeing as I don't really drink alcohol besides on the weekend and I eat really healthy, it's a vice I allow myself."

She took a small sip, holding the coffee on her tongue for a moment before letting it slide down her throat. It really was spectacular.

Better than the caffeinated swill she was forced to buy and drink at home. It was all she could afford. The bigger the can, the better. No amount of creamer or sweetener could make it passable. But she needed something to help her stay awake at work and burn the candle at both ends.

Junior partners didn't sleep on the job.

Junior partners could afford decent coffee.

Eyes on the prize.

She looked forward to the day she was a partner at the firm and could grab her coffee from the partner's lunchroom.

They had one of those fancy Tassimo things, while the first-year associates were subjected to a lunchroom the size of a bathtub and the coffee maker was always empty, filthy or the dregs at the bottom were weaker than tea.

"What kind of coffee do you drink?" he asked, setting a pot of water to boil.

Um ...

Her lips twisted in thought as her brain scanned the coffee aisle at her local grocery store. What was a fancy coffee he might know? Ah, fuck it, she didn't know any, and she really hated lying. "I buy the biggest, cheapest can I can find, and some days I reheat the coffee from the day before if there is any left in the carafe. Though I'd love to get my hands on some beans from that little gourmet shop in Pike Place."

"Bean Around the Block?" he asked, his eyebrows lifting on his forehead. "That place is pricey."

She pouted. "Don't I know it. It takes far too much no-name brand hazelnut creamer to make the swamp juice I brew taste like anything even remotely resembling coffee. But it keeps me awake, and in the end, that's all that matters."

He nodded before opening the breadbox on the counter next to the fridge and pulling out a loaf of artisan bread—because, of course, it was artisan.

She had Wonder Bread in her freezer at home.

"Well, then, Miss Lawyer Lady who needs to stay awake so she can win all her cases, save the world and all that jazz, drink up. My good stuff is your good stuff while you're here."

Her heart did a heavy *thump, thump* in her chest.

What's mine is yours ...

He plopped four slices of bread into the toaster. "Butter?"

"Is the Pope Catholic?"

He shrugged and grinned. "Wouldn't know."

Once again, her smile hurt her face.

The clock on the microwave said it was closing in on one o'clock. They'd slept and sexed the morning away.

Why couldn't every morning start out that way?

"So, Miss ... " Zak paused with an egg carton in his hand. "Shit, I don't even know your last name." He ran his free hand through his hair and then scrubbed it over his rust-colored beard. "I feel like a real ass now."

"A real ass with a *fine* ass," she quipped. "You're forgiven."

His smile made her insides liquefy.

"Besides, I don't know yours either."

"Eastwood."

She rolled it around on her tongue. "Zak Eastwood."

It suited him.

"Zachary Ryan Eastwood, to be exact. Now your turn."

She thrust her hand out. "Aurora Leanne Stratford. Nice to meet you, Zachary Ryan Eastwood. Thank you for having me in your house and for all the sex."

He snorted, then smiled, taking her hand and shaking it. "The pleasure was *all* mine."

A big grin split her face before she released his hand, then tucked a strand of hair behind her ear. "Well, some of it was mine."

"Touché."

She kicked her legs playfully beneath the counter. "So, besides bang until the cows come home, what should we do today? Watch a movie? Read books? Bake cookies?"

He went back to work preparing breakfast—or more accurately, lunch. "Whatever you want, darlin'."

She rolled her eyes. "You're quite the charmer. Tossing around that twang like it's no big *thang*."

He bobbed his eyebrows up and down. "Is it working? Are you *charmed*?"

She'd been charmed the moment she walked into the

gym and spotted him. He could speak in binary code and she'd still be madly in love with him.

"I'm going to assume that you are, based on that salacious look you're giving me right now. Down, woman. I need to feed you before I fuck you." He chuckled as he pulled out a countertop griddle from beneath the island and plugged it in. Then he grabbed a pack of turkey bacon from the fridge and opened it. "We should bake cookies. I haven't baked anything in years, but it seems like the Christmassy thing to do." He wrinkled his nose and looked around himself. "Though I'm not even sure I have everything needed to bake cookies. I seriously keep a pretty healthy household. If the temptation isn't there, then you can't fall off the wagon, right?"

She slid off the chair and wandered around the island to stand next to him. "Where's your *baking* cupboard? I'll see what I can dig up, and then we can improvise from there if need be."

He pointed her to the slatted pantry door beside the fridge and then went to work laying the bacon on the griddle. Aurora snatched the apron she spotted on the hook next to where Zak had grabbed his and draped it around her neck before heading to the pantry.

She had a hankering for gingerbread and hoped he had what they needed. Otherwise, they'd probably have to settle for something more basic, like shortbread. Still good, but it was no gingerbread.

She opened up the pantry door, expecting to see just a row of shelves, but was stunned when it turned out to be an entire small room. A room that was in fact bigger than the entire bathroom back in her apartment.

She stepped inside, flicked on the light and went in search of the baking necessities. Baking powder: check. Vanilla: check. Brown sugar—would coconut sugar work? Because that was all he had. It would have to do. She tucked that under her arm along with the other ingredients. Thankfully, his spice rack was decked to the nines, so she had no problem coming up with all the necessary gingerbread spices. She managed to find some whole wheat flour tucked behind the three unopened tubs of protein powder, and then finally the molasses. The ingredient that made gingerbread what it was.

Wiping her brow with the back of her wrist and reorganizing everything in her arms, she headed back out into the kitchen.

"Found what we need to make gingerbread." She beamed, setting it all down on the counter far enough away from Zak's workstation that she shouldn't be in the way.

He nodded with a grin as he cracked an egg into the boiling pot of water. "Breakfast won't be long, then we'll get to work on the cookies."

She walked up behind him and cupped his butt in her hands, loving how the cheeks tightened beneath her fingers, then tightened even more when she dug her nails into the hardened muscle.

"You're playing with fire, young lady," he joked, cracking another egg into the water. "I am not against shutting off everything right now, throwing you over my shoulder and hauling you upstairs. I'd love nothing more than to toss you over my knee and ... " His breath hitched.

She'd reached under his apron and over his boxers. She had him in her palm now.

"And what?" she purred, planting kisses across his back.

"And attach some nipple clamps to your tits and then paddle that ass of yours," he replied, the timber of his voice rough, dark and laden with promise.

Nipple clamps? Yes, yes please!

Her pussy tightened at the thought of Zak spanking her ... of Zak punishing her.

She steadied her breathing, grateful that she was behind him and he couldn't see her intense reaction to his suggestion. "Sounds like a great plan," she said, releasing him and backing away. "But first make me breakfast. I'm famished." Then she slapped his butt and skipped back around the island, loving the gleam in his eyes as he watched her.

She didn't really recognize herself and the way she was behaving. Flirty and seductive. Aroused at the mention of being spanked and decked out with nipple clamps. But if this was who she was when she was with Zak, then she had no plans of introducing him to the real, boring Aurora that all her other boyfriends quickly grew tired of. Zak liked this Aurora. Aurora liked this Aurora, and if Zak decided he liked her enough to keep her more than just through the blizzard, then she was going to kick the old Aurora to the curb and not look back.

9

"YOU'RE DOING IT WRONG," Aurora said, a giggle in her tone as she hip-checked Zak out of the way and grabbed the piping bag of icing from his hands. "You're just adding genitalia to all the gingerbread people. You need to add faces and buttons."

"But they're naked," he said, reaching for the piping bag again. "Why do they need buttons?"

She held the bag out of his reach, which was cute because she was a short little thing and he could easily snatch it from her. But he didn't, and instead he wiped a dollop of icing off the counter and plopped it onto her nose.

Her mouth went wide in shock.

He did it again, this time getting her cheek.

Using the bag, she squirted a bunch of frosting onto his naked arm, then the hollow of his throat.

Before he knew it, they were having an icing fight, him with the bowl of icing, spatula and his fingers and her with the piping bag.

She squealed and giggled as he continued to try to get her face. Her apron shifted, pulling her tank top with it and a nipple peeked around the edge. He scooped a tablespoon or more of white icing onto his index finger and smeared it on her nipple.

She gasped, then crooned, her eyelids immediately dropping to half-mast.

She reached behind her neck and pulled the apron over her head.

Zak smeared more icing all over her chest, then bent his head and licked it off, pulling her breasts free over the top of her tank top. The sugar rush combined with Aurora made him heady and clouded his brain.

The woman had cast a spell on him.

"We should go wash up," she said, leaning her elbows on the counter and lifting her head toward the ceiling, pushing her breast against his face.

He cupped the other breast, then moved his mouth to that nipple, giving it the same devotion as its twin. "You go start the Jacuzzi tub. I'll clean up here and bring up some wine," he said, not releasing her tight nub, but rather sucking it farther into his mouth until her sharp inhale and drifting hand down between his legs made him bite down.

He'd love to make her come solely from breast and nipple stimulation. He bet she could do it. If anybody could, it would be Aurora. She was so sensitive, so responsive.

He pulled his mouth from her, her whimper of reluctance making his cock jerk beneath his apron. "Go." He spun her around and slapped her butt, loving the way it jiggled as she skipped and squealed off toward the staircase.

She paused on the bottom step, her hand on the rail. "You're a bit of a kinky fucker, aren't you?" she asked, no judgment in her tone, just open curiosity.

His mouth slid up into a sly grin. "Not much I won't do, if that's what you're asking. As long as everyone is a consenting adult, I'm game." He pursed his lips in thought for a moment. "I don't do dudes, though. I think the penis is fucking ugly."

She tossed her head back and whooped out a laugh, her long, blonde hair falling down her back. "I dunno about that. I've seen a pretty handsome one recently, nothing to complain about."

He grinned back at her, stepped away from the island, lifted his apron and pulled down his boxers, flashing her the hard penis she was speaking about.

"Oh, I don't mean that one."

Zak's face fell, and he dropped the apron.

Aurora's laugh became even louder, making her whole body shake. "I'd like to know all the depraved things you've done," she said, running her tongue over her bottom lip.

"Should we play *Never have I ever?*" he asked. "Take a drink for each thing you've done."

Her eyes widened along with her smile. "Sounds like a plan." She began to climb the stairs. "Though something tells me you're going to be drunk mighty fast, my friend." Then she disappeared up the stairs, laughing.

THE TUB WAS FULL, complete with bubbles and a few candles Aurora had found in one of the bathroom cabinets. She really hoped that Zak hadn't used those with his ex-wife way back when, but she also didn't want to think about it for very long, so she lit them and then pushed the other thought out of her mind.

Wrapped up in nothing but a big, fluffy towel, she was just about to head back downstairs to check on her ginger-bread muscle man when the doorbell chimed.

Who in the what now?

She glanced outside the bathroom window. It was growing dark, but it had also stopped snowing. Had the plow finally come through? Was she going to have to head home?

She switched rooms and pulled back the drapes in her room—the room she'd never used—and saw a big, dark green diesel truck parked in the driveway. It looked as though the snow plow had gone through, but there was more snow on top of the roads. It'd gone through a while ago while it was still coming down.

But who was at the door?

She raced back into Zak's bedroom, ripped off the towel, grabbed his shirt off the floor and threw it over her head before she found her yoga pants on a nearby chair and pulled those onto her legs. Once she was covered, she crept to the top of the stairs, her ears practically aching from how hard she was straining to listen.

But there wasn't a peep.

Carefully, she tiptoed down a few stairs, then a few more, until she was finally at the bottom. She kept herself hidden though.

"It was your turn to have them anyway," a female voice said with enough impatience in the tone, Aurora could feel it all the way in the stairwell. "Craig's friend has a cabin on Mount Baker. Craig usually goes for Christmas and New Year's, but because it's our first Christmas as a family, he wanted to take the kids to Disneyland."

"You're not a family," Aurora heard Zak grind out. "If spending Christmas with them is so important to you, then go back to your house."

His ex-wife made a dismissive noise. "But now that we're not going to Disneyland, we can go to the cabin. It's a no-kid thing. Besides, it's your year. You threw such a big stink about not getting them, I figured you'd be thrilled."

"Of course I'm thrilled," Zak said, both happiness and fear shaking in his voice. "It's just ... "

"Just what?" she asked, more impatience in her tone. "Why do you have to make things so difficult, Zak? Just take them. Merry Christmas. We'll be by to get them on January second."

"What?" Zak asked.

Oh, what Aurora would give to be a fly on the wall and not just as eavesdropper. She needed to see the woman's facial expressions. She could only imagine her lips were turned up into a sneer or a smug smile of satisfaction.

"We're going to stay at the cabin through the new year. May as well."

Aurora shut her eyes and shook her head. Zak's ex was a real piece of work. It seemed as though she only wanted her children when it was convenient for her or when she could stick it to Zak. Otherwise, they were a burden to her freedom.

"Who are you?" a small feminine voice asked. "Is that my dad's shirt?"

Aurora's eyes blinked open, and her mouth resembled that of a hungry codfish.

"Are you my dad's girlfriend?" the little girl continued, wrinkling her nose the same way Zak did when he was confused. Her bright amber eyes squinted at Aurora as she tilted her head to one side.

Aurora swallowed. "I'm, uh ... "

"Who are you?" A boy the spitting image of Zak, only a bit shorter and without any tattoos, appeared around the corner. Red hair, sharp blue eyes, freckles on his cheeks, forehead and down his arms. "What's your name?"

"I'm Aurora," she finally managed to say. "But you can call me Rory."

The little girl shook her head, jostling her red waves that floated around her shoulders. "Nope, I'm calling you Aurora. That's the same name as Sleeping Beauty, and I *love* Sleeping Beauty."

"Are you Dad's new girlfriend?" the boy asked, leaning his

arm on the stair rail. If she remembered correctly, Zak had said that Aiden was ten and Tia was eight.

They each wore a backpack, and the little girl had a stuffed panda bear beneath her arm. "Are you spending Christmas with us?"

"I, uh ... "

"We were supposed to be at Disneyland, but our flight was canceled. Mom and Craig want to head to Craig's friend's cabin, so now we're back with Dad." She scratched her head. "I was excited for Disneyland but not spending all that time with Craig. He's weird."

The boy nodded. "And he smells funny."

His sister nodded in agreement. "Like bad cough syrup."

Aurora swallowed. "Can you tell me your names?" She was going to avoid answering their question about her being their father's girlfriend as best she could.

No, I'm not your father's girlfriend, just his friendly neighborhood stalker who's been having an obscene amount of sex with him for the past eighteen hours. No big deal. Merry Christmas, kids!

"I'm Aiden, and this is Tia," the boy said, pointing at his sister. "Could we please get by you so we can go and put our bags in our rooms?"

Wow, what great manners.

Aurora shifted on the stairs until her knee hit the wall. "Yeah, totally. Sorry 'bout that."

He lifted one shoulder and ascended the stairs. "No problem. Thanks."

Tia remained standing in front of her. She clutched her panda tight to her chest. "Did you and my dad bake cookies?" She angled her head back around the corner toward the kitchen. "It smells like cookies, but this house never smells like cookies. Spinach and protein muffins maybe but *never* cookies."

Aurora smiled. She liked Tia. She liked both of Zak's kids.

"We did. And I bet he'll let you have one if you run upstairs like your brother and put your bag away."

The little girl's eyes went wide. "Okay. You'll tell him you said it was okay?"

Aurora's lips contorted. "It's not my place to say. But your dad seems like a pretty reasonable guy, so if you ask him politely, he might say yes to you having one."

Tia's nose wrinkled. "Okay. I'll be right back." Then she thundered up the stairs like her big brother just had, leaving Aurora sitting on the stairs, wondering how she was going to get out of this jam.

———

Zak slammed his front door shut and locked it.

He clenched his jaw until he was close to chipping a tooth and pulled violently on the ends of his hair.

He would not stoop to her level. He would not call his children's mother names. Not even in his head. He would not.

He.

Would.

Not.

But Craig was a motherfucking douche-canoe with a bad haircut, boy-band streaks and the smile of a goddamn sociopath. He reeked like Drakkar Noir and cherry-flavored vape and drank motherfucking light beer. Who the fuck drank light beer?

Douche-canoes! That's who.

And the guy wore a jeweled pinky ring.

A. Pinky. Ring.

If there was anything he planned to teach Tia and have her carry through life as she grew into a young woman, it was that she should *never* ever trust a man, let alone go near a man who wore a goddamn bedazzled pinky ring.

Not to mention, the guy was a fucking jet ski and speed-boat salesman. Was there a smarmier, more lowlife job on the planet? No, there was not.

Craig was an asswipe. Craig was a prick. Craig was shit for brains.

Phew.

He let go of his hair.

That felt better.

He would never in a million years speak ill of the mother of his children, because that would be speaking ill of his kids, but he had no love lost or otherwise toward Craig. Craig was a tool with a capital T.

The first time Zak met him, Craig had pulled into Zak's driveway, blasting music from his dark blue racing-striped Dodge Charger with the personalized license plate that said *LDISMAN*. Yes. Ladies' Man. Loni was in the front seat, and they were there to pick up the kids.

At first, Craig hadn't gotten out of the vehicle. He remained behind the steering wheel, engine still running, music still playing.

But then Zak refused to let his children leave with a man he'd never met, so Loni made Craig get out of the car.

Zak had had to stop himself from snorting a laugh.

The guy was at least six inches shorter than Zak and almost a hundred pounds lighter.

He watched as Craig took in Zak's size, his height, his tattoos and then finally Zak's truck.

Not one week later, when Craig and Loni came to pick up the kids again, Craig had traded in his Charger for a truck just a touch bigger than Zak's.

Snort.

Yeah. He was *that* kind of a tool.

Compensating for much there, buddy?

Like how small his *tool* was, perhaps?

Poor little Craigy, not quite six feet, with size eight shoes and hands the size of a sixth grader's.

Yeah, Zak had checked the man's shoe size when he dropped the kids off at Loni's one day and saw Craig's biking clip shoes on the front stoop, caked in mud.

Poor little Craigy.

The thought of Craig's tiny feet eased the rage in Zak's heart just a tad.

Ordinarily he never would have mocked a man for his size or made fun of him in any way. Zak had been bullied enough as a kid for ten lifetimes and didn't take kindly to bullying of any kind.

But Craig was different.

Craig had assisted in the dissolution of Zak's marriage, and Craig never once showed Zak or his children an ounce of respect, so in turn Craig got no respect from Zak. The man was fair game for Zak's belittling thoughts. Besides, it's not like Zak ever said anything he thought out loud. They were just his way of keeping his anger in check without breaking the man's nose.

His thoughts—and his punching bag downstairs—were all he had.

Speaking of his punching bag, he was feeling the itch, feeling the need to duck downstairs to his home gym and pound out a few rounds on the speed bag to release the tension that was building up in his shoulders.

At the moment, though, he had bigger fish to fry.

Like the woman who was probably sitting upstairs in his Jacuzzi tub waiting for him and how he was going to explain her to his two children.

Swallowing, he turned the corner into the kitchen only to nearly trip over his own feet as he slid to a stop, finding Aurora standing behind the island chatting with Tia and Aiden, who were both sitting on the bar stools.

"Dad, can we have a cookie, please?" Tia asked. "Aurora said we needed to ask you first, that it's not her place."

Zak's pace was cautious as he approached the island, surveying the woman he'd come to know intimately over the last day and how she was with his children.

He'd never introduced them to anybody before.

Probably because he hadn't been with anybody since Loni. Hadn't dated or slept with a soul since the divorce. He just wasn't ready.

Was he ready now?

Were the kids ready?

"She has the same name as Sleeping Beauty," Tia added with a big grin that warmed his heart. "We like her."

Tia was the easy one to win over. Aiden was the one who would remain a touch more guarded. He'd been the one who found out about his mother's infidelity—and not in the best or gentlest of ways. Aiden was protective of Zak. Aiden was the most incredible son in the world.

"You can each have *one* cookie," Zak finally said, making his way between his children and running his hands down each of their heads before pecking them on the temples.

Gleefully, his kids thanked him, then leaned over the counter, and each grabbed the biggest gingerbread man they could find.

Tia's eyes suddenly went wide as she studied her cookie. Then she glanced back up at Zak. "Dad, what is on these cookies? Is that a *penis?*"

Oh shit!

He forgot about his R-rated icing job.

Aurora chuckled. "Your dad was just being silly. Yes, a few of them do have *body* parts." She reached over and grabbed two cookies that had no more than buttons and smiley faces and exchanged them with the two suggestive cookies Tia and

Aiden had grabbed. "Here, these ones have clothes on. See, buttons."

Tia gave Zak a curious look. "You're weird, Dad."

Zak inhaled through his nose and nodded. "That I am. But you love me anyway."

His daughter simply rolled her eyes. "I kind of have to."

"I don't care if my cookie had a penis," Aiden piped up, picking off an icing button with his fingers and popping it into his mouth. "A cookie is a cookie. It's just icing."

Aurora snorted. "A cookie is just a cookie."

"These are good," Tia said, having immediately snapped off the gingerbread man's head, crumbs tumbling out of her mouth.

"Don't speak with food in your mouth, please," Zak said, resting his hand on her warm little back again.

She glanced at him, then nodded. "Sorry, Dad," she muffled through the cookie, sending more crumbs flying.

Zak rolled his eyes.

Aurora's soft chuckle made his eyes finally drift up to hers.

"You changed," she mouthed, pointing to his now clothed body.

He nodded stiffly.

When he saw through the living room window that it was Craig's truck, he'd ducked into the garage and pulled a pair of clean sweats and a T-shirt out of the dryer.

"Are you happy we're here for Christmas, Dad?" Aiden asked, his eyes darting back and forth between Zak and Aurora. "Or did we interrupt something?"

Fuck.

Aiden had always had a sixth sense for picking up on the undertones of tension in a room or the low humming vibe of something just a touch off.

Zak grabbed the cooling rack that held the gingerbread cookies and picked one up for himself, snapping off the head just like his daughter had. "Of course I'm happy you're here, buddy. If I could spend every Christmas with you, every day with you, I'd be a happy Dad. But I didn't think I'd be spending it with you, so I made plans with my friend Aurora and some of the single dads."

Aiden nodded. His hair was just a touch darker than Zak's, with natural darker, almost auburn streaks throughout. It'd be interesting to see what color his facial hair turned out to be and whether his beard went darker as well or bright red like Zak's grandfather.

"That's okay, Dad," Tia piped up, licking a crumb off her thumb. "Christmas is about being together. The more the merrier, right?" She lifted her head back up, pinning her gaze on him. "Can I have another cookie ... please?"

Zak narrowed his eyes at her. "What have you eaten today?"

She wrinkled her nose in thought, her amber eyes—the same shade as Loni's—squinting at the same time. "Umm-mmmm ... toast and jam for breakfast with apple slices. Then McDonalds for lunch—I had a cheeseburger. Aiden had nuggets. And then we had pretzels and grape juice."

Zak pushed down the fury that threatened to bubble over. Had that been Craig or Loni feeding them garbage all day?

He shook his head. "I'm sorry, sweetie, but no more cookies today. You've had a fair bit of treats already, it sounds like. Thanks for being honest with me, though. Let's have a really healthy dinner, and then we can talk about maybe having a couple of cookies tomorrow."

His daughter made a face that said she was upset but understood.

This was the way it was in Zak's house.

Clean eating and honesty. He also got the kids out doing

regular exercise, or if the weather was foul, he took them downstairs into his home gym and had them do some fun, age-appropriate exercises.

Having finally finished his cookie, Aiden got up from his seat and wandered into the kitchen, grabbed two glasses from the cupboard and poured both him and his sister water from the fridge dispenser. He slid Tia's glass over to her.

Zak loved how independent and thoughtful his son was growing up to be.

"Is Aurora sleeping over?" Aiden asked.

Zak nodded. "She is. It was too snowy for me to take her home. Do you guys mind if she stays over?"

Both his children shook their heads.

"In your room?" Tia asked, her wide-eyed innocence causing tingles of nervousness to traverse the length of Zak's arms.

"Of course in his room, silly," Aiden said, taking a seat next to his sister again. "I think Aurora is Dad's new girl-friend, we just hadn't met her yet. She's wearing Dad's shirt. They're dating."

Aurora had been awfully quiet this entire time, and Zak had done his best to avoid looking at her too often, out of fear his children might read into something.

But apparently, they were just too damn clever for their own good—or Zak's good.

"Your dad and I are friends," Aurora finally spoke. "I will sleep wherever you guys are more comfortable with me sleeping. This is your home, your dad, and your Christmas. I don't want to make either of you feel uncomfortable."

Wow!

Zak's bottom lip dropped open, and his eyes went wide.

Could this woman get any more amazing?

Tia shrugged. "You can sleep wherever. Dad's bed is

bigger and crazy comfy. No sense dirtying another set of sheets, anyway."

Aurora's mouth twitched.

Was she thinking what he was thinking? That his sheets in his bed were fucking filthy?

Probably.

"Yeah," Aiden added. "Sleep in Dad's bed. I don't really mind. We appreciate that you guys gave us the option though. Mom and Craig didn't."

Motherfucking Craig.

"Yeah, Craig just moved all his junk into the spare room but started sleeping in Mom's room right away," Tia added, shaking her head and making a frustrated face. "And he takes *sooooo* long in the bathroom." She held up her hands in confusion. "What's he doing in there anyway? He's not that big of a guy."

Zak stared directly ahead at Aurora's face and bit his lip to keep himself from laughing. She appeared to be doing something similar.

Out of the mouths of babes.

He'd never once spoken ill of Craig to his children either, or even within their earshot, and he'd certainly never commented on his height.

Tia was an observant little one, though. Always had been.

"Craig's probably putting gel in his hair," Aiden added. "The guy's head is like a helmet. Have you ever touched it? Hard as a rock from all that gunk."

Zak was about to open his mouth and say something about being nice to people when the doorbell chimed again.

Who the hell was it now?

If it was Loni and Craig back to ask for his children, he was going to blow a fucking gasket.

Both his children slid off their stools and followed Zak to the front door.

"Who's driving in this stuff?" Tia asked. "They better have a truck, otherwise they shouldn't be out in the snow. It's treacherous."

His little dictionary child. Tia had always loved words. Was talking circles around Aiden by the time she was two.

Zak peered through the window next to the door and once again nearly lost his balance.

He flung open the door to find his grandparents from freaking South Carolina standing on the welcome mat, suitcases by their sides, snow flurries in their hair.

"Grammy! Papa!" Tia and Aiden shouted, hurling themselves forward and into the waiting arms of Zak's grandparents.

"Dad's got a new girlfriend," Tia said, pulling out of her great-grandmother's arms and then catapulting herself into Zak's grandfather's arms.

"Does he now?" Zak's grandfather asked, lifting his gaze to Zak and quirking up an eyebrow.

"Yeah." Tia nodded. "Her name's Aurora, which is just like Sleeping Beauty, and she's in the kitchen. She and Dad baked cookies. Dad never bakes cookies, so we already like her more than we like *Craig*."

Zak's grandfather's mouth slid up into a big smile, his blue eyes fixed on Zak. "I can't wait to meet her."

Zak let out a slow breath as panic swelled up inside him and threatened to swallow him belly first.

This was not at all how things were supposed to go.

This was not the plan.

This was too much too soon, wasn't it?

It had to be.

Now he had to decide if he was going to just go with the flow and let Christmas take its course, allowing Aurora to stay and spend Christmas with his family and friends, or figure out a way to get her home and not hurt her feelings or crush any potential for something more with her.

Because one thing was for sure, he definitely wanted more with the woman who had broken his dry spell and then some. He just wasn't sure if he was ready to have her spend Christmas with his family.

10

AURORA HELD her breath as she heard the commotion at the front door make its way through the house toward the kitchen. When she heard Aiden and Tia yell "Grammy! Papa!" she knew it had to be Zak's grandparents.

The house just went from two to six very fast.

Was Zak feeling overwhelmed?

Was he ready for his entire family to meet someone he'd just started sleeping with—yesterday?

Aurora knew she wouldn't be if the roles were reversed.

Perhaps she should just run upstairs and pack her bag, make the decision for him.

But oh, her heart.

Her Christmas gift to herself. Her birthday wish. It wasn't complete. It wasn't over, not yet. It couldn't be.

Was that selfish of her?

She was about to climb the stairs when Tia, dragging a comely woman with silver-gray hair in a stylish bob and dark green eyes, came rushing around the corner.

"Grammy, this is Sleeping Beauty. Dad's new girlfriend," Tia said with a giggle. She tilted her head to the side, her smile wide and silly. "Just kidding. Her name's Aurora." She held up a finger, her face suddenly growing serious. "But technically that is also the name of Sleeping Beauty, so I'm not wrong."

Zak's grandmother's smile was equally wide as Tia's, and her eyes held a glimmer of amusement to them. "Well, Sleeping Beauty or not, I'm pleased to meet you, Aurora."

Aurora smiled as she stepped down off the bottom step. "You as well ... Mrs. ... ?"

"Mrs. Fraser," Tia added. "Grammy and Papa are Mr. and Mrs. Fraser."

Mrs. Fraser's eyes sparkled. "That's true, but please call me Daphne. My husband is Sherman, but we all just call him Papa or Sherm. Whatever you prefer."

A small, cool hand took Aurora's, and when she looked down, she found Tia smiling up at her. "Come on, let's go meet Papa."

"It's all right, dear," Daphne said with a laugh. "We don't bite. But I'm guessing whatever it is between you and Zachary, that it's quite new and you hadn't anticipated meeting the whole Fraser-Eastwood clan so soon."

The woman was a mind reader.

Tia pulled both Aurora and Daphne back into the kitchen where Zak, his grandfather and Aiden stood behind the island. Sherman was chewing on a gingerbread cookie.

"Papa, should you be eating that with your diabetes?" Tia asked, a look of concern falling across her young face.

Her great-grandfather rolled his eyes. "I'll be fine, love. Don't you worry about your old Papa here."

He seemed to have a wordless conversation with his wife before they both broke eye contact and smiled at the rest of the people in the room.

Aurora's parents had those kinds of conversations too. The kind where you didn't need to speak a word to say a million things. They were the kinds of conversations you could only have with someone you were truly in sync with, truly connected with.

She hoped to have those conversations with someone one day.

"I'm so excited that Grammy and Papa are here for Christmas," Tia said, bouncing up and down on her toes, jostling both Aurora and her grandmother, as she was still holding each of their hands. "It's going to be better than Disneyland!"

"I still can't believe you guys braved that blizzard," Zak said, offering Aurora a sheepish smile before turning back to his grandfather. "What were you two old coots thinking?"

Sherman's head reared back as if he were affronted, but then his mouth spread into a big smile as he chewed his cookie. "Ah, it wasn't that bad. Our flight was diverted to Vancouver due to the storm. Not such a big deal. It's a beautiful airport and nice people. Then we rented a truck and after a short drive across the border—badabing, badaboom —we're here. Nothing these two *old coots* can't handle." He grabbed another cookie, stared at it for a moment—it was obviously one of the ones with genitalia on it—but he did nothing but shrug and take a bite, scratching at his bright red but silver-speckled beard as he spoke. "Besides, we were thinking that we didn't want one of our favorite grandsons to be all lonesome for Christmas. Figured we'd surprise you. But you surprised us with a houseful. Not that we're complaining. We'll never complain when we get to see Tia and Aiden." He grabbed two more cookies off the cooling rack and passed them to each of his great-grandchildren, all before Zak could say a word.

But both children simply held the cookies in front of them.

"Dad?" Aiden asked.

Zak rolled his eyes. "Fine, whatever. But it's broccoli for

breakfast, lunch and dinner after the new year. Need to purge the sugar from your systems."

Daphne made a dismissive noise in her throat, her green eyes rolling. "You need to lighten up, dear. I'm on board with being healthy, but you take it to the next level." She grabbed a cookie for herself off the counter. "And that level can get annoying."

"I'm going to take our bags upstairs to the guest room," Sherman said, having finished his second cookie. "Aiden, be a good lad and help your Papa. I'm an old coot, after all." He shot Zak a sarcastic look over his shoulder, his blue eyes full of humor and defiance. "Only got one good leg left." And as if to prove a point, Sherman grabbed two suitcases and limped —though just slightly—toward the stairs.

"You only have one *real* leg left, Papa," Aiden said with a chuckle, grabbing the two remaining bags and slinging them over his shoulder. "Will you show me your stump when we get upstairs? It's so cool."

"We'll see," Papa said, already a quarter of the way up the stairs.

"Papa lost his leg to diabetes when we were kids," Zak said, his mouth next to Aurora's ear. "Hasn't really slowed him down much, though. Still a stubborn old codger who insists upon doing everything without a cane—even though he really should have one."

"Oh, he's a stubborn one, that's for sure," Daphne said, standing behind Tia and playing with her hair. "Can still mow the lawn and buck wood, but somehow dancing with me just makes his leg ache. Good thing Adam was willing to fill your grandfather's dancing shoes."

"Always willing to save the day. That's Adam for you." Zak grinned.

Daphne's smile was wide before she tickled Tia's neck. "Come, darling, come show Grammy the Christmas tree in the living room. I spied it on our way into the kitchen, and it looks to have a bunch of gifts already beneath it." Daphne must have known Zak and Aurora needed a moment alone to regroup.

Tia nodded, oblivious to Daphne's true ploy, and led her great-grandmother into the other room.

Once they were alone, Zak stepped around the island and into Aurora's space. His hands fell to her hips. "I am so sorry."

She closed her eyes for a moment and shook her head, happy to have him touching her again. "It's okay. It's not like you planned any of this. And they're your family. People should be with family on Christmas. I'll understand if you'd like me to go."

Please don't make me go.

His eyes narrowed, and his brows pinched. "Why would you go? I invited you to join me for Christmas. I'm not going to rescind my invitation. That would make me a pretty terrible person, don't you think?"

Was he only keeping her around so he didn't look or feel bad?

His fingers on her hips tightened, and he tugged her against him and dipped his head until his mouth hovered just above hers, their bodies now touching, breaths mingling. "I want to spend Christmas with you. Is it going to happen the way I'd hoped? No. But the kids are okay with you staying in my room. My grandparents are two of the nicest and most accepting people in the entire world. You really have nothing to worry about."

Nothing to worry about.

Ha!

"I never intended for your kids to discover me," she whispered, her body betraying her mind as she melted into his muscular embrace. "I hid on the stairs when I heard the doorbell. Then when I realized it was your kids, I got dressed.

They found me. I honestly didn't tell them that I was your girlfriend."

Not that she was his girlfriend.

Erm. Awkward.

Had he noticed her slip?

He didn't seem to.

With worry rattling around in her belly like a stone in a jar, she continued. "I told them as little as humanly possible. I even told them that it wasn't my place to say whether they could have a cookie."

She felt his lips twitch as he tried to hold back a laugh.

Her bottom lip jutted out, and she exhaled. "It might just be easier if I go."

But I don't want to go.

He shook his head. "You're not allowed to leave. I won't let you. I'm your ride, remember, and I don't plan on driving anywhere for a while." The gleam in his diamond-blue eyes was practically diabolical. "Now, there'll be no more kitchen or living room sex, but I still have a fair few things that I'd like to do to you before I'm forced to take you home. Kids and grandparents across the hall be damned."

Kids and grandparents across the hall be damned.

Her knees were about to buckle.

Finally, she summoned the courage to wrap her arms around his neck. She needed to hold on to something.

"I like you, Aurora. And no, this is not how I would have introduced you to my kids, let alone this early. But it is what it is. So far they seem to like you."

"I like them too. Tia is such a sweetheart, and Aiden is a real charmer."

The pride that flashed behind his eyes was unmistakable.

"We'll take it slow," he said. "If the family stuff gets over-whelming, just say you have to check some work emails and duck upstairs for a bit. I already told my grandfather that you're this big powerful attorney, so they know that you're a busy person."

Big powerful attorney. Right.

That lie just kept coming back to haunt her, didn't it?

Well, it wasn't so much a lie, as she hadn't bothered to correct his assumption.

Was that still a lie?

You're a freaking lawyer! You know damn well it's a lie! A lie of omission. Dear God, how did you ever pass the bar? By the skin of your teeth and horseshoes up your ass, that's how.

His tongue darted out and ran along her bottom lip. "Say you'll stay," he whispered, pressing his pelvis against hers, letting her know just how much he wanted her to stay. "Don't let me wake up Christmas morning without you in the bed next to me. It's all I want for Christmas. Santa can leave me coal in my stocking as long as you're in my bed." He pulled away and tossed his head back, the back of his hand falling to his forehead as if he were some Southern belle on the verge of fainting. "I simply could not bear it if you left now. I must wake up with your lips around my cock come Christmas morning. 'Tis what I asked Santa for."

A big, ugly laugh flew from Aurora's mouth before she could stop it. She pushed out of his grasp and turned away, rolling her eyes as she continued to laugh.

"You'll stay for the jokes at the very least, right?" he asked, smiling like a gorgeous tattooed idiot as he drew her back into his embrace with his hands once again on her hips.

She exhaled, her eyes roaming across his much too handsome, much too chiseled face. "Do I really have a choice?"

Before she could blink, she was off her feet and dipped, her head just inches from the ground. "No, you really don't," he growled before taking her mouth ... and her heart.

ZAK WAS JUST as surprised with himself as Aurora seemed to be. He'd been on the fence about having her stay until he saw her with his family. Until he saw her with his children, with his grandparents and how right she looked standing in his kitchen, smiling and laughing and eating Christmas cookies.

She belonged there. She was meant to spend Christmas with him, to spend Christmas with them.

Noise on the stairs and around the corner in the living room had him breaking their kiss and standing the woman in his arms back up on her two feet. She wasn't wearing a bra, and he could feel her hard nipples poking out beneath his shirt.

"All set up in the guest room," Zak's grandfather, or Papa, said, stepping off the last of the stairs and entering the kitchen.

His limp appeared more severe than normal. Hopefully it was just a bit of temporary discomfort from all the sitting he'd done on the plane and on the drive from Vancouver.

"We moved the rest of Aurora's stuff to Zak's room," his grandfather went on. "Hope you don't mind?"

Aurora tucked a strand of hair behind her ear, her cheeks flushed, lips puffy. She shook her head. "No, thank you. I meant to do that, but I, uh ... "

"Unexpected guests threw you off your game," Zak's grandmother, or Grammy, finished, holding hands with Tia and reentering the kitchen.

Aurora's cheeks burned an even deeper shade of pink. "Something like that."

Aurora's phone buzzed in the pocket of her hoodie, and she pulled it out, glancing at it. Zak watched her, hoping that it wasn't the same person from earlier who had set her into a funk.

She made a face, one that he couldn't quite place but knew, beyond a shadow of a doubt, held no glee.

"Everything okay?" he asked, his hand landing on Aurora's back as he leaned in just slightly to see if he could get a peek at the screen.

She flinched beneath his touch, glancing up at him, her eyes going wide at the same time she angled the screen of the phone away from him. "It's fine. Just work stuff. Nothing that can't wait until the twenty-sixth, though." She scanned his face and the obvious shock. "But it's confidential, so ... " Her mouth thinned into a grim line as she glanced back at her phone before turning the screen to black and shoving it back into her pocket. "Sorry, it's just ... "

He rested his other hand on her arm. "No need to explain. Client-lawyer confidentiality. I get it. Say no more."

The nod of her head was tight and her smile small. "Something like that."

Zak studied her face for a moment. He wanted to pry more, find out what made her mood do such a complete one-eighty, but now was not the time or the place. Maybe she'd open up to him more when they were alone. Away from the prying eyes and ears of his children and grandparents.

"Dad, what's for dinner?" Aiden asked, breaking the tension that seemed to be bouncing back and forth between Aurora and Zak.

Aiden sidled up next to his grandfather, his eyes darting to the cookies on the counter.

"Yeah, I'm hungry," Tia added, her eyes also falling to the cookies.

"Well, it's not cookies," Zak said, his tone stern but his smile kind.

He and Aurora had only just eaten breakfast/brunch/lunch or whatever they were calling it just a few hours ago. He wasn't overly hungry. The clock on the stove said it was closing in on dinnertime soon.

He needed to come up with something to feed his family.

"Why don't I whip something up?" Aurora offered, slipping out of his grasp and wandering around to the other side of the island, her hand landing on the fridge handle.

Her sullen mood seemed to be fading. Maybe that message really had been a work thing and she was just trying to power down for a few days but found it difficult to truly shut out work.

He understood that all too well. The kids said he often lived on his phone or his laptop, and if he wasn't on one of his devices dealing with work, he was at the gym or talking about the gym and the business.

When it was your livelihood, your life and what the success of your family's survival was riding on, you did everything you could to make it flourish.

"You don't have to cook," Zak said. "You're my guest. I'm sure I can figure something out.

But she shook her head, a defiant twinkle emerging in her eyes. "You all go into the living room and chat. I'm guessing it's been a while since you've seen your grandparents. I insist." She pulled open the fridge door. "Fridge looks pretty stocked. I'm sure I can come up with something. Doesn't look to be enough of last night's dinner for everyone, but I'll figure something out."

She lifted her eyebrow at Zak as if to tell him to *git*, then she showed him her back and bent down to explore the fridge.

"I guess we have our orders," Papa said with a chuckle. "I like her."

"Me too," Tia added, following Papa and Aiden into the living room.

A warm hand landed on Zak's shoulder, and he turned to face his grandmother.

"She seems sweet," she said, dropping her voice down to just above a whisper. They continued to walk into the living room, so hopefully they were out of Aurora's earshot. "I'm guessing things between you two are still quite new, though."

That was the understatement of the century if there ever was one.

Zak nodded. "Yeah, it's pretty new."

"But you like her?"

He nodded again. "I do. She's a lawyer, high up in her law firm. Seems to have her head on straight. Knows what she wants in life. No head games ... from what I can tell."

From what I can tell of the last eighteen hours ...

"Where did you meet?"

They were standing next to the fireplace now. Zak's kids and grandfather were playing with the electric train set beneath the tree.

"At the gym. She's a member."

His grandmother's mouth twitched at the corner. "I thought you had a rule about that?"

Zak snorted. "Yeah, I thought so too."

She put her hand on his shoulder again, her smile warm —grandmotherly. "Some rules are made to be broken, sweetheart. I hope she makes you happy. You deserve to be happy. Why, you and your brother and the stress in your lives these last few years have really tested our blood pressures. We started talking with a Realtor about selling our place and moving out west. Help you and Adam with the kids, get your lives back on track."

Zak leaned down and pecked his grandmother on the cheek. "Thank you, Grammy. But Adam is doing great, as you know. He's with Violet. They're expecting. Paige is doing well with Mitch. Mira is healthy and happy."

"And you? You're happy now too?"

He nodded, leaning his hand on the mantle and glancing in the direction of the kitchen. "I'm getting there. The kids keep me grounded. They make me happy. And my business is booming. I think this year will definitely be better than last year. And most certainly better than the year before that."

She took his hand. "You need love too, Zachary."

He shifted his gaze down to his children and then back up toward the kitchen, a small smile catching on his lips. "I know, Grammy. And I think maybe now I'm ready to start looking for it."

———

"THIS IS AWESOME," Aiden said, using his finger to wipe up his plate. "Can we have veggie tacos every Christmas Eve?" He reached into the middle of the table and grabbed a cut-up piece of bell pepper. "And can we make more cookies tomorrow?"

"Yeah, can we make cookies tomorrow?" Tia chimed in, finishing her veggie taco as well.

"We'll see," Zak replied, finishing up his own taco.

"I agree," Papa added, "these tacos are delicious. Did you make the tortillas yourself?"

Aurora nodded, her body growing a touch warm from all the compliments being thrown at her. "Yeah, I couldn't find any wraps in the fridge or freezer, but making them yourself is easy enough. And Zak's pantry is like a grocery store, so it was easy to find beans and rice and corn. Didn't want to wait for ground meat to thaw out though."

"Nothing wrong with a vegetarian meal," Grammy said with a nod. "We should all eat less meat."

"Can I have more?" Tia asked. "I need healthy food after the crap we ate today."

Aurora grabbed her drinking glass and hid her face, struggling not to smile or laugh. She glanced up and noticed that Zak and his grandparents were looking for ways to stem their amusement as well.

"Absolutely you can have more, sweetie," Grammy piped up, the first to regain her composure. She grabbed another tortilla off the plate and passed it to Tia, then pushed all the taco fixings in Tia's direction. "Why don't you make your own?"

Tia nodded. "Okay, thanks."

"Well, I say we get an early night's sleep tonight," Papa said, leaning back in his chair and resting his hands on his belly. "We'll have a busy day ahead of us tomorrow. Need to shovel the driveway, bang the snow from the gutters, sweep it off the back steps. Then we need to watch Christmas movies, play board games and wait for Santa Claus."

Zak's mouth twisted. "You've got it all planned out, have you?"

Papa nodded. "I certainly do. Haven't spent Christmas Eve with my kiddos in a long time, need to make the most of it." He pushed himself up to standing with a groan that only made sense coming from a man of advanced age, then he took his plate and Grammy's plate to the dishwasher.

"And we can bake more cookies, too, right?" Tia asked. "To leave for Santa."

Zak and Aiden exchanged looks.

Zak's eyebrows lifted just slightly on his head. Aiden nodded.

Ah, okay. So Tia still believed in Santa; Aiden knew the truth. Good to know.

Aurora nodded. "I'm sure we can carve out some time for that. What do you guys usually eat on Christmas Eve?"

"Homemade pizza," Aiden said, standing up as well, taking his and then his father's plate to the dishwasher. Both he and his grandfather began to clear the table and clean up.

Such gentlemen. Such domestics.

"Yeah, we each get our own mini pizza to put whatever we want on it," Tia added. "Then we play board games. Then we each get to open one present, then we go to bed. Then Santa comes."

Aurora smiled, loving her enthusiasm and the childhood wonder that surrounded Christmas. "Sounds like quite the lovely tradition."

"And you get to be a part of it this year." Tia beamed. Then her face fell as if she'd just been informed of the true identity of Santa Claus. Her eyes shifted warily to her dad. She hopped off her chair and went to whisper in Zak's ear.

He listened intently, his brows furrowing, then lifting. All the while his blue eyes continued to sparkle beneath the ornate light hanging above the kitchen table. Finally, he patted Tia on the back and nodded. "We'll figure something out, sweetheart. Don't worry."

Tia didn't seem nearly as convinced, but she nodded anyway and then returned to her seat to finish building her taco.

Aurora squinted in query at Zak across the table, but he made the lip-zip motion with his thumb and finger, then dramatically tossed the pretend key behind his shoulder.

Aurora rolled her eyes.

"Well," Daphne said, stretching in her seat before pushing her chair away from the table and standing. "I think I might actually retire to our room. It was a long flight with many stopovers and then a white-knuckle drive across the border." She cupped Tia's head in her palms and planted a kiss on the little girl's wavy crown. "I'm probably going to have nightmares about all that plane turbulence going over the Rocky Mountains."

Tia grinned, chewing her taco. "You can come sleep in my bed if you're scared, Grammy. I don't mind."

Daphne chuckled, then kissed Tia again before releasing her head. "Thank you, my love. I just might take you up on that."

Daphne made her way around the table and rested her hand on Aurora's shoulder. "It's so nice to have you here, dear. I look forward to getting to know you better tomorrow. Sweet dreams." Then she did something rather unexpected, at least for Aurora. She cupped Aurora's head just like she had Tia's and kissed her crown, the same way she'd done to the little girl.

Aurora smiled, her cheeks flooding with heat. "And I you, Daphne."

Daphne's smile was wide and warm. "I'm off to bed, my loves." She turned to Sherman. "Try not to make too much noise when you come into the room, dear."

Sherman and Aiden had their heads together over the kitchen sink. He glanced over his shoulder. "Aiden and I are going to watch a movie, so I'll be a while."

"Night, Grammy," Aiden tossed over his shoulder before he went back to his task of drying dishes.

Daphne simply shook her head and smiled. "I swear that husband of mine turns into a child the moment he's around all the kids." Her green eyes grew soft, and she took a detour back around the table to stand next to Zak. "All the kids. Big and small." Then she patted his big tattooed arm, pecked him on the side of the head and retired to bed.

"Can I watch a movie too?" Tia asked as she licked taco sauce off her thumb and stood up to take her plate to the dishwasher.

"You're not going to like it," Aiden chimed in, intercepting his sister before she could open up the dishwasher. "It's scary."

"Then I don't think *either* of you should be watching it," Zak said, standing up to his full height and making his way behind the island. "Papa, what movie are you two planning to watch?"

Aurora loved watching Zak in his element with his grandparents and children. It was a whole other side to him, a whole other part of him that she was quickly falling hard for.

Sherman pulled the plug in the sink, set it on the back and then dried his hand on a dish towel. "We were going to watch *The Grinch,* but the one with Jim Carrey."

Aurora spun in her seat. That movie wasn't scary.

Zak's broad shoulders visibly relaxed. "Oh."

"But Tia is a scaredy-cat," Aiden said. "She freaked out during the lava scene in *Aladdin,* remember. She doesn't like scary stuff, and *The Grinch* can be a bit scary."

Zak stroked his beard. "T, what do you think?"

Tia planted her hands on her hips, her mouth in a deep frown and her eyes fierce. "I'm not a scaredy-cat. I want to watch it."

Aiden rolled his eyes. "Fine, but don't say I didn't warn you. When you come knocking on my door tonight asking to sleep in my trundle bed, I'm going to say *I told you so.*"

Tia huffed. "I won't be scared, I promise. And I'll stay in my own room."

Aiden wandered into the living room. "Yeah, we'll see about that."

Sherman and Tia followed Aiden into the living room, but Zak hung back with Aurora. She finally stood up. She hadn't even noticed, but someone had taken her plate away for her. The whole kitchen was clean and everything put away.

She liked the efficiency in this family. Everyone had a job; everyone pitched in.

Once they were alone, Zak wrapped an arm around her waist. "You feel like watching a movie?"

She shook her head and bit her lip. "Sure don't."

His smile made her nipples pebble beneath his T-shirt.

She still wasn't wearing a bra—or panties. Oh God, had

her headlights been blazing the entire time she sat across the table with Zak's grandparents and children? How mortifying.

"Thank you for being so cool about everything," he said, his hand traversing her butt, then pinching the bottom of her left cheek. "And for dinner. That was amazing. You really didn't have to do it, though."

She smiled up at him, turning so that she was now in his arms. Her new favorite place to be. "I was happy to do it. Thank you for allowing me to spend Christmas with your family. I really like them—all of them."

He dipped his head and brushed his lips over hers. It was a sweet kiss, a gentle kiss, unlike the majority of the kisses they'd shared so far, which had been lust-fueled and laden with deep-seated passion. But this kiss was no less earth-shattering. In fact, it was more. It was a kiss that spoke of his acceptance of her into his life, into the fold of his family. She wasn't an Eastwood or a Fraser, but she was welcomed into their world, even if just for a short while. She could already tell that Zak was heavily guarded and protective of his children, but that only made her love him even more. Because she did love him. She hadn't known him for long—only known of him, watched him, lusted after him—but she'd quickly fallen head over heels into a snowbank for the man as she observed him with his children, with his family and saw how fiercely loyal and protective he was of those he loved.

She wrapped her arms around his neck, pushed up on her tiptoes and kissed him back, mimicking the light brush of lips against lips that he'd given her. Her tongue darted out and caressed his bottom lip, tasting him and his beer from dinner.

Her phone vibrated in her hoodie pocket.

Pressley was getting insistent. He was getting demanding.

Why couldn't he just leave her alone? Let her spend her Christmas in peace.

"You want to get that?" Zak asked, pulling away from her slightly, his eyebrows lifting up on his head just a fraction.

Swallowing, she nodded, reached into her pocket and brought out her phone.

The bubble message on her home screen.

When I can see you? When can I come by?

She shut her eyes, then turned the screen back to black and shoved the phone back into her hoodie pocket, flashing as big a smile as she could muster at a curious-faced Zak. "Let's go watch the movie," she whispered. Then she dropped her hand to his and led him into the living room. "It's Christmas. You need to spend time with your children."

He squeezed her hand back, pulled her back against his chest and dipped his mouth next to her ear. "You're incredible, you know that? I don't care what *your* rules are. *My* rules are no pajamas, and I expect you to obey. I want to be able to dip my head between your legs at any point in the middle of the night and have zero obstacles." Then he nipped the shell of her ear and pinched her butt with his free hand.

Aurora's heart beat rapidly inside her chest, and her nipples now ached from how hard they were. She released his hand and wiped her sweaty palms on her pants. The man was going to turn her into a puddle right in front of his family. She craned her neck around and grinned at Zak behind her, her smile now wide and real because he made it so easy for her to be happy.

"Did Dad tell a funny joke?" Tia asked, all curled up in a blanket on the couch next to Sherman.

Aurora swallowed, then took a seat in the big chair, her whole body warmer than the pavement in the peak of summer. She nodded and smiled. "Something like that."

Tia pulled up her blanket. "Come sit with me. There's

plenty of room." She nodded her head in encouragement. "Dad, you sit in the chair. I want Aurora to sit with me."

Zak grinned, taking Aurora's place in the chair as she made her way around the coffee table to sit next to Tia. Tia draped the blanket over Aurora's legs and snuggled in next to her.

"I like this," the little girl said, yawning.

Zak's eyes met Aurora's over the top of his daughter's head. Fire burned behind the dark, intense blue.

Aurora swallowed again, certain that Tia could hear her wildly beating heart.

Yeah, she liked this too.

11

IT WAS ROUGHLY four o'clock on Christmas Eve, and Aurora was rummaging through Zak's closet.

Because he'd told her to go and grab one of his shirts—not because she was taking her stalking to the next level and searching for stray strands of his hair so she could slowly fashion her own Zak doll. No, that wasn't it.

But that was a very specific thought.

She'd put on a load of laundry, so she needed something warm to change into before a rigorous night of pizza-making and board games. Zak had whisked her downstairs after she'd made cookies with Tia and Aiden, and the two of them did a little sex workout, starting with his head between her legs as she did sit-ups. All to the most heinous rap blasting from the high-end sound system he had hooked up.

Best. Workout. Ever.

She'd never done more crunches or orgasmed as she did crunches before in her life.

There was no going back now.

She'd never be able to do a normal sit-up again.

Zak was ruining her—but in the absolute best possible way.

Sweaty from their workout-sex-out, she left her dirty, dirty personal trainer downstairs with his kids and grandparents and she hopped in the shower.

Only she wasn't alone for long.

Best. Christmas. Ever.

Their shower was *extra* long. She was sure Zak's grandparents knew exactly what they were up to, so she was doing her best to take her time before she headed back downstairs. Which was why she was deep into Zak's walk-in closet, rummaging through his shirts and letting his manly smell wash over her.

She found a lovely plaid pattern and pulled it off the hanger, expecting it to be a nice cozy shirt she could toss over another one of Zak's tank tops and stay warm in.

It was no shirt though.

It was a kilt.

A kilt.

Her mouth flooded with moisture, as did the fresh pair of Zak's boxers she was wearing.

"Whatcha got my kilt out for?" Zak asked, wandering into the closet behind her, a towel slung sexily around his shoulder and *nothing* around his waist. He claimed his beard needed a trim, so he'd hung back in the bathroom to tidy up his scruff.

She thought he looked delicious no matter the length of his beard. It certainly felt amazing against her inner thighs and *other* places.

Aurora licked her lips. "You. Have. A. Kilt?"

He nodded, grabbing a pair of jeans from one of his closet drawers. "Sure do, darlin'. I'm half Fraser, after all. Papa came over to America when he was twelve, but the man was born in Sterling. Still has family there."

Her nipples tightened to painfully hard points beneath her bra. "But why do *you* have a kilt?"

With the carefree gait of a man who knew he was sex on a candy cane any red-blooded woman within a hundred miles would want to lick until she was in a sugar coma, he headed to his other dresser in the bedroom and pulled out a pair of boxers. He tucked his fine ass into the briefs. "Because back when I was in high school, Papa and Granny took Adam and I back to Scotland for a few weeks. There was a big family wedding. We met all our kin, or *clan* Fraser, if you will. We got the family tartan, ate haggis. You know, the usual." He slipped his toned legs into his jeans.

"Did you wear it?" she asked, following him out into the bedroom, her fantasies cannoning around inside her head like a kaleidoscope of butterflies suddenly tossed from a tree into the wind. They were all madly flapping their wings. They were all looking for purchase.

But *this* fantasy, this butterfly needed to happen. This butterfly needed to rest its tired wings and take a break. On a kilt!

"You okay?" he asked, pulling a tight black T-shirt over his frame, showcasing his tattoos and *well*-defined pecs. He stalked toward her, a knowing smirk now on his oh-so-talented mouth. "You one of those *Outlander* lovers? Got a penchant for redheads in kilts there, *lassie?*"

He stood mere inches in front of her, gently pried the kilt from her hands and held it up against his waist. "I reckon it probably still fits." He was bouncing between accents. One minute he was laying on that Southern charm; the next he was hitting the brogue hard. Her nipples and brain didn't know what do to. But what they did know was that they liked it all.

"Should I try it on later? See if it fits," he asked, his accent sliding back into a sexy brogue.

Oh lord, yes, please say it still fits.

Unless, of course, it was just too short ... nothing wrong with that. Absolutely nothing.

"Get dressed and head on downstairs, Rory." The deep command in his voice made her knees wobble. His Southern twang was back, and he sounded like a cowboy ready to ride the range.

The range being her!

He pushed past her and headed back into the closet, coming out seconds later with a pair of his sweat pants, a plaid shirt and a tank top. "Put these on and then head downstairs. I'll join you in a moment."

She nodded, taking the clothes from him.

He didn't smile but simply said, "Good girl." Which made her nearly come on the spot. He took the kilt back into the closet and didn't return before she'd gotten herself dressed, having to cinch the drawstring on the sweatpants super-tight around her waist. They were also crazy long on her. She looked ridiculous.

Rolling her eyes at her bag-lady appearance, she headed downstairs, her body still on fire from the thought of him in a kilt, from his rough demand and the way he called her a *good girl*. Was she going to get to see him in a kilt later, or would she be forced to shut her eyes during sex and simply pretend he was wearing one? She could do that. She would do that. But she'd much prefer the real deal. Because the real deal was perfection.

BACK AT THE TABLE, with personal pizzas half eaten and the game of Candy Land sitting in the center, everyone drank wine, sparkling flavored water and beer and laughed until their sides hurt.

It was one of the most wonderful Christmas Eves Aurora had had in a long time. It reminded her of when she and Brecken were small, her parents had been healthy and working and things in life were good. Things in life made sense.

Every Christmas Eve in the Stratford house, she and Brecken would spend the afternoon with their dad handing out socks, sandwiches and blankets to the homeless while their mom prepared her famous Stratford family nachos and wrapped presents. Then they'd all sit down on the living room floor, spread a blanket out and have a "picnic" indoors while they watched old Christmas movie classics like *A Christmas Story* and *It's a Wonderful Life*. Then Brecken would put the porcelain baby Jesus figurine in the manger—not that they were religious, they just had a nativity scene they put out —and Aurora would place the angel atop the tree, and they'd go to bed.

It was one of the days she'd most looked forward to each year because her family was together—which wasn't very often, given how much both her parents had to work. Her mother had been a hospice nurse but primarily worked nights, and her father had been a heavy-duty mechanic for a construction company, but the company had fallen on hard times during the recession, and he'd lost his job.

Despite his education and experience, he struggled to find work and ended up taking odd jobs until he landed a truck-driving gig, hauling milk products up and down the Eastern seaboard.

Then he was rarely home.

The last great Christmas she could remember when they'd picnicked in the living room had been when she was about thirteen. Brecken was sixteen, and their father had just lost his job, but her parents had decided to wait until after Christmas to tell their children. She remembered her dad's sad eyes, the looks of worry that passed back and forth between her parents as they tried to smile and laugh through it all. She knew something was up—Brecken did too—but even then, her parents had put on big smiles and given Aurora and her brother a wonderful Christmas to remember.

A hand squeezed hers beneath the table, drawing her out of her thoughts.

"You okay?" Zak asked, his eyes dark with worry. "You looked about a million miles away."

Nope. Just seventeen years in the past and three thousand miles away.

She shook her head and grinned a big cheesy grin. "I'm right here. Exactly where I want to be."

"What are your parents up to this holiday season?" Sherman asked, taking a bite of his pizza. "Are they here in Seattle?"

Aurora shook her head. "No. They're back in New Hampshire, which is where I'm from."

He nodded. "Lovely state."

"I think so."

"What are they doing for Christmas? They didn't want to come out and visit you?" He continued to munch on his pizza, washing it down with a sip of beer.

They can barely afford electricity right now. A flight was out of the question.

"They wanted to, but it's not really in the cards right now. My dad suffered a heart attack earlier this year, so he's not feeling too hot. Lots of doctors' appointments and medications. It's also only our second Christmas without my brother, so ... " She swallowed past the hard lump in her throat, averting her eyes away from the people staring back at her with curious expressions on their faces.

"We lost a child too," Daphne said quietly. "Just because Laura's been gone for thirty-one years doesn't mean the holidays aren't the hardest times of all. Christmas was her absolute favorite time of the year." She dabbed at the corners of her eyes with her napkin. "Became a little girl on Christmas morning, bouncing around, unable to contain her excitement."

Zak made an unidentifiable noise in his throat and awkwardly shifted in his seat next to her. Did he remember much about his mother? He'd been so young when his parents passed away.

Aurora's smile was small. She also wasn't ready to lift her head. "Brecken's death was really hard on them—was hard on all of us. I know I should be home with them for Christmas this year, but we just can't afford it. Not with my dad's medical bills now and my student loan debt."

Sherman groaned, which caused her to finally lift her head. "I'm truly sorry, Aurora. That's never easy. Why, if I didn't have a decent pension or medical plan, my insulin would have put us in the poorhouse long ago."

"We'd never let that happen," Zak said, his voice deep and slightly strained. His hand landed on Aurora's thigh beneath the table and gave her knee a gentle squeeze.

"How did your brother die?" Tia asked.

"T, we don't ask that," Zak quickly said, squeezing Aurora's knee once again.

"But Dad, I—"

"It's okay," Aurora said, her throat now feeling tighter than ever. "He was sick, and he didn't think there was any other way to get better, so he made a very difficult decision to end his life."

Did the kids know about suicide? Was she overstepping explaining such a thing to Zak's kids? Her head hurt.

Daphne gasped and crossed herself.

Zak squeezed her knee again.

"I'm sorry," Tia whispered. She turned to face Aiden, her

face a mix of sadness and conviction. "As much as you bug me sometimes, don't you dare do that."

Hot tears stung the corners of Aurora's eyes, her emotions forcing her to once again turn away, focusing on the fridge magnets across the room.

She could see out of the corner of her eye Aiden's reaction though. His eyes went wide, his mouth open like a guppy. But after a moment, he closed his mouth and nodded once. "I won't."

Sherman cleared his throat. "Well, we're so happy you could join us for Christmas this year, Aurora. And I hope that kind people invite your parents over for turkey dinner so that they're not all alone."

Aurora hoped so too.

"We'll have to make a point of getting them out this way next year, though," Sherman went on. "Could even road trip out here with us. We've got a motorhome. Could make it a real *old coot* party." He moved his board game piece up to a Licorice Space, where he was now forced to lose a turn. "Have a big family shindig once we all get here. Lord knows, Zak's got the space." He slapped his grandson on the shoulder, taking hold and giving Zak a loving shake. "Couldn't be prouder of you, son. You've built yourself quite the empire."

Zak's cheeks burned a sexy red. "Trying to, Papa. Not there quite yet. Need to expand into more states before I can consider it an empire. Right now, it's just a city domination. We need to take Club Z statewide, then national, then international." He took a bite of his pizza, his grin wide and boyish.

Aurora was happy for the change of topic. She hadn't been prepared to share so much about her family, and yet, now that she had, her heart felt just a touch lighter. She moved her gaze from the fridge back to the board game. A hand beneath the table linked with hers. She was sitting next to Tia.

The little girl gave her a small smile and squeezed her hand. "I'm happy you're here with us," she said softly. "I am really sorry about your brother and your dad."

Aurora's lip wobbled, and fresh tears welled up in her eyes. She squeezed Tia's hand back. Could these children get any more amazing?

Was it too late to write her wish list to Santa Claus? Because at the very top of that list would be being a part of these kids' lives. They were truly wonderful little human beings.

"Thank you," Aurora managed to say. "Just like yours, Brecken was a really terrific big brother."

Tia smiled at her. Their hands remained linked beneath the table, and even more of the pain that had been sitting like an elephant on Aurora's chest for so long finally began to slip away.

"I'm pleased to see that the snow finally ebbed," Daphne said. "And that the plows came through. The children and I had quite a nice time outside building a snowman this afternoon, but there comes a point where enough is enough." Her green eyes went a touch buggy. "I mean it was nearly up to poor Tia's navel. Girl could hardly move."

"Yeah, but it was fun, Granny," Tia said, smiling. "I could flop right back into the snow and almost disappear."

They continued to laugh and play, eat and drink, when the doorbell interrupted Zak's victory dance over his epic Candy Land win.

He stood up from the table and checked his phone. "Why do I think that seven o'clock is late?" he asked, making a face of disbelief. "I was about to ask who was here at this hour. I'm turning into an old coot." He made his way to the door.

"Plenty of room at the old coot table, son," Sherman called behind him. "Lots of fresh prune juice too."

Aurora snorted a laugh. She really liked everyone in Zak's family, but Sherman was a real character through and through.

The rest of them around the table went quiet as they heard Zak open the front door. Eyes of curiosity darted from person to person.

Who was at the door?

Was it Zak's ex and that Craig guy?

Voices Aurora didn't recognize besides Zak's drifted into the kitchen. She heard the front door close, and Zak appeared moments later, a gaggle of men, women and children in his wake.

Aurora counted two men, both tall and handsome, one another redhead like Zak, the other tall with dark hair and dark green eyes.

The women looked like they could be sisters with the same dark hair and blue eyes as well. One woman had a baby on her hip, while the other had a little boy of about five by the hand.

The longer she studied all of them, the more she realized she recognized them. Particularly the taller man with red hair. It was Dina's brother, Aaron.

All four of these people had been at Dina's service.

Heat pooled in her belly and began to bubble up, unease taking over.

Would they recognize her? Would they start to ask questions about her, about how she knew Dina? Would they blow her cover? Tell Zak that she wasn't the powerful fourth-year associate with the fancy corner office he thought she was?

Tia and Aiden both leapt off their seats, distracting her.

"Gabe!" Tia cheered, approaching the little boy. "Can I have a Christmas hug, buddy?"

The little boy nodded, his smile wide and infectious before he released the woman's hand and threw his arms around Tia. Even though she wasn't much bigger than him, she picked him up anyway, causing them both to start laughing.

"Mark, Aaron, Tori and Iz popped by for a quick visit," Zak said, his face more relaxed than Aurora had seen in a while.

Daphne's eyes went wide. "Is that a baby? Can I hold her? I haven't had a baby in my arms since Tia." She stood and rushed the woman carrying the baby. "May I?"

The woman laughed, passing off said baby. "Of course. Sophie isn't stranger-shy yet. She just woke up, so she should be in a good mood."

Sophie.

Why did that baby's name sound so familiar?

Wait, did Dina's brother get custody of her baby when she died? That must have been it. Sophie was Dina's daughter, and now Aaron had gone from uncle to father literally at the speed of a bullet.

Tia, Aiden and Gabe had already disappeared into the living room, the sound of the train starting up drifting around the corner, while Aurora and Sherman still sat at the table, staring at the newcomers.

Still beaming, Zak proceeded with the introductions.

"Papa, Aurora, these are my friends Mark and Aaron. Mark is dating Tori." He gestured to the slightly taller of the two women who had come in holding Gabe's hand. "And Aaron is with Isobel. Tori and Isobel are also sisters."

She knew it. They looked far too much alike to not be related somehow.

She held her breath, waiting for them to recognize her.

But there was no pique to any of their eyes as they smiled and said *hello* to her. Maybe a small pause on Aaron's end, but nothing that said they would all blow her cover any time soon.

"Just doing the rounds now that the streets are plowed and the clouds have taken a break. Had to pop into the hospital quick to play Santa in the children's ward, decided to make a family affair of it. Now we've just been stopping in to say *hi* to a few of our nearest and dearest," the man who'd been introduced as Mark said. "Thought Zak was all by himself, but it looks like you guys are having quite the rager. Pizza *and* Candy Land." He shook his head. "Take it easy, man."

Zak snickered. "Let's go sit in the living room. I'll grab some drinks."

Aaron, who seemed to be a quiet beast with piercing blue eyes and a dangerous aura hanging around him, hadn't taken his gaze off Daphne with Sophie. A protective father if ever there was one. Isobel rested her hand on his chest and said something quietly to him. He made a face of protest, but then his eyes softened slightly and he turned and left.

Aurora finally stood when she saw the two sisters approach her, both of them wearing matching, knowing grins.

"We had no idea Zak was seeing anybody," Isobel said. "How long have you two been together?"

Was forty-eight hours the correct response?

Aurora wandered around the island, grabbed two more wineglasses down from the cupboard and twisted off the cap of the wine bottle. She paused, waiting for the women to nod. They both did with enthusiasm.

"It's quite new then?" Tori said, a teasing smile causing the corners of her eyes to crinkle. "Been there."

"Me too," Isobel said with a snort. She and Tori both accepted their wineglasses. "To shtupping the boss," she said, clinking her glass with her sister.

"Hear, hear," Tori said with a chuckle.

"They were your bosses?" Aurora asked, nearly choking on her wine.

Both women nodded.

"I was Gabe's therapist when Mark and I started sleeping together. Iz was Aaron's nanny. Do you work for Zak?"

Aurora shook her head. "No. I, uh ... I go to one of his gyms. We met there."

"Saw him in a tank top with all those tattoos and rippling muscles and you forgot your own name, right?" Isobel asked. "Been there."

Aurora's eyes went wide. Been there, as in she'd been *there* with Zak?

She must have read Aurora's mind. "I mean the man is fine, and when you see those muscles, your ovaries explode. But Zak and I have never been anything more than friends. Have you seen the sexy redhead I showed up with? I got my own Highland warrior to ride." She tossed her head back and laughed. "Though the look in your eyes said you were ready to take me to the mat and fight for him. Girl, you got it bad."

Aurora hid her face in her wineglass.

No shit.

Aurora had it the absolute worst.

"I'm still here, you know?"

Tori and Isobel spun around, and Aurora's head jerked to the left. Daphne was sitting next to the window in a high-back chair, quietly playing with a smiling Sophie. The woman was a phantom. How had they not noticed her?

"Shit," Tori murmured.

"Whoops," Isobel said.

Aurora's face was on fire.

"Sorry," Tori said with a giggle to her voice. "You do have one very hunky grandson though. You can't argue with that."

Daphne stood up, adjusting Sophie on her shoulder. "I

won't argue with that." She grabbed her wineglass off the table, set it on the counter and lifted her eyebrow at Aurora. "Fill me up, please, dear."

Tori and Isobel both snorted.

Aurora did as she was told, draining the bottle into the glass.

"I believe there is another bottle of the same to the left of the pantry," Daphne said, adjusting Sophie in her arms once again before she picked up her wineglass. "Have fun, ladies." Then she took the baby and her wine to the living room, where male voices dominated the air, punctuated once in a while by the *woo-woo* of the electric train.

Once they knew Daphne was around the corner, Tori, Isobel and Aurora all began to laugh.

"Whoops!" Isobel said, taking a sip of her wine. "Good thing I didn't say anything *too* embarrassing, like how Aaron has the sexual appetite of a submariner finally on the surface after a year at sea. Even the Energizer Bunny takes a break once in a while. But not my SEAL. He just keeps going and going and going and going ... "

Tori's lips twitched. "I'm sure Zak's grandmother has heard it all." She leaned on the kitchen counter, grabbed a piece of pizza off the pan and took a bite. "What's your story, Aurora? How long *have* you and Zak been *working out* together?"

Isobel's eyebrows bobbed as she grabbed her own slice of pizza and leaned on the counter next to her sister. "Yeah, woman. Dish. And don't leave out *any* details."

12

ZAK HADN'T BEEN EXPECTING company for Christmas Eve, let alone a houseful.

But he loved it.

First Aurora, then his kids, then his grandparents, and now finally his not-so-single-anymore single dad friends.

He grabbed Mark and Aaron's empty beer bottles off the coffee table and headed into the kitchen, resting his hand affectionately on Aurora's knee as he passed her where she sat on the couch chatting animatedly with Tori and Isobel.

He couldn't have asked for two nicer women to show up at his front door and befriend Aurora. Mark and Aaron had lucked out by landing the Jones sisters. Any man would be lucky to have either woman in his life, house or bed.

Zak pulled open the fridge to check to see if he needed to restock it from the beer fridge in the garage. There were four left. He grabbed them all, then shut the refrigerator door.

"She's cute," Mark said, entering the kitchen and grabbing a slice of pizza off the counter. Aaron was right behind him. "Where'd you meet her?"

"Gym," Zak said, passing his buddy another cold one. "Went against my own rules."

Aaron's dark red eyebrows drew down into a tight V as he accepted his beer from Zak. "Didn't we all?" He used his teeth to pop the cap; meanwhile, Mark used the bottle opener on the counter like a civilized human.

Aaron was a bit of an odd duck.

"I mean, Mark screwed his kid's therapist. I started banging my nanny. And now you're giving it to a client." Aaron took a swig of his beer.

"Member," Zak corrected. "And it wasn't like I pursued her. Her car died the other night during the start of the snowstorm. She lives across town in Greenwood, and I wasn't about to get myself caught in that shit if I didn't have to. Offered her the spare room and then ... " He shrugged and lifted his hands up in a *I don't know* gesture.

"She seems good with the kids," Mark added. "Early to introduce her to them though." He snorted as he tipped his beer to his lips. "I'm one to talk though, I guess. Seems like none of us are really doing this whole reentering the dating world in an orthodox way."

"That's because the dating scene is fucked up now," Aaron added. "I much prefer how I did it. Didn't have to put on airs. Iz has seen me at my fucking worst and the woman still loves me—God only knows why."

Both Mark and Zak bobbed their heads in agreement.

Aaron was a retired Navy SEAL who now ran his own construction company. His sister had died a month after her daughter Sophie was born, leaving Aaron to raise his niece all alone. Until he found Isobel, that is. Nanny of the millennium. The woman had saved his ass—and his soul, then finally his heart. And now they were raising Sophie together. It'd taken Aaron a while to dig himself out of his well of grief though. And understandably so. If Zak lost

Adam the way Aaron lost Dina, Zak would be a fucking wreck too.

"She looks familiar," Aaron said, scratching the back of his neck. "I can't put my finger on how, but she does."

Zak lifted a shoulder. "She's a lawyer. Maybe Dina knew her?"

Aaron's jaw grew tight, but he nodded. "Maybe. She might have been at the service. The place was packed to the rafters with lawyers that day."

"It was packed to the rafters with people who loved Dina and love you and Sophie," Mark corrected.

Aaron made a noise in his throat, took a sip of his beer and turned his face away from the other two men. "Anyway." He cleared his throat again, still not bothering to look at them. "Should probably get going soon. Would prefer Soph not to fall asleep in the truck, otherwise she'll be up for a few hours and, well ... " He drew his eyes back up to the other men, color staining his cheeks from the earlier mention of his sister.

"Santa wants to come down the chimney?" Mark asked with a wicked laugh, draining his beer and setting the empty bottle on the counter.

Aaron nodded. "You know it."

Zak rolled his eyes and shook his head. "Glad I'm past the baby stage. Kids are fucking cock-blockers at any age as long as they're under your roof, but it does get better as they get older."

"Fucking hope so," Aaron mumbled, finishing his own beer and setting it down next to Mark's.

"And here your brother is headed right back down that rabbit hole," Mark said. "Poor Adam," he mocked.

Zak guzzled his own beer. "Yeah, he and Vi are still a bit shell-shocked, but I think they're finally coming around to the idea of a baby."

Aaron scratched the back of his neck. "Not a lot of sleep ... or sex, but I will say it's a fun time too."

Zak's head reared back from Aaron's words. The man was not known for having a softer side. At least not when around the other single dads. He had a hard shell and had been tough to get to know.

The man rolled his eyes, dismissing Zak's reaction. "You know what I mean. Babies *can* be fun. Until they start crying or shit on you."

There he was.

"Tori wants to start talking about babies," Mark said, reluctance not only in his tone but also painted clear across his face. "I'm not ready to jump down that rabbit hole yet. I'm happy just doing what rabbits do best—but outside the hole." His brows dropped and his mouth pursed, his face taking on a confused expression. "You know what I mean. In the hole ... her hole, but not down the rabbit—"

"Yeah, yeah, we get it," Aaron said. "I'm going to go get Iz, let her know we should hit the road." Then the tight-lipped SEAL lumbered his big frame off toward the living room.

"Are you going to keep seeing her?" Mark asked, bringing their conversation full circle and back to Aurora. "I mean if the weather is your main problem right now, the roads are clear. We could take her home tonight."

Zak could tell that his friend was testing him. The glint in Mark's eyes and the way the corner of his mouth ticked said he was making the offer of getting rid of Aurora to see how far gone Zak really was.

Oh, he was so fucking far gone.

Zak shook his head, making sure to keep his voice neutral. "Naw, man, she can stay. Would disappoint the kids to send her home now. Besides, Tia made her a Christmas present this afternoon. Kid was pretty upset when she realized Aurora was going to wake up tomorrow morning and not have anything to open."

"Did you get her anything?" Mark asked.

Zak's lips twisted. He had a *gift* in mind, though Aurora would be "opening" it tonight once they were in his room and the door was closed—and locked. He took another sip of his beer.

"Your dick in a box doesn't count." Mark rolled his eyes. "Believe me, I asked Tori if she would accept that as a gift from me, and she told me she'd rather just unwrap a bag of baby carrots. Said it'd pretty much be the same thing, but at least the carrots tasted good dipped in ranch."

Zak choked on the beer in his mouth, half of it spitting out and the other half making him cough.

That Tori was a real ball-buster.

"That's my woman," Mark said sarcastically.

"What about me?" Tori emerged from around the corner and wrapped her arm around Mark's waist. "Speaking my praises, are you?"

Mark wrapped his arm around her and pecked her on the side of the head. "But of course, my love."

Tori was all smiles. "Thanks for the wine, Zak. We approve of Aurora." Her blue eyes narrowed. "Don't fuck it up."

Zak reared back. "What makes you think—"

"Just listen to the woman," Isobel said, coming to stand next to her sister. Aaron was right behind her with a drowsy-looking Sophie on his shoulder.

"Uh-oh, man," Mark said. "Better get that baby home if Santa wants to fulfill his mission down the chimney. She looks sleepy."

Aaron grumbled and gently patted Sophie on her round, chubby cheek. "Wake up, baby."

Tia, Aiden and Gabe rounded the corner, all of them

yawning. The grandparents and Aurora were right behind them, all yawning as well.

"Looks like everyone is ready for bed," Tori said, joining in on the communal yawn. "Need to get to sleep, that way Santa can come." Gabe slid his hand into hers and leaned his head against her hip. She glanced down at him. "You excited for Santa?"

The little boy seemed too exhausted to do anything but blink and nod.

"All right." Mark pulled his arm out from behind Tori and clapped his hands. "And we're going to head out. Thanks for the drinks, man. Merry Christmas, everyone, and we shall see you all in a few days." He nodded at Zak. "Poker next Saturday?"

Zak nodded. "Of course. Adam and Mitch will be back by then too. Should be a full group."

Mark grinned. "Good. I'm feeling fleeced after this holiday and all the gift buying. Could use a win."

Aaron snorted as he led the group to the front door. "Says Mr. Moneybags."

"That's *Dr.* Moneybags," Mark corrected.

There were hugs all around, including Tori and Isobel with Aurora. Then they wished their guests a final goodnight and a Merry Christmas and shut the door.

Zak clapped his hands loudly. "All right." He glanced at his watch. It was nearly ten thirty. No wonder the kids looked so exhausted. "Tia—angel on the tree. Aiden—baby in the manger. Papa and Granny—get your old coot butts to bed. Aurora—" His tone softened, as did his eyes. "Would you mind helping me tidy up?"

Her smile warmed him from head to toe.

"I would be happy to," she said, playing with Tia's hair as she walked behind Zak's daughter toward the living room.

"But first she needs to help me put the angel on the tree," Tia said.

Zak nearly tripped and fell into his grandfather.

Tia had asked Aurora to help her with her angel?

Tia had never asked anybody to *ever* help her. It was Tia's thing. Had always been Tia's thing. She wouldn't even let Zak lift her up. The stubborn little monkey required a ladder or for the tree to be angled down far enough to her small stature on the floor.

Zak had to see this for himself.

They all headed into the living room, where Tia's angel lay in her box beneath the tree. His daughter knelt down and pulled the box to her, then she motioned for Aurora to kneel down next to her. She slid the box over to Aurora. "You can open it," Tia offered.

Gently, as if unwrapping not just a porcelain-faced doll that sat on the top of a tree, but a doll made of fragile crystal, Aurora lifted the lid. Tears welled up at the corners of her eyes and her jaw appeared clenched as if she were trying to keep more emotions from surging forward.

"This was our family tradition too," she whispered. "I put the angel on the tree. My ... " She swallowed. "My brother put baby Jesus in the manger." She lifted her gaze up to Tia's. "I had no idea other families did the same thing."

Zak could feel Aurora's pain through the air. She'd been vague about her brother's passing, obviously for the sake of Zak's kids—which he appreciated—but he wanted to know more.

He wanted to know everything.

He had so many questions for the woman he was falling for, and yet he wasn't sure she'd open up to him about any of them. She didn't seem like she wanted him to get to know her, didn't seem like she wanted to lay it all out like he had.

Was that dishonesty or self-preservation?

Was this just a fling to her, and she didn't get attached or open up to flings?

You're reading into this shit too much. Chill out. It's been two days.

"You can take her out of the box," Tia encouraged. "You won't hurt her."

With a stiff, forced smile and a nod, Aurora lifted the beautiful little doll out of the box. "She's lovely. Where did you get her?"

"She was a gift from my dad for my first Christmas."

Aurora ran her hand lightly over the doll's hair. "That's a really special present. And I can see you take great care of her, so you must really love her."

Tia gently asked for the doll back and clutched her to her chest. "I do love her." Her eyes traveled the length of the tree. "She only comes out once a year, but for that little bit of time, she makes the whole house feel more special."

Aurora's smile was a touch wider and seemed to be making its way to her eyes. "I bet she does. I can already feel her Christmas magic working."

Tia's eyes sparkled as she continued to stare up at the top of the tree. "Yeah," she said on a slow breath. She turned back to face Aurora. "You can put her on the top this year if you like. If it's your family tradition too and you don't get to do it this year with your own angel, you can use mine."

Aurora shook her head and held her hands out in protest. "Oh, no, no, no. I couldn't. That's your tradition. She's your doll. Thank you for the offer, sweetheart, but I can't take that away from you." She glanced behind her at Zak, who was standing behind them watching it all, watching in awe as his daughter embraced Aurora like she'd never embraced anyone in her life.

Tia craned around, and her eyes fell on Zak. "Dad, can you lift me up, please?" She stood up and stepped toward her father. Still surprised by his little girl's complete one-eighty, he gently placed his hands on her waist. "Not yet, though, mmkay?"

Aurora was still sitting in front of the tree, her brown eyes full of curiosity. Zak probably looked the exact same way. He glanced around at his grandparents and son. They, too, seemed eager to know what Tia had up her sleeve.

"Aurora," Tia started, "if Dad says it's okay, you can stand on the arm of that chair, and we can put the angel on top of the tree together." She turned around to face Zak. "Can she, Dad? Can she stand on the arm of the chair just this one time?"

Zak's eyes softened as he stared down into the eyes of his daughter, a hopeless romantic, a pure optimist and an absolutely wonderful person. "Sure, sweetheart, just this once."

Tia's smile pulled at every single string in his heart. Her head spun around to face Aurora, and she held out her hand to help the woman up. "Come on. Dad said you can."

Aurora took her hand and stood, then she gingerly stepped up onto the chair cushion and then finally on to the wide arm. It would easily hold her weight—that wasn't why the kids weren't allowed to climb on it. Zak just liked his kids and his furniture in one piece, and it was easier to make them horse around outside or downstairs in the gym on the mats than in his expensively furnished living room.

"Up please, Dad," Tia commanded, jumping a little to help Zak with the takeoff, not that he needed her to. His child weighed less than half of what he deadlifted.

He lifted her up until she was able to reach the top of the tree, then he skirted around so that Aurora could hold on to the doll as well. Then the two of them carefully, placed Tia's porcelain Christmas angel atop the tree—both of them smiling and giggling as they did.

"Now the tree looks perfect," Daphne said. "I'll get the lights so we can see it in all its glory."

Once the angel was secure, Zak brought Tia back down to her feet, then he held out a hand for Aurora to step down off the chair at the same time the living room went dark. The Christmas tree shone like a bright beacon before them, with tiny rainbow lights, popcorn garland, ornaments the children made and Tia's angel.

It was the perfect tree.

He felt a small body lean against his leg, and he wrapped his arm around Tia, stroking the length of her hair down her back. "Great job, kiddo," he said.

"Thanks, Dad," Tia said with a yawn. "Now Aurora's officially part of the family. It's not just *my* tradition anymore, it's *ours*."

13

AURORA GRABBED the empty wineglasses off the kitchen table and brought them over to the dishwasher. After the emotional moment in the living room when Tia had asked Aurora for her help putting the angel on the tree, they'd all watched Aiden put the baby Jesus figure in the manger—Aurora's eyes once again wet and her heart heavy as she thought of Brecken—and then everybody but Aurora and Zak went to bed. Tears had pricked Aurora's eyes at Tia's heartfelt words, the way she'd welcomed Aurora into their family with open arms and a beautiful smile.

It made her miss her own family and their traditions more, but it also eased the ache inside her chest at how much this new family embraced her.

"I'm going to go and grab all the Christmas presents in the garage," Zak said, having tidied up the board games and helped her put away the leftover pizza. "I didn't think I'd have to bring the gifts out until later, when the kids got home from Disneyland, but I'm glad that I get to see them open everything tomorrow morning."

Aurora's heart beat heavy at the thought of Zak not being

with his kids on Christmas. She'd never been so thankful for snow in her life—for more reasons than one.

He headed off in the direction of the garage, and Aurora continued to clean up.

She was busy humming "Jingle Bells" in her head when a creak on the steps caused her to pause from where she'd been wiping the counter. It was Aiden on the stairs.

"Hey, buddy," she said. "Everything okay?"

He nodded, rubbing his eyes and yawning. "I'm okay. Can't sleep though."

"Too excited for tomorrow?"

He scratched the back of his neck the way she'd noticed Zak did when he was uncomfortable. He slogged his way into the kitchen. "No. I don't believe in Santa anymore. I know that the presents come from Mom and Dad. Tia still thinks he's real though, so we pretend for her."

She nodded, then continued to wipe up the counter. "That's very sweet of you to continue pretending so your sister still gets to enjoy it a bit longer."

He made a noise in his throat.

It was insane how similar he was to his father, not only in appearance, but also mannerisms and facial expressions. "Some kid at school last year came to class one day saying how his parents refused to lie to him, so they told him there was no such thing as Santa from the very beginning. He decided to tell the class one day. Said our parents were all a bunch of liars."

Aurora's hand paused on the countertop. "He did what?"

Aiden nodded, walked around behind her and grabbed a fresh drinking glass from the cabinet. He filled it up from the fridge dispenser. "Yeah. Lots of parents were upset when their kids went home crying about no Santa."

"But not you?"

He shook his head and shrugged before he took a sip. "I

wasn't sure if he was real or not, but I kept pretending for Tia. I know my parents are liars though, so that didn't bother me —at least my mom is." His blue eyes, the same shade as his father's, grew dark and stormy. "Promise me you'll never lie to my dad the way my mom did ... please."

Holy shit.

Where was this coming from?

Wasn't this kid like ten?

His gaze narrowed, and his glass paused in front of his mouth as he waited for her response.

Swallowing, she nodded. "I promise. Th-though I have no idea what kind of lies your mom told your dad ... "

Did she want to know?

Even if she did, it wasn't right for Aiden of all people to be filling her in.

The door leading out to the garage opened. Aiden's eyes shifted in that direction, as did Aurora's. Zak came fumbling through, his arms loaded up past the top of his head with boxes of gifts. He spied Aiden, and his eyebrows lifted. "What are you doing up, buddy? Everything okay?"

Aiden lifted his drinking glass, and he nodded, which seemed to be enough for Zak because he continued on into the living room. Aiden swung his hawklike stare back to Aurora. "I like you," he finally said. "You make our dad smile and laugh, but just please don't hurt him. Our mom really hurt him, and I don't want to see him like that again."

Aurora blinked back hot tears.

Zak was raising some pretty unbelievable kids.

"I'll do my best," she said, feeling that sense of unease begin to gurgle deep in her belly again. She shoved it down, reached out and rested her hand on his shoulder. "For the record, I like you too." She let go of him. "Now get on to bed." She made a clicking sound with her tongue the way one would for a horse. "You don't want Santa to find you still awake, do you?"

Aiden rolled his eyes and smiled as he headed back in the direction of the stairs. "Santa, Dad, whoever. I'm just hoping there's a microscope under the tree."

Aurora smiled back. "You'll need to go to sleep to find out. Now *shoo*."

He smiled once more, then climbed the stairs, waving to her before he disappeared.

Please don't hurt him. Don't lie to him.

Why did she feel like she was not only going to break her promise to Aiden, but she was also going to break his heart?

"You head on upstairs and wait for me," Zak said, joining Aurora in the kitchen after he'd finished putting all the Christmas presents beneath the tree. "I have one more thing I need to take care of, then I'll come join you." He wrapped his arms around her waist and buried his nose in her hair.

She pressed her nose to his pec and inhaled.

Dear God, the man smelled good.

"Don't be too long," she said, resisting the urge to bite him. "That's an awfully big bed for just me. And I'm quite tired. I'd hate to fall asleep before you came to kiss me goodnight." She made sure her pouty face was extra pouty, then batted her lashes at him.

His deep, throaty laugh made her nipples pearl. "Don't worry, I'll be but a minute." He dropped his hand from her waist to her butt and gave her a gentle pat. "Head on up."

She did as she was told. She washed her face, brushed her teeth and then ignored the voice in her head telling her to put pajamas on and climbed into bed in her birthday suit.

She was sitting up against the headboard, reading

through the text messages from Pressley and his growing insistence to see her, when the bedroom door opened.

Aurora's phone dropped into her lap, Pressley and his desire to see her forgotten.

Zak stepped into the room and shut the door behind him, his strides slow and cocky—so it was more like a swagger—as he approached her. His smile was carefree and relaxed, almost arrogant—and it made everything inside her melt.

But as lazy as his gait and smile were, his eyes told a different story. Purpose and desire burned hot in the dark blue of his irises. With just a look, just a saunter and an amused grin the man was capable of turning her into total mush, a fuzzy-headed fool with only one thing on her mind. Thankfully, it looked like Zak had that same thing on his mind as well. He had a plan, and it was going to be her job to follow it. To acquiesce and do as she was told. Like a good girl.

She loved it when he called her a *good girl*. Because even though she was doing as he asked, she somehow felt bad being his good girl.

How weird was that?

He stopped next to her side of the bed, a slight smile lifting the corner of his mouth. "Evenin', lass," he said.

Aurora's pulse sped up to the rate of a hamster's.

Her eyes slowly raked him from toe to tip, lingering extra, extra long on the center area, where a box wrapped in Christmas paper sat in his hands. And of course, what was behind that box? A kilt.

A mother-effing freaking kilt—and nothing else.

And boy, did he wear it well.

She licked her lips, her eyes continuing to roam across his body, around each hardened pec, down the washboard of his stomach, the sexy V-line of his hips that pointed to the secret beneath the kilt.

The kilt.

Oh dear lord, he'd put on the kilt.

She still couldn't believe it.

He also had a present for her. How did he manage that? He hadn't left the house.

She felt like a complete tool now. Here he'd miraculously managed to get her a Christmas present and even wrap it, and she had nothing but her naked body and a smile to give him.

"What say ye, lass? It's gettin' a wee bit chilly. Might I share yer bed wit ya?" His arm extended forward, and he cupped her cheek, the other hand still holding the box.

She nodded. "I'd like nothing more."

"But first ye need to open yer present. I made it myself. I hope you like it."

She shook her head, which caused him to remove his hand from her cheek. "Zak, you really shouldn't have. I didn't get you anything. We've only known each other for a few days. I wasn't expecting anything. Please." She made to push it away. "It's too much."

"Lass, just open it." Man, he really was not breaking character, not for anything. "I swear I didn't spend a quid on it."

Letting out an exhale of frustration, she rolled her eyes and lifted the lid, peering inside.

Aurora's eyes flew up to Zak's face. His smile was the size of Jupiter. Then he started to dance. *"It's my dick in a box ... "*

Aurora threw her head back and laughed harder than she'd ever laughed before. She released the lid and toppled back on to the bed, tears streaming down her cheeks as her sides began to ache and her whole body shook.

That's when she noticed just how *low* the kilt was pulled down at the front, allowing for his cock to spring out and be tucked inside the box. His red, neatly trimmed pubic hair was peeking out over the top of the kilt and box. She hadn't noticed it before because well, the man had rippling muscles everywhere and gorgeous tattoos, she'd been a bit distracted. She glanced back up at him, and he was still jiving, humming the tune to the *Saturday Night Live* parody song "Dick in a Box."

His eyes were closed, his mouth bunched and his fists tight as he unapologetically got down to the beat.

Could this man get any more amazing?

She hadn't laughed like that in a while—it felt good.

And no man she'd ever dated had made her laugh like that, played games or did silly pranks and stunts the way Zak did. He took life seriously when it mattered, but otherwise he was just a big kid. And she loved that about him.

He stopped dancing and opened his eyes. "Do you like it, lass?" he asked, the brogue still strong. "I made it myself ... well ... *grew* it myself."

Aurora snorted and sat up, grabbing the lip of the box and tugging, forcing him to climb on to the bed. "I love it," she said, gently pulling the box off him. "It's the best Christmas gift I've ever received. How did you know it was exactly what I wanted?"

He flashed her another wide and sexy grin. "Intercepted your letter to Santa." He tucked himself back beneath the kilt and pulled it up. Though the tent he created was unmistakable.

God, he looked good in that kilt. Like a sexy Highland warrior with all his tattoos and rippling muscles. He just needed a swath of blue paint across his face and she'd probably spontaneously orgasm right then and there.

She reached beneath the kilt and took his hard length in her palm, stroking him. He cupped the back of her head. "Take me in your mouth, lass. That's my Christmas wish, then I'll give you yours ... over and over and over again."

She smiled up at him, flicked her tongue out and licked

off the bead of precum from the crown of his cock. "With pleasure."

THEY WERE both breathing heavy and Aurora's leg was cramping by the time Zak rolled off her. He removed the condom, tied it and quickly nipped off to the bathroom to dispose of it. Seconds later, he was crawling into bed beside her and scooping her into his arms.

He kissed the top of her head as she lay next to him, cradled against the hard length of his body, her hand over his heart, head on his shoulder.

"Can I ask you something?" she said, glancing up at him. "It's about Aiden."

He grunted, nodding once. "Did he say something to you?"

"Yeah." But then she quickly shook her head. "I mean he did, but it wasn't anything offensive or anything. Just something that made me wonder a few things."

"What did he say?"

"He made me promise that I wouldn't hurt you. He said that his mom really hurt you and that he doesn't want to see you like that again. Can I ask what happened? Why a ten-year-old knows so much?"

Zak didn't strike her as the type of dad who filled his kids in on the details of his divorce. That was not something the children should be privy to—even though she saw it all the time in her job.

Zak let out a long sigh, his chest expanding as he inhaled again, held his breath, then released it once more. "Things in my marriage to Loni were a little strained. I was working a lot trying to get my business up to a new level. We were expanding the gym to its second location and siting places for its third. I was branching into merchandise and on-site dieti-tians. I was working a lot. I was trying to make a better life for my family. Loni wanted the big house in the ritzy neighbor-hood, so even though I wanted to wait a few more years until the business was in a better place, I gave in, and we bought this house and moved here. Which meant that the pressure was on for me to expand the business. I needed to pay the mortgage."

"That must have been really stressful for you," she said.

He nodded. "It was. But my kids were happy. They go to a really great school. They want for nothing. And my wife had a really great life too—or so I thought. I rarely said no to her. Figured she was home with the kids, taking care of the house and of our family—the least I could do was provide for them but let her take care of the rest. She'd quit her job as an inte-rior designer to be a full-time mom, so I made sure she was comfortable. Just like the kids, she wanted for nothing."

"But that wasn't enough, was it?"

God, she could see where this was going.

"Apparently," he said stiffly. "It was a Tuesday afternoon in the summer. I was home with Tia helping her plant some seeds for her garden, and Loni was off at her *book club,* or so she said. Aiden asked if he could go a few doors down to the neighbors' and play in his friend's new backyard treehouse. It was July, hot, and we're longtime friends with the neighbors, so I saw no problem with it."

Apprehension tingled across Aurora's limbs. What was Zak going to say next? What did Aiden see? What did he hear? Was this why Aiden had warned her not to hurt Zak, because he'd witnessed his mother do something horrible?

"It wasn't until dinner that night that Loni's true where-abouts were revealed," he went on. "Aiden simply asked her why she was naked wandering around Mr. and Mrs. Sharpe's bedroom and why Mr. and Mrs. Sharpe were naked too. Then he asked who the other people were and why they were naked too. He saw her from the treehouse. She was at the neighbor's house behind the house where Aiden was playing."

Aurora's hand flew to her mouth.

"His question was innocent. No accusation in his tone, just simple curiosity. We've always been very open and accepting of the human body in our house. Nakedness is normal. But they also know that it's inappropriate to be naked in someone else's house unless you're having a bath or shower or something. The human body is beautiful in all forms, but there are certain times and places when you need to keep your private parts covered. My kids know that. I've drilled that shit into their heads since before they could walk." He glanced down at her. "I'm crazy protective of them, if you haven't already noticed?"

She blinked up at him and smiled. "I noticed, and I think it's wonderful."

He squeezed her tighter against him, then continued, "Aiden just didn't understand why his mother was naked in the neighbor's bedroom in the middle of the day."

"An understandable conundrum for a, what, nine-year-old boy?"

He nodded. "Yeah, he was almost nine at the time. Kid never should have seen that shit."

"He discovered his mother was having an affair." She shook her head. "That's terrible."

"He discovered his mother was having an orgy, actually. She belongs to a swingers' club. And had for nearly a year. That's where she met Craig. That motherfucker helped end my marriage. They're probably up on the mountain in that fucking cabin right now with every hole in her body filled by a different guy." He made a disgusted face and shook his head. "She brought up a threesome with me once, and I shot it right down. I'll get as kinky as they come in bed, but I don't fucking share. Not with a man, not with a woman. When you're my woman, you're mine and *only* mine."

Everything inside Aurora tightened. Her breasts suddenly ached, and her pussy throbbed.

When you're my woman, you're mine and only mine.

Yes, please.

"It was after Aiden asked her that I began to put the pieces together. I'd been oblivious or ignorant or too caught up in building my business to really take notice. I mean I knew she was gone a lot, claimed she was reasserting her independence, finding herself again now that the kids were in school. Here I thought she was taking a pottery class, going to hot yoga, taking part in a book club. Meanwhile, she was getting stuffed by half the fucking neighbors."

Aurora's fingers clenched over his chest, her nails digging slight half-moons into his skin. He didn't seem to mind. "I'm so sorry," she whispered, kissing his shoulder. "And poor Aiden. Did you ever tell him what she was really doing?"

He shook his head. "Not really. But he figured out enough. He knows that his mother was lying to me and that it hurt me and it broke up our family. I didn't tell him that *she* was the one who broke up the family. I'd never blame his mother to his face or where he could hear. But he's a smart kid. He figured it out."

"He's a brilliant kid. And he loves you so much." She released her fingernails from his pec and kissed the spot where she'd left marks. "I'm really sorry."

"I should have known though, should have paid more attention. She was a liar from the beginning. Our whole relationship, whole family was built on a lie." His fists bunched. "I fucking hate liars. Hate them. I've had so many of them in my life. Never again."

She straightened the bedsheets at her waist with long,

nervous strokes as a pit the size of a watermelon opened up in her belly.

"Aiden was created out of a lie." He ran his hand over his face. "My son was born because she'd lied to me. Loni lied about being on the pill, which was why Aiden was conceived only three months after we started dating. She wanted to trap me. I was only twenty-four, had just lost my wrestling scholarship and didn't know what I was going to do. I was getting my degree in kinesiology, but after an injury, I lost my scholarship. I lost my drive. I didn't want to be up to my neck in student loans with a baby on the way, so I made the decision to quit college and get my personal training certification instead. I took business classes at night and then eventually made enough money to buy a hole-in-the-wall gym in the bad part of town, where I trained MMA fighters and fitness competitors."

"That's amazing. And from there your success just skyrocketed?"

"I guess you could say that. But Loni was never content. Always wanted more. I thought for a while she was trying to seduce one or two of the guys I trained, but they told me they'd never touch my woman and gave me their word, so I let her flirtations slide. I shouldn't have though, should have checked in more, made sure she was happy. Tried to fix things if she wasn't."

"No marriage is perfect," she whispered. "No relationship is perfect."

She could attest to that—and then some.

"But what she did was wrong," she added. "Even if you were a workaholic, it wasn't your fault she cheated."

"Yeah," he breathed. "I know. Still feels like I could have done more though. She lied about waiting to introduce the kids to Craig, too. She didn't fucking wait. She—" He glanced down at her when she'd re-dug her nails into him. His kissably soft lips dipped into a deep frown. His eyebrows followed suit. "I'm sorry. This is different. You—us, it all took me by surprise. Had we done things the conventional way, I would have waited a while before you met the kids."

She released her nails again, then flopped back against the pillows. "I understand, and I wasn't upset. Is your ex going to give you a hard time for introducing me to your kids so soon?"

He lifted one shoulder and made a face that said *probably*. "She might. I won't lie to her if she asks about how we met or why you met the kids so early." He held up a hand. His index and middle fingers were crossed. "Let's just hope she doesn't ask."

A lie of omission.

Aurora was getting good at those.

Her stomach rolled over, and she pushed down the taste of bile.

"You have to admit though," she said, taking a deep breath to steady herself, "this is kind of surreal. I mean I *just* met you, and now I've met your kids and am spending Christmas with you. It's all so backward."

"Only if we choose it to be. I mean, are you wanting to call it quits after tomorrow?" He rolled over and faced her, propping himself up on his elbow. "We never really discussed a timeline for ... *us*."

Us.

She glanced down between them, and he grabbed her hand. "Is there an *us*? Or is there just a Christmas we'll never forget?"

"Can't we have both?" he asked, running his big, strong thumb over the back of her knuckles. "I really like you, Aurora ... *Rory*, and I don't want this to just be a Christmas fling. I haven't been with anybody since Loni because I wasn't ready. I carried a lot of anger and knew that it wasn't healthy to start a new relationship so pissed off with my ex. But I'm in a good place right now, and I really like you."

And I'm in love with you.

"Will you tell me about your brother?" he asked, his deep blue eyes boring past the façade that she was carefully constructing around her and seeing right down to what made her tick—which was family, love and Zak.

She closed her eyes for a moment. "Brecken was diagnosed with bipolar disorder when he was twenty-three. He had episodes, but not many. But when he did have them, they were severe. He went on medication right away, and that seemed to help. Or so we thought. It was the summer between my second and third year of law school. I was busy *summering,* as they call it. Working my nose to the grindstone for a legal clinic in Seattle, so I wasn't able to make it home for a visit since the summer before. He called me one afternoon, wanting to talk, but I was too caught up with work to really give him the time of day. I ended the call after only a few minutes." Her words became strangled in her throat. "Had I known he was calling to ask for help, I never would have ... "

God, she didn't want to ruin the moment with heartache and painful memories. Being with Zak made her have hope for the future—something she'd been far too long without— and even if their pipe dream of turning this into something more fizzled out, she wanted to store this moment in her memory bank for eternity.

"He walked out into the lake by our house and never resurfaced. They found his body a few days later."

Zak made a deep, pained noise in his throat.

A knuckle came under her chin. "I hope you don't blame yourself."

"But I do," she whispered, blinking back warm tears. "I was so busy with work that I didn't have time for my own brother. Maybe if I'd taken just an extra five minutes to talk to my brother, I would have been able to prevent him from ... " She wiped at a tear that had slipped down her cheek. "I could have convinced him to get some help."

He shook his head. "No. It's not your fault. And I bet your brother would say the same thing."

Brecken most definitely would, because he was that kind of a selfless, extraordinary person. Didn't mean she still didn't wish she could have given him more of herself, more of her time—maybe things would have turned out differently. Maybe her dad never would have had his heart attack and instead all four of them would be putting the angel on the tree and baby Jesus in the manger this evening back in New Hampshire.

But then you never would have met Zak.

As much as it gutted her to think such a thing, it was a small price to pay for having her brother back. But it was one she'd hope Zak would also choose if in her shoes.

For a long time, anger had been her only emotion. She was angry with her brother. Angry with their country's broken medical system and the way mental health was swept under the rug as if it wasn't a real problem and the people afflicted just needed to get outside and go for a run.

Most of all, though, she'd been angry with herself. Still was.

"Promise me something," Zak said, his voice soft and gentle.

She turned to face him, sniffling. "Hmm?"

"Promise me that you won't continue to beat yourself up over this. I know it's going to take time, but know that it wasn't your fault. Nobody blames you but you, and you're wrong."

Pain funneled into her heart. How did he already understand her so well? They'd only known each other for a few days, and yet he seemed to just get her the way no man ever had.

She squeezed her eyes shut, causing another tear to drip down her cheek. She needed to calm her heart, calm her breathing and allow the thundering thoughts and harsh words of blame and criticism in her head to fade away.

"You're thinking awfully hard there, lass," he purred, the brogue back. "Care to share?"

She shook her head and wiped the tears out from beneath her eyes. "It's nothing. Just reminding myself of how lucky I was to be rescued in the snowstorm by such a capable, generous and *sexy* man. I could still be stuck out there if it wasn't for you."

"I'm the lucky one," he purred, rolling on top of her. His smile was carefree, but there was a storm behind his eyes. They'd gotten into some pretty heavy stuff in just a few days. Much like her, he probably had a lot on his mind. "I don't want what's starting between us to end when the tree comes down and the snow melts." His mouth was now less than an inch above hers.

"This all feels like a dream," she whispered.

"Better than a nightmare." His voice now a husky whisper.

"I keep pinching myself hoping that I won't suddenly wake up and be stranded in my car buried by a mound of snow, freezing to death all alone on Christmas."

"I'd never let that happen."

She chuckled beneath him. "My hero."

"Damn straight," he said with a growl, grinding his pelvis against her, pulling her once again from her dark thoughts and into his dirty ones. "Do I need to put the kilt back on to convince you?"

She made sure her smile was brighter than the sun.

The kilt again? Um, yes please!

She snagged her bottom lip with her top teeth, but he was quick to pull it free. "Ah, ah, no biting, remember? That lip is mine."

She batted her lashes at him. "Maybe you should put the kilt back on, and bring back the brogue too. I might just need a bit more convincing."

His smile grew, as did something else that was nestled between her legs. "Oh, lass, you dinna have any idea what I have in store for you tonight." He stood up and helped her to her feet before he wandered around to the other side of the bed and grabbed the discarded kilt off the floor. "Bend over the bed, lass," he said, the brogue thick and making her pussy grow wetter by the second. "Stick that bonnie arse up in the air."

Bonnie arse.

Oh lord, he was enjoying this too much.

He re-wrapped his kilt and fastened it. Aurora stared at him. Never had she seen anything so drop-dead incredible in her life ... wait, yes, she had. Just an hour ago when he'd walked into the bedroom wearing that the first time—with his dick in a box.

"You canna come until I say so, all right, lass?" he asked, positioning himself behind her, his fingers trailing down the cheeks of her ass or *arse,* then between her crease until he found her wet and waiting for him—impatient for him.

A harsh *thwack* to her left cheek made her yelp. She craned her neck around to look at him, her mouth open in shock.

His eyes blazed back at her. "You need to answer me, lass, otherwise I'll give you another." He lifted his palm in the air.

Did she dare defy him again? She kind of liked the spank.

Hell, she didn't just kind of like it—she freaking loved it.

Then she remembered his mention of nipple clamps. Did she dare ask him about them?

She bit her lip and wiggled her bottom in front of him. "And what if I don't answer you?"

Zak's smile alone was enough to push her to the verge of orgasm—well, that and the fingers that were now rubbing circles around her clit.

Another loud and hard smack landed on her other butt cheek. "You're a wee bit of a scamp, aren't you, Rory? A little brat. Might need to take you over my knee and teach you a real lesson."

Yes, please!

She swallowed, her pussy tightening with every swirl of his fingers. She was already really close.

"You canna come until I say, lass. Say you understand, or I'll tan yer arse again."

She nodded, and at the same time, her body shuddered from whatever he was doing to her clit now. "I—I understand."

He nodded. "Good. Now drop to your knees, lass, and help me with the condom." He removed his fingers from her, which made her whimper far too loudly and caused him to chuckle, then he helped her turn around. With a forceful but still kind hand on her shoulder, he pushed her to the ground. Then he handed her the condom.

This was probably one of her favorite parts, lifting up the kilt to see what was hidden beneath. Though with the ten-man tent he was pitching at the moment, she only had one guess.

She licked her lips and lifted the kilt, taking him in her palm and stroking him, feeling him continue to grow in her hand.

"Slip it on, lass," he said, his voice hoarse and strained. "Need to be inside ya."

She tore open the foil packet and placed it over him,

allowing him to hold the base while she used both hands to roll it down his length.

His breath hitched above her as she nudged his hand away and gripped him.

"Ya dinna kin how sexy you look right now, Rory. On yer knees like that. Right bonnie."

Her lips tightened as she tried not to smile. His brogue was hot, albeit fake as hell. But she loved how into the role he got, never breaking character, never abandoning the accent. She could just imagine that they'd have some real fun role-playing. She'd never done it before, but that didn't mean she was against it.

Once she had the condom in place, he offered her his hand and helped her stand up, a gentle but firm hand to her back encouraging her to bend back over the bed.

She did as she was told, a slight tremor of disappointment spooling through her at the thought of not being able to see him in his kilt as he made love to her.

Made love.

Yeesh, she really needed to get ahold of herself.

He gripped her hips, poised himself at her core and eased inside, taking his time as he slid across the sensitive nerve endings of her channel.

"Look to the right, lass," he said, seating himself to the hilt inside her. "The mirror."

She did as she was told, and sure enough, there they were. Her, bent at the waist, hands gripping the duvet cover of the bed as Zak held her by the hips and slid inside her, his kilt resting on her lower back, his abs contracting and popping with each measured thrust.

Holy God.

Why hadn't she noticed that mirror before?

He grinned at her in the mirror, his eyes a dark blue storm, his skin faintly flushed across his cheeks and forehead.

"Nothing sexier, lass." He pumped hard but steady, making sure he drove into her all the way to the base only to then ease his way out, teasing her entrance with the tip.

She rested her forehead on top of her palm and squeezed her eyes shut.

"No, lass, watch us," he ordered. "Watch me take you. Watch me fill you."

Watch me fill you.

She did as she was told, opening her eyes and tilting her head so she could watch them in the mirror.

He nodded, bared his teeth and grunted as his cadence picked up fervor and his grasp on her hips tightened. She squeezed her internal muscles around him, feeling every inch of him possess her, consume her.

She wasn't going to last much longer. The image of Zak behind her, a tattooed sex god in a fucking kilt, was enough to make any woman cream her jeans.

Only Aurora wasn't wearing any jeans.

She wasn't wearing a damn thing—except Zak that is. Or maybe he was wearing her.

Either way, his insatiability was wearing her out in the best way possible.

"Gonna come, Rory," he ground out, hunching over her and reaching beneath her body and between her legs until he found her clit. She was a sopping wet mess between her legs, and his fingers on her slippery nub were enough to kick her over the ledge.

Her body went rigid, her pussy quivered and squeezed, and her toes curled where she stood. The orgasm took hold of her from the center and exploded outward like a starburst, hitting the top of her head, the tips of her fingers and bottoms of her feet. Every cell sang; every nerve tingled.

She opened her eyes, only realizing then that she'd shut them again, to find Zak behind her, still pumping. His brows were furrowed into a deep V and his lips curled back, making him look more animal than warrior. His flush now spanned the broadness of his chest and up his thick neck, getting lost in the ruddy beard that clung to his chiseled jaw.

"Gonna come, lass." He grunted, began to hammer into her even harder, and then he stilled. His eyes slammed shut, and his toes curled on the rug beneath his feet.

She loved him in a kilt, but at that moment she kind of wished he was naked so she could see his ass cheeks flex and bunch. The man had a rockin' ass. The most amazing ass on a man—on a human being—she'd ever seen.

Oh well, another time. She could always ask him to lift the kilt next time as he took her in front of the mirror.

Next time. God, how she hoped there would always be a next time.

His cock twitched and jerked inside her as he came, his breathing ragged and hitched behind her as he pumped out the last of his release.

His fingers on her hips relaxed, and he exhaled. She watched in the mirror as every one of his heavily toned muscles unclenched and his eyes fluttered open.

A small, serene smile coasted across his lips as he leaned forward and kissed down the length of her spine. Then he pulled his fingers free from between her legs and held on to the base of the condom as he slid from her body.

She immediately mourned the loss of him inside her, and she must have made a noise of protest because his deep chuckle and a light pinch to the bottom of her butt cheek had him helping her stand up. "Trust me, lass," he said, the brogue still thick, "dinna fret. That wilna be the last time I take ya. Far from it." Then he tied off the condom and headed to the bathroom, still in his kilt and whistling "Jingle Bells" as he went.

14

"You're still wearing it," Tia said to Aurora with a giant smile as the young girl made her way down the stairs, dressed in a beautiful red skirt and shimmery gold top. "You like it?"

Aurora paused what she was doing in the kitchen with the Brussels sprouts in the roasting pan and grabbed at the beaded necklace around her neck. "I absolutely love it, Tia. I told you that. It's one of the most thoughtful Christmas presents I've ever received. Thank you. How'd you find time to make it?"

She suspected that the little girl had a stash of beaded necklaces and bracelets in her room and simply pulled one out for Aurora so that Aurora wasn't left being one of the only people without something to open Christmas morning. Either way, it was very thoughtful.

Tia plopped down into one of the bar stools across the island from Aurora. "Dad helped me. He has the special wire in his shop that makes it easier to bead quickly. Otherwise it takes a while with fishing line."

Aurora's eyes softened. "Well, I really appreciate it. It's really beautiful. You're quite crafty."

Tia fished beneath the neckline of her shirt and brought out a necklace that matched Aurora's. "See, I made myself a matching one. Now we match. Matching friendship necklaces. Cool, huh?"

Aurora's heart swelled just like the Grinch's did after he rescued the sleigh full of gifts from tumbling into the ravine. This little girl was incredible.

"I love that, thank you, Tia."

Tia's smile widened, and she tugged at her ears. "I like your earrings. I really want to get my ears pierced one day. Dad says I'm too young."

"You're beautiful enough without the bling," Aurora said, finishing up the Brussels sprouts by slathering them with olive oil and spices before sliding the pan into the oven. Zak was out shoveling the driveway, Sherman and Daphne were taking a nap, and Aiden had ducked upstairs to his room, claiming he had a top-secret project he needed to take care of. Aurora had offered to assume the chef role, once Zak told her exactly how he planned to prepare Christmas dinner. His guests, Liam and Emmett, were set to arrive any minute, so she wanted to make sure she had as much done as possible.

"I like your sweater," Tia said, slipping off the bar stool to come around and stand next to Aurora, reaching up and gently rubbing the soft fabric of Aurora's sweater. "It's really soft."

She'd been either wearing some of Zak's clothes, like his boxers and tank tops—which were huge on her— or making due with her hoodie and yoga pants. "Thank you. It's what I wore to work the other day, but your dad was kind enough to let me do a load of laundry. Now I don't feel *so* out of place, as the rest of you like to dress up for Christmas dinner." Aurora passed the little girl a peeler and a bowl of potatoes.

"Dad says we need to dress up for dinners like Christmas

and Thanksgiving and stuff to pay respect to the chef," Tia said, stepping away to grab an apron, then tying it around her waist and over her neck before resuming her position beside Aurora and beginning to peel potatoes. "Granny taught him that."

"Your Granny and Papa are very wise people," Aurora said, washing the olive oil from her hands in the big sink.

Noise on the stairs had both Aurora and Tia looking up from their place next to the sink. Unlike Tia, who was light on her feet, tiptoeing and prancing gently around the house, Aiden was a herd of elephants wearing chain mail, the way he made a ruckus wherever he went.

"Here," he said, practically running up to the counter and holding up a beautiful picture in front of his face. "I made you this for Christmas."

Aurora's face grew warm. These kids ...

"Aiden," she started, "you didn't have to get me anything for Christmas. Just getting to spend the holiday with kind people who make me feel welcome is gift enough. If your dad hadn't invited me to spend Christmas with you, I would be spending it all alone with my dead goldfish and dead cactus."

"Why don't you flush your goldfish down the toilet?" Tia asked, her nose wrinkling. "That's weird to keep a dead fish."

Aurora fought the urge to snort.

She'd flushed the fish ages ago.

"It's the Aurora Borealis," Aiden went on, ignoring Aurora's earlier declaration that he needn't get her anything. "You know, the northern lights. That's what your name means, right?"

Aurora nodded. "More or less. Yes." She dried her hands on a dish towel and took the picture from him. It was well done. It appeared as though he'd used pastels, not just your run-of-the-mill forty-pack of Crayola crayons. There was blending and smudging—real skill had gone into the picture. "Aiden, this is beautiful," she said, her throat growing tight and tears stinging the back of her eyes. "I'm going to frame this for sure, put it up on my wall."

He shuffled back and forth on his feet and let his eyes drift down to the floor. "It's nothing. I kind of rushed the last part there where the snow meets the horizon. I just didn't want to run out of time and be called for dinner." He lifted his eyes to meet hers. "Merry Christmas, Aurora."

"Merry Christmas, Aiden," she said, making her way around the island and offering her open arms to him. It was up to him if he wanted to hug her—he did.

He smelled like fresh soap and pastels, and his hug was tight and genuine. "I'm sorry if what I said the other night was rude," he whispered, his own voice sounding slightly choked. "I didn't mean to be rude. You make my dad smile. I just don't want to see him get hurt."

She squeezed him even tighter. "I don't want to see him get hurt either, buddy." She sniffed and pulled away from him, quickly wiping beneath her eyes and clearing her throat. She glanced behind them at Tia. "You two are pretty incredible kids, you know that?"

"I couldn't agree more," Zak's voice said, breaking the moment she was having with the kids.

Aurora spun around to find Zak standing next to the garage door, a handsome man beside him.

"You need to be nice to her," Zak had warned Emmett as he led his friend into the garage after meeting him in the driveway. Zak was just finishing up shoveling the driveway when Emmett showed up. Liam had texted earlier that day to say he was going to be late.

"She's honest and sweet. Not a bad or lying bone in her body."

Emmett cocked a dark brow. "And you've done a *thorough* job checking that body, right? No stone unturned, no inch of flesh untouched."

"Just be fucking nice," Zak growled, hating the idea of Emmett treating Aurora with even an ounce of negativity. The woman just didn't deserve it.

"I will be nice," Emmett said, stomping his feet to free the snow.

"Like you were nice to Tori?" Zak asked. He pulled off his knit cap and hung it over the heater in the garage. "We all know how *nice* you were to her when she started seeing Mark. Took all your anger about Tiff and Huntley out on Mark and Tori. Projected the shit out of them or onto them … or … " He scratched his chin in thought, then grunted. "You know what the fuck I mean."

Emmett cleared his throat and hung up his coat. "I know, and I apologized to everyone involved. I shouldn't have been so rude to Tori, especially since she's without a doubt the best thing to have ever happened to Mark and Gabe, and I shouldn't have let my own shit affect my reaction to Mark dating."

"No shit." Zak snorted. "We were starting to think you needed like anger management or counseling or something."

Emmett nodded. "Aaron introduced me to the Rage Room. You know that place right by Violet's dance studio, Mitch's photography studio and Paige's restaurant?"

Zak nodded. "Oh, I know the place. Been there a couple of times myself. Luna, who runs the place, is a gem. Gave her a free month's pass to the gym, she's been so accommodating to me. Nothing like smashing shit to help you get your head on straight."

Emmett made a noise of agreement in his throat. "Ain't that the truth."

"So, you'll be nice?" Zak asked, his hand resting on the doorknob. "Because I never intended for any of this to happen. Wasn't looking to hook up or date, didn't think I'd have the kids. It was all unplanned."

"Sometimes the unplanned things are the things that bring us the most joy," Emmett said.

Zak's head reared back and his lip curled up. "What the fuck? You the Dalai Lama now?"

Emmett rolled his eyes. "Fortune cookie last night, actually." He nodded. "But it fits, no?"

Zak tossed his head back and laughed. "You know those cookies were invented here in America, right?" He opened the door from the garage to the house, only to find his son wrapped in a warm embrace with the woman he was growing to deeply care for. Tia was standing next to them, smiling.

"Well, she's certainly won the kids over," Emmett said under his breath.

"You two are pretty incredible kids, you know that?" Aurora said.

You're incredible.

But instead, he simply said, "I couldn't agree more," interrupting their moment and letting his presence be known.

Aurora's light brown eyes flew up from Aiden's face to Zak and Emmett. Those eyes nearly grew twice in size as she stood up and wiped her hands on her apron. She seemed nervous. Why was she nervous?

Besides Adam, she'd met every truly important person in his life. All the single dads were just a bonus, but their opinion of her didn't really matter to him in the end. If he liked her, if his kids liked her, that was what mattered.

"Rory," he said, stepping forward and moving into the

kitchen, "this is my buddy, Emmett, and one of the fellow Single Dads of Seattle."

Emmett stepped forward and extended his hand. "Nice to meet you, Rory. I've heard great things ... at least as much as Zak was able to tell me from the driveway through the garage."

So far, so good. Emmett seemed to be genuinely giving Aurora the benefit of the doubt. There was no chip on his shoulder, no edge to his tone. The Rage Room appeared to be working.

Aurora shook his hand back. "Nice to meet you too." Her cheeks pinked up real nice like a schoolgirl's. "I'm afraid I haven't heard anything about you, though."

Emmett laughed and released her hand. "Probably for the better, actually."

Sounds of footsteps on the stairs had them all turning their heads. Two sleepy-eyed *old coots* came down, smiling when they saw Emmett.

"Emmett, nice to see you again," Grammy said with a yawn, coming up to give Emmett a big hug.

Emmett had actually looked up Zak and Adam's grandparents last spring when he was in South Carolina at a medical conference, so there were no introductions needed.

"Where's JoJo?" Grammy glanced around the room in an attempt to see Josie, or JoJo, Emmett's five-year-old daughter.

"She's with her mom for Christmas dinner," Emmett said with palpable pain. "I had her last night and this morning though."

Grammy nodded as she pulled away to allow Papa to shake Emmett's hand.

"At least you got to see her," Papa said. "Zak here almost missed out on Christmas with the kiddos entirely."

"Thank goodness for canceled flights," Grammy added, stepping next to Tia and wrapping an arm around her.

Emmett nodded and smiled, though Zak could see the ache inside his friend from not getting to be with his daughter all day on Christmas.

Zak clapped his hands once. "All right, Chef Rory," he said, addressing his woman in her sexy red sweater and tight black dress pants. "Where are we with dinner? Put me back to work." He wandered toward the fridge and pulled out three beers, popping the tops before he handed one to his grandfather and the other to Emmett.

"Tia's peeled the potatoes for me," Aurora said. "Sprouts are in the oven. Turkey is resting. Stuffing is still inside the turkey. I was just about to check on the yams and put the potatoes on to boil."

He leaned over and pecked her on the temple, pinching her butt where nobody could see. "Thank you, co-Chef. I couldn't have done it without you."

She chuckled. "You'd planned to, so yes, you could have. But thank you for the compliment."

"Are we having dessert?" Tia asked, grabbing herself a drinking glass from the cupboard. "I know we're generally a sugar-free house, but come on, it's Christmas." She glanced at Aurora. "I guess we have the cookies you and dad made and the ones we made yesterday."

Aurora nodded. "That we do." She shot a glare in Zak's direction. "Though some health freak doesn't have a sprinkle to his name in the house, so they're undecorated." She batted Zak playfully on the chest. "Who doesn't have sprinkles? M&M's or candy I understand, but *sprinkles?*"

"Uncle Liam is bringing the pies," Zak said, giving his daughter a sympathetic smile. "He said he picked up a lemon meringue and a chocolate orange pie from Emerald City Bakery yesterday before they closed. He ordered them special for dinner tonight. And Uncle Emmett brought his mama's famous figgy pudding. It's just out in the garage in a big cooler bag. Ice cream is in the freezer out there."

Tia's eyes went wide. "Figgy pudding, like in the song?"

"*We won't go until we get some ...* " Papa started to sing.

Emmett nodded once and lifted his index finger, pointing it at Tia. "The very same. My mom's recipe is the best in the land."

Tia licked her lips. "I can't wait."

Zak grumbled. "After New Year's Eve, it's broccoli for every meal until Valentine's Day, you guys hear me?"

There were groans from everyone, including Emmett.

"You really need to ease up," Grammy said. "It's just pudding."

"WHAT ARE your plans for New Year's Eve, Emmett?" Zak asked as he stood at the counter with the big electric carving knife in his hand. Aurora had helped him into his apron so as not to muck up the dress clothes he'd run upstairs and changed into.

"Daisy and Riley are throwing a party," Emmett said. "I've got JoJo, but apparently their party is kid-friendly. They said to bring her, that other people will be bringing their kids too. They're going to have a room set up for the kids to play in, watch movies and stuff." He scrunched up his face. "We'll see how it goes. If JoJo isn't having fun, we can bail and just head home and have our own little celebration."

"Where's Tiff going?"

Emmett's lip curled up. "She and *Huntley* are going to some fancy party at The Ludo Lounge. A masquerade thing. I wasn't *supposed* to have JoJo, but Huntley surprised Tiff with the tickets to the party, so they asked me if I could take her."

"Did you have plans?" Zak asked, knowing that this wasn't

the first time Emmett's ex had pulled something like this on him. Considered her plans more important than his because he was single and she was not, so therefore he shouldn't have a life outside of work.

Emmett shook his head. "I was going to go in to work, but now I'll just go to work until five or so, then swing by Tiff's, grab JoJo and take her to Riley and Daisy's party."

"What do you do for work?" Aurora asked, scooping the stuffing out of the turkey. Zak was waiting for her to finish before he started to cut into the bird.

"I'm an ER doctor," Emmett said. "I work with Mark, who Zak said you met yesterday."

Understanding dawned in her eyes. "Ah, yes, we did. Along with Isobel, Tori and Aaron. And of course, baby Sophie and sweet little Gabe."

Emmett's dark amber eyes softened, and he smiled wide at Aurora. He was one of Mark's best friends and extremely protective of Mark's autistic son Gabe, so to hear Aurora talk so affectionately about Gabe, Zak knew that was earning major bonus points with Emmett.

"Yeah, and Riley is a doctor as well, and our buddy, Will. Though Will and Amber are off on their friend's island in Belize."

Zak made a noise in this throat. "Must be nice."

Emmett's lips pursed, and he nodded. "Right?" He glanced at his watch. "Where the hell is Liam? He wasn't going into the office today, was he?"

Zak shook his head. "No. I think he had Jordie until noon or so and then he was going to spend some time with Scott and his kid. Scott has Freddie for Christmas, but he wants to do something with just the two of them. Scott and Liam's parents are in Palm Springs visiting their sister and her family."

Emmett's head bobbed in understanding, and he took a sip of his beer. "What about Mason and Atlas?"

"Mason and Willow are with his parents. It's Willow's first Christmas, so his parents are making a big deal. Understandable—first grandbaby and all. Atlas and Aria are in Oregon visiting his parents. Apparently, some shit is hitting the fan with one of Atlas's cousins or something and she might lose custody of her kid. Atlas was going to go see what he could do to help."

Emmett blew out a long breath and raked his fingers through his short, dark curly hair, scrubbing his hand down his face. "Shit, man. Poor Atlas."

Zak nodded. "Right."

"All right," Aurora said, running her hands beneath the faucet. "That turkey is empty."

Zak leaned forward and kissed her on the cheek. "There isn't anybody else I'd trust to unstuff my bird."

Emmett snorted across the island.

Aurora rolled her eyes. "Was that supposed to be dirty?"

Zak shrugged. He was in too good a mood to care. "I dunno. It sounded better in my head than it did out loud." He pressed the button for the electric carving knife, and it began to vibrate and *whirr* in his hand. He bugged out his eyes. "Muahaha, prepare to be carved, Mr. Turkey. Your breasts shall be mine. Get in my belly!"

Aurora snorted and shook her head.

He flashed her a big grin. "You love it."

Her eyes softened. "I do."

And fuck, I might be falling in love with you.

THEY WERE JUST SITTING down to eat when there was a ring and a knock at the door.

Zak rolled his eyes. "Shows up just in time to eat," he grumbled. "If he wasn't bringing the pies, I'd pretend we weren't home. Make him freeze his ass off out there."

"Dad, let him in. I want lemon meringue pie," Tia said. "It's my favorite."

Aurora smiled at Tia. "Mine too."

Zak got up from his spot at the head of the table and ran his hand over Aurora's shoulder as he made his way to the front door. She loved how affectionate he was becoming—even out of the bedroom. His kids had accepted her, his grandparents had, so now he must have felt it was okay to show them all that he accepted her as well. He accepted her as more than just a person to warm his bed and body for the last few days.

Would he ask her for more once the whimsy of the holiday wore off? Would he want to date?

Did she have time to date?

It's Zak. You will make time.

"Always show up just as we're about to sit down and eat, huh?" Zak said after he heaved open the door, his voice loud enough that they all heard him loud and clear in the dining room. "Typical Liam."

"Had things to do, man."

That voice.

Why did she recognize that voice?

"Had to spoil my kid rotten, then spoil my nephew rotten. Finally, I spoiled myself rotten. Ordered a new set of wheels."

"Just the wheels?" Zak asked, their voices drifting closer to the dining room after the sound of boots stomping and the hallway closet being opened to hang up his coat.

Liam's coat.

Liam.

Liam Dixon.

Aurora froze. Ice trickled in thick tributaries down her

spine, and her gut roiled and churned. Bile burned the back of her throat.

"No, the whole shebang," Liam continued. "New Audi should be arriving in a week or two. Santa didn't bring me what I wanted, so I said fuck it and decided to be my own Santa." Liam rounded the corner, a huge smile on his face, mischief twinkling in his dark brown eyes—just like it always did.

Because Aurora knew Liam.

Aurora worked with Liam.

Liam was her boss.

"Rory, this is Liam," Zak started, wandering behind her and planting his warm hands on her shoulders, giving them a gentle, loving squeeze. "Liam, this is Rory."

Confusion flashed behind Liam's dark, almost black eyes. "Yeah, I know."

Puzzled expressions flitted around the table. She was glad she couldn't see Zak's face at the moment. She wasn't sure she could bear it.

"I'm her boss," Liam went on, his dark eyes narrowing.

Zak's fingers tightened just a touch on her shoulders, but not in an angry sort of way. "I didn't know you two worked together!"

Aurora could only nod. Her heart pounded wildly inside her chest, and her palms were slick with sweat.

Neither Liam nor Zak seemed to be aware of how she was feeling though.

"Nice to see you, Aurora," Liam went on. "How are you?"

"I'm well, thank you," she croaked, feeling the sudden urge to leap up from the table and go puke.

He sat down directly across from her. Zak released her shoulders and took his position at the head of the table once again after he placed the pies Liam had brought on the buffet ledge behind him.

"All right, now that we're all here, let's eat," Zak said, rubbing his hands together. "I'm starved."

Aurora couldn't imagine eating anything. Not when she knew in just mere moments every lie she'd ever told Zak was about to come flying back in her face, was about to ruin what had been the greatest three days of her life.

"So," Liam started, scooping mashed potatoes onto his plate, "how did you two meet?"

"At the gym," Zak said, jabbing a fork into the turkey meat and then transferring it to his plate. "Don't normally date members"—he lifted one shoulder—"but when Aurora's car wouldn't start, I helped her and, well ... now we're having a wonderful Christmas." Zak passed his friend the plate of turkey.

"You're ... dating?" Liam asked slowly.

Zak made a dismissive face before he shrugged. "Sure. It's still new, haven't *really* put a label on things yet, but sure. Why not?"

Liam pinned his dark eyes on Aurora, one eyebrow slowly ascending on his forehead before he spoke. "You really need to trade in that lemon of a car." His gaze shifted from curious to fatherly. "It's only a matter of time before it dies on you for good."

Aurora's smile was tight and forced at the same time a prickle of unease slithered down her spine. "I know. Have other things sucking my money though."

Liam's eyes softened. "Right."

Aurora swallowed, and an ache began deep in her chest.

Zak's gaze narrowed. "If you work at Wallace, Dixon and Travers, why did you tell me you work close to the Rainier Vista gym location? That law firm is nowhere near Rainier Vista. It's nowhere near Greenwood either." Confusion filled his eyes. "Do you even live in Greenwood?"

That ache intensified.

She knew he hated liars. And even though her lies were small, they were still lies.

Slowly, she nodded, feeling like a bug under the magnifying glass just seconds from the sunbeam ready to fry her to a crisp. "I do."

"Why did you lie about where you worked?"

She swallowed hard again when her throat tightened, and a sting in her eyes began to blur her vision. A tear slipped down her cheek, and she finally brought her head up to look at him. "I don't know."

"What else have you lied about?"

"Zak ... " Emmett's voice was soft and gentle. "This isn't the place, buddy."

Zak shot his friend a look that said *shut up.*

"I agree with Emmett," Liam said. "I never meant to blow up Christmas dinner."

"Better I find out now that she's a liar than six months from now," Zak said, his tone wooden. He turned back to face Aurora.

"Enough, Zachary," Daphne said, her soft green eyes flitting back and forth between Aurora and Zak. "This is not the time."

A muscle in Zak's cheek jiggled, and he did a slow blink before opening his mouth, but Sherman cleared his throat at the other head of the table and let his utensils clatter noisily to his plate, causing Zak's mouth to snap shut. Heat rushed to his eyes and his cheeks, but it wasn't a boyish blush or the flames of lust—no. The fire that stared back at her was that of hell, was that of fury

"Your grandmother is right, Zachary. This is Christmas dinner. Don't ruin it." Sherman fixed Zak with a fatherly glare. "Enough."

Zak's jaw grew ever tighter, and red filled his cheeks.

Aurora felt smaller than a gnat.

Then his expression became blank, which made the hairs on the back of her neck stand up even more than they already were. Because it was at that moment that she knew there was no going back. There would be no forgiveness, no reconciliation. Zak was done with her.

She's ruined Christmas.

She'd ruined everything.

THE REST of the meal was eaten in tense, awkward and excruciating silence.

Zak wouldn't even look in Aurora's direction, wouldn't even glance at her. And she was sitting right next to him, so it wasn't easy—but he managed.

He managed to ignore her.

He managed to finish his meal. Eat a second helping, and then take his plate to the kitchen, all without so much as acknowledging even Aurora's pinky finger.

She'd barely touched her own meal, the pain in her heart making her want to curl up in a ball and cry her eyes out.

She'd ruined everything.

She'd ruined Christmas, Zak's affections for her, any potential future they might have had. She'd lied her way right into hell. And there she would stay.

Unable to eat anything else due to the tight knots in her gut, she picked up her plate and took it to the kitchen. Daphne was in there, putting foil over the rest of the turkey. She paused her efforts, her eyes sad as she looked up at Aurora. "He's very set in his ways. A stubborn ass with deep-seated rules and values. I'm not excusing how he spoke to you, I'm just explaining to you who he is." She rested her cool hand on Aurora's shoulder. "I hope the two of you can work through this, dear. We all really like you."

Her eyes flicked up behind Aurora, her smile turning grim.

Zak?

She turned around to find Liam standing there, worry written all over his face, his shoulders unusually hunched. Normally the man appeared larger than life, in charge of the room and with all eyes on him—and loving it. Not so much now.

He stepped forward, gripped her forearm and wheeled her back around and over to the far corner of the kitchen with a strength and speed that startled her. "We need to talk," he murmured.

"I'm going to go grab more dirty dishes," Daphne said, excusing herself.

"Are you not with Pressley anymore?" Liam asked, his voice low and almost accusatory. "You're not ... *cheating* on him, are you?" Color rushed to his face, and restrained anger filled his eyes. His hold on her forearm tightened. "Why are you here? Where is Pressley?"

Aurora clenched her jaw. "I ... we ... "

She hadn't wanted anybody to find out. Let alone anybody at work. Most of all her boss. Her big boss. And Liam Dixon was one of the *big* bosses. A name partner.

A throat cleared behind them. Liam stilled. Aurora's body turned to ice.

"Can you give us a minute?" Zak's deep voice sent Aurora's whole body into a nervous tremble.

Aurora didn't turn around to face him, but she heard Liam murmur something to his friend before her boss's footsteps retreated into the living room, where the rest of the family and Emmett had reconvened—all of them laughing, all of them having a great time enjoying what was left of Christmas day.

Once she knew they were alone in the kitchen, Aurora slowly turned around.

His angry gaze sliced her face, made her knees buckle and her heart shatter. "So you have a boyfriend? Is *he* who's been texting you all weekend? Your irritation spurred by his interruption into your little *tryst.*" His mouth turned up into a furious sneer. "Am I *other* man? What else have you been lying about?" he asked, his tone hard, his words clipped. "Are you even a lawyer? Or are you a legal secretary or a paralegal? Maybe just the janitor at Wallace, Dixon and Travers?"

"I'm a lawyer," she whispered, tears burning the back of her eyes, her throat aching as she fought back the emotions that struggled to ransack her. "I'm a first-year associate at Wallace, Dixon and Travers."

"You're a *first*-year?" Zak asked, exasperation in his tone, his fingers threading their way into his hair as he spun on his heel and paced away from her. "A *first*-year! Man, it's just one lie after the next with you, isn't it?"

"To be fair, I never lied about being a first-year. I just never corrected you when you assumed that I was a fourth-year."

A lie of omission is still a lie, counselor. You know that!

But her words seemed to strike a chord with him, and he reared back, his eyes going wide.

Yes, she had lied, but in the grand scheme of things, her lies had been small, and he was treating her as though she'd just told him she was the party planner for all of his ex-wife's orgies and had convinced Loni to leave Zak.

He regained his composure, and his eyes squeezed into thin slits. "Are you even from New Hampshire? Are your parents busy throwing Christmas parties? Or is there some big secret there too? You're actually from Milwaukee and your parents are flying out tomorrow. Is your brother even dead?"

She drew in a quick, pained breath. "Watch it, Zak. Yes, I

lied but I've never been cruel. I never went out of my way to hurt you, to hurt any of you. But right now, you're being cruel. You're deliberately being mean and hurtful and I don't deserve it."

His expression remained blank, but the slight jump in his jaw muscle said he wasn't immune to her standing up for herself.

Good. She was tired of being treated like a doormat by men. Pressley, Zak and all the boyfriends before them. She was tired of being dumped, tossed aside like yesterday's trash.

No more.

She fixed him with the best eye contact she could, even though deep down it hurt her heart to look at him. "I'm from New Hampshire, yes. And, yes, my brother is dead. He killed himself last summer. My parents are struggling to stay in their house after my father's heart attack and all of his medical bills. Any extra money I make goes to them. That's why I can't afford a new car. I do not have a boyfriend ... *anymore*. He dumped me the day after our company Christmas party a few weeks ago. Right before my birthday, right before Christmas. Because they all dump me. He's been texting because he wants to talk. He wants his stuff back ... a jacket and couple of books or something. I've never cheated on anything or anyone in my life."

A tear dripped down her cheek, and she reached out to the edge of the island to keep herself standing. Emotions warred inside her. She needed to remain strong. Show him her strength and let him see that she was more than the white lies she'd told. But at the same time, she also wanted to crumple to her knees and beg him to give her another chance. A chance to explain her lies, to explain why she didn't want him to know all her shortcomings, all her tragedies. That there was more to her than all her glaringly enormous flaws—though most days she struggled to see anything but those flaws when she looked in the mirror.

Her past boyfriends saw those flaws though. Saw them all.

She was always the dumpee. She'd only had four boyfriends in her life, but they'd all ended things with her. And Pressley was no different. Only, unlike the other three, Pressley had said being with Aurora reminded him of how much he missed his ex-girlfriend. So after attending Aurora's law firm Christmas party with her as his date, inviting her back to his place to spend the night and sleeping with her, he dumped her the next morning. Kicked her out of his apartment and didn't even offer to drive her home.

She had to take the bus.

Pressley went and proposed to his ex-girlfriend two days later. Their engagement announcement flooded her newsfeed because she stupidly forgot to *unfriend* him.

She was embarrassed for how things had played out. Didn't want anybody to know she'd been dumped—again. She didn't need the reminder that being with her only reminded men of what they could have elsewhere. There was obviously something wrong with her if she kept getting dumped, if she couldn't keep a man.

He was a ways away from her in the kitchen now. She hated the gulf between them. Missed his warmth and the strength she drew from his presence. But she needed to find a way to draw strength without him, to draw on her own strength, no one else's. Stand tall and strong alone and on her own two feet. It seemed impossible though.

He rounded on her. "Let me get this straight. You lied about where you work, saying that you worked closer to the gym than you do. That's lie one." He began counting on his fingers. "You lied about what year associate you are. That's two. You lied about who was messaging you all weekend, telling me it was work, when it was actually your boyfriend. That's three." He wiggled the two remaining fingers. "Am I missing any?" His blue eyes were wide, nostrils flaring, his talented mouth set in an angry, hateful scowl.

She shook her head, determined to look him in the eye no matter how much it killed her. "No, I don't think so." Her bottom lip quivered. "I'm really sorry for the lies, Zak. I just wanted to forget about my shitty life for a couple days and have a nice Christmas with a man I've been attracted to for such a long time. I didn't think I was hurting anybody with my omissions." A small part of her wanted to roll her eyes at how angry he was about such piddly little lies. He was blowing this all out of proportion. And yet, her love for him and how furious he was with her made all that so confusing and all the more painful. The way he was looking at her was gut-wrenching.

"Pfft." He shook his head, glancing down at the floor. He obviously couldn't stand to look at her any longer. "*Omission?* Is that what you lawyers call them? Well, I call them fucking *lies.*" His chin jutted forward. "I told you what I think of liars. Big or small, a lie is a lie. It's a betrayal. Loni's lies, your lies, they're no different. A lie is disrespectful to the person you're lying to. It says you don't value them enough to tell them the truth. Is that how you feel about me? I wasn't worthy of the truth?"

She shook her head again, and she chomped down hard on the inside of her cheek. "That wasn't it at all." Her pulse began to thunder in her ears, and her breathing grew shallow, creating an awful, painful ache right where her heart had been, before he'd ripped it out just now, stomping on it with his hurtful words. "I think I should go. I'm going to call myself a cab and leave." The ache inside her chest was near fatal as she dropped her head and stared at her feet, unable to look at the disappointment and anger on his face any longer.

"I think that's a good idea," he said, not bothering to look at her. "The roads are clear. You shouldn't have any problem getting a cab now." His head jerked, which caused her to lift her eyes from the floor, regretting it instantly when he fixed her with one final glare, a glare that made everything inside her crumple and wither. It made the remaining fragments of her heart, of her soul disintegrate, leaving nothing but a vast hollow she knew could never be filled. Then, just to twist the knife in her gut one more time, he turned around and showed her his back, preferring to stare out the kitchen window into the empty darkness of the backyard than at her for another second.

"Dad, no!" Tia burst into the kitchen, and she wrapped her arms around Aurora's waist. "Aurora, you can't leave." She turned back to face Zak. "Dad, she didn't mean it. Don't let her leave. It's Christmas!"

Zak still hadn't bothered to turn around, but she did notice his shoulders lift closer to his ears and his fingers clench white-knuckled fists at his sides.

"Dad?" Aiden whispered, having followed his sister into the kitchen, coming to stand on the other side of Aurora. "She's got nobody to go home to. This isn't fair."

Aurora shook her head again and swallowed past the painful lump in her throat, blinked back the tears and willed the throb in her now empty, heartless chest to ebb. She rested a hand on Aiden's shoulder. "It's okay, kids. I'll be okay. Thank you though." She put her head down, pulled out of Tia's embrace and turned to go, but she stopped herself and lifted her head to face him. "I'm sorry, Zak. I really am. I didn't think my lies were hurting anybody, they were just protecting my pride, protecting my heart. But I understand how you feel about liars, and I'm sorry. A lie is a lie, no matter how big or how small. Thank you for welcoming me into your home." Her eyes fell to the two teary-eyed children standing in the kitchen. "I'm sorry, guys. I'm sorry I ruined Christmas." Then she headed upstairs and packed her bag, tears streaming down her face as she fought to keep herself standing and not buckle to the ground in a heap of sobs.

She swung her bag over her shoulder and drew her phone out of her purse only to find Emmett standing on the threshold of Zak's bedroom door. "I'll drive you home," he said, then he turned and headed down the stairs, leaving her standing there with a hole where her heart should be and more tears in her eyes.

15

Aurora stared blankly out the window of Emmett's SUV as they made their way across town. The streets were fairly quiet and the roads plowed, the harsh orange glare from all the streetlights only intensified as it bounced off the big snow drifts.

"Wanna talk?" Emmett asked, pulling up to a red light.

Aurora's gaze slid to his. "Why are you being so nice to me?"

His lips twisted. "Because I was a dick to Tori when I first met her, and I feel really bad about that. I let issues from my divorce cloud my judgment about Mark's relationship, and I projected shit." His mouth crooked up into a half smile. "Or at least that's what my therapist says. I'm trying to make amends with the universe. I'm giving you the benefit of the doubt. Tia and Aiden really like you. Zak really likes you. Liam really likes you. So I'm guessing you're not the devil and in fact a pretty great person."

"I doubt Zak thinks so anymore," she murmured, focusing on her gloved hands in her lap. "I lied to him. He hates liars."

"And rightfully so. I'm assuming he filled you in on Loni?"

"Yes."

"You get where his anger is coming from, then?"

"I do. And I knew not telling the truth was wrong ... I'm a lawyer, for Christ's sakes. It's just ... "

"Your pride?"

She lifted her gaze to his. "Yeah. I've been through a lot these last couple years, and I just wanted a few days to forget about it all. To not be that person with all that baggage. I didn't want him to look at me with pity in his eyes or as a charity case."

The light turned green, and he continued on. "What do you mean, with pity and as a charity case?"

Aurora let out a long, slow exhale. Greenwood was at least another twenty minutes. They had time.

"Well," she started, "it all started a year and a half ago when I was summering at a legal clinic here in Seattle ... "

Twenty minutes later, Emmett pulled up in front of her apartment building, his jaw slack, his eyes wide. He put the SUV in park and turned to face her. "I'm really sorry, Aurora. For all of it."

She clenched her jaw tight, desperate to wait until she got inside before she let more tears fall. "Yeah, well ... you win some, you lose some, right?"

He shook his head, his amber eyes showing signs of that thing she hated—pity. "No. You don't deserve to lose anymore. You just deserve wins from here on out."

She choked out a half laugh, half sob. "From your mouth to the ears of the universe."

"And you didn't think you could share this with Zak? Seems like he shared his pain and past with you."

She shook her head and glanced out the window at her little two-story cube-shaped apartment building. "I know he did, but I don't work like that. I don't just spill my guts to a complete stranger."

The snort though his nose caused her to glance his way. He lifted one dark, bushy eyebrow.

She couldn't stop the laugh that broke free. "Okay, well, I don't *normally* spill my guts. I wanted him to see me for *me*. You know, the chick who's been stalking him for the past six months." She rolled her eyes.

His grin was wide and genuine. "I wouldn't go so far as to call you a *stalker*. Just an admirer. A fangirl. And I know Zak has quite the fan club."

She cringed. "I'm not sure that's any better."

His light chuckle eased a bit of the tension that had been caught up in her shoulders. He turned off the ignition of the vehicle just enough to stop it from running, but not so much as the heated seats stopped warming her butt into melted butter. "If your relationship had progressed further, into weeks, months or more, would you have told him the truth?"

She lifted one shoulder. "He'd have found out a lot on his own eventually, but yeah, probably. I hated lying to him. Even my lies of omission. I get serious stomach pains whenever I lie. I've never liked it. Never been good at it. But for some reason, they came out of me before I could stop them. I'm ashamed of how I treated my brother, of how I handled his death, letting it affect my last year of law school. I also hate that I can't help my parents more, that they're struggling and the insurance company is doing everything they can to deny my father coverage. I found them a lawyer in New Hampshire that was supposed to help them fight the insurance company, but he's a joke. Has done nothing to help them."

His smile slid into more of a thin line. "You have nothing to be ashamed of, Aurora. Nothing. You're an incredible daughter, and you were the best sister you could be. Your brother wouldn't blame you, and I don't think your parents do either."

She knew he was trying to comfort her, but his words didn't mean much at the moment. She was hurting too much. Her therapist—at Dina's insistence—had said as much to her as well, but no matter what, she couldn't stop blaming herself for Brecken's death.

"Zak's marriage ended rough," Emmett went on. "I empathize with him because so did mine. I understand where you are both coming from, him from a betrayal stand-point and you from a place of self-preservation and pride. Liam and I will try to talk some sense into him, help him see where you were coming from and that even though, yes, you did lie, they weren't like Loni's lies. Just because he spilled his guts to you doesn't mean it's quid pro quo."

She shook her head and put her hand on the door handle. "Thank you, but I don't need you guys to fight my battles for me. I messed up, and I need to own my mistakes. Maybe in a few days once he cools off, he will be willing to talk to me." She snorted and shook her head at her reckless behavior and how out of character she'd behaved these past few days. "I don't even have his number."

"Easily fixable," he said calmly. "I can give you that."

She shook her head again. "Maybe it's for the best that I don't have it. I don't think we were meant to be." She pulled on the door handle, the frosty air from outside hitting her cheek and tossing her hair against her face. "A Christmas fling was all we were ever meant to have. No more. I was deluding myself thinking I could have more with him, be enough for him. Guys always get bored with me, find a reason to end it." She shrugged her tight shoulders. "It just is what it is. We're from different worlds. It could never work."

"This isn't *West Side Story*," Emmett said dryly. "You're not from different sides of the tracks. Stop romanticizing it, *coun-*

selor, and admit that you've fallen for him, he's fallen for you and you want to be with him."

"Now who's romanticizing things?" she said, her fingers tightening around the door handle.

He shook his head, his dark amber eyes holding what she could only discern as a warning. "I'm not romanticizing, I'm stating fact. Liam and I will talk to him. Just hold tight, Aurora, and in the meantime, take care and call your parents." He turned the key in the ignition again and the engine roared to life. She took that as her cue to get out.

"Thank you for the ride, Emmett. I really appreciate it." Blowing out a breath, she dropped her gaze to the seat where she'd just been sitting. "Lord knows I couldn't have afforded the cab."

He smiled. "My pleasure, Rory. I'm sorry for how things played out, but take heart that it'll all work out."

She tried to smile, but her mouth just wouldn't work that way. The weight in her chest held too strong a pull to let any joy break through.

"Merry Christmas, Aurora, and Happy New Year. I promise next year will be better."

A sarcastic laugh burst forth from her lungs through her nose. "Can't get any worse than this year, can it?"

His smile was grim. "Good night."

"Good night, Emmett." Then she shut the door and headed toward her lobby, her tears once again falling freely as she thought of the warm welcome her dead cactus would give her when she turned the key and stepped inside.

———

IT WAS Saturday night once again, and the guys were back at poker.

Aurora's car hadn't moved from the gym parking lot all

week. Probably because she couldn't afford a tow truck—or to get it fixed. How was she getting to work? The bus?

"How was everyone's Christmas?" Mason asked, settling down into his seat with his beer.

Smiles and nods drifted around the table. Along with a few grumbles.

Zak could feel Liam and Emmett's eyes on him.

"Care to share?" Mark asked slowly, elbowing Zak. "When we left you Christmas Eve, things seemed to be going great. What happened?"

"In case you're wondering, she's been working from home," Liam said, sitting across the poker table from Zak and giving him a knowing look. "We gave all our associates that option if the snow made it too hard to travel. Particularly since we got hit with another eight inches of that fluffy white crap on Wednesday."

Zak cleared his throat. "I wasn't wondering."

"Bullshit," Emmett said with a snort. "It's written all over your fucking face."

"Yep," Mitch added. "Plain as day."

"Like Sharpie marker, bro," Mark cut in. "Emmett and Liam filled me in." He clicked his tongue and shook his head. "You need to relax. If there's anything I've learned from the way I treated Tori after what happened with Gabe, it's that good women don't mean to hurt us and we need to stop and realize that before we hurt them. And we all know how I fucked up with Tori, how badly I hurt her." He shook his head, his eyes wide in bewilderment. "That woman is a saint to forgive me and give me another chance."

"Amen to that," Liam agreed. "You were a dick."

"Yep," Adam chimed in. "If you ever spoke to me like that, I'd have given you two fucking black eyes and then called it a day."

Mark made a sheepish face. "Believe me, I'm still making

amends for it. We're together, but her forgiveness wasn't immediate. She still holds that shit over me from time to time, reminds me how much of an ass I was." He glanced at Zak. "Don't make the same mistake I did. I got lucky, Tori took me back, but Aurora might not be as forgiving."

"She lied," Zak ground out, taking a sip of his scotch. He hadn't had a drop to drink all week, but once he got to Liam's that night, he knew beer just wouldn't cut it.

"Yeah, but they weren't heinous lies," Liam countered. "They were lies of self-preservation. She didn't cheat on anybody. She didn't hurt anybody. She told you she worked closer to the gym so that you wouldn't think she was some creepy stalker-chick. She let you believe she was a fourth-year rather than a first-year, and she didn't tell you that her ex-boyfriend was harassing her. All pretty minor in the grand scheme of things, don't you think?"

"They were still lies," Zak challenged. "And after the shit Loni put me through with all her deceit and cheating, I vowed I'd never be with a liar again. Once a liar, always a liar. A white lie today, a cheating lie tomorrow."

"Bullshit," Aaron said, shaking his head like he was tired of this topic. "Get off your fucking high horse, dude. Fuck."

Zak ignored Aaron. Aaron could be abrupt sometimes; that was just who he was. "I just don't understand why she didn't tell me all that stuff right from the beginning. I was honest with her."

"Because not everybody vomits their life story on the first date, bro," Adam said, shaking his head.

He, Violet, Mira, Mitch, Paige and Jayda had all returned from Hawaii two days ago. The motherfucker was tanned and happy. Zak wanted to punch his brother in his smug, tanned face.

Adam tipped up his beer. "You've been out of the dating game a while. Did you forget how it goes?"

Zak's eyes drifted down to the cards in his hand. "I just prefer to lay my cards on the table right off the bat, so to speak. I want to do the relationship thing different this time. No lies, just honesty from the beginning. If the woman can't do that too, then she's not the one for me."

"And that's all well and good, but you can't force other people to adhere to your timeline or your philosophies. She was embarrassed about where she came from. She was embarrassed that she's been essentially stalking you—which she wasn't, by the way. Maybe she just wanted you to like her and then she'd tell you the truth, who knows. Only *she* knows why she did what she did," Liam added. "But what we all know, and I think you know it too, is that you overreacted. Aurora is a sweet person and one hell of a lawyer, and she likes your kids and they like her. I'd go and fix things before it's too far gone and unfixable."

"Where's Atlas when we need him to get all angry and pound his fist on the table?" Mark asked, glancing down at the cards in his own hand before moving a stack of chips into the center.

"He's still in Oregon," Liam said, raising the stakes with an even bigger stack of chips. "Scott says Freddie gave him his cold, so he's in bed with his NyQuil and Dristan."

"Kids are gross," Adam said, shaking his head before exchanging glances with Mitch. "I'm sure we're all going to be sick in a few days from that airplane ride. All that recycled air and shit. We should have bathed Mira and Jayda in Purell every twenty minutes while we were in the airport." He shuddered and then crossed his fingers. "Please don't let it be a gastro bug. I can deal with a runny nose and a cough, but I can't handle the shits."

Mitch made a face that said he was right there with Adam. "The guy sitting behind us on the plane was sneezing like he'd just inhaled a whole cup of pepper."

"Ah, fuck," Adam groaned.

"Just pray your pregnant girlfriend doesn't get it," Liam offered.

Adam's eyes went wide. "Ah, fuck. I didn't even think of that."

"Tell those effers to keep their snot-nosed kids away from my Willow," Mason chimed in. "The last thing I need is a sick baby on my hands. The bar has been slammed. I'm supposed to be taking quote, unquote paternity leave, only working part-time, but I've been at the bar every fucking day but Christmas day. My poor baby's not going to recognize her daddy if things keep going the way they are."

"Who's got her now?" Mitch asked.

Mason, was busy spinning a beer bottle cap in his fingers, staring blankly at it. "My mom. Willow loves her nana, so it makes it easy to get a break or work, but still. I don't want my kid being raised by my parents. I also don't want to abuse them."

"Maybe let Adam and Violet take her once in a while. They're going to need to get used to changing a shitty diaper again," Liam said, snickering.

Adam rolled his eyes. "I can remember how to change a diaper, thank you." He turned to Mason, his eyes earnest. "But we will take her whenever. Love that little squirt."

Emmett cleared his throat. "Anyway, back to the topic at hand. Which is Zak being an info-barfer and expecting everyone he meets to follow suit."

"I don't expect them to barf info," Zak countered, getting frustrated with how they were twisting his words. "I just don't want to be lied to."

"And I don't want to have to pay my ex-wife alimony," Liam said, rolling his eyes. "But sometimes life doesn't go the way you want it to. She didn't lie to hurt you. She's been through a lot these past two years and didn't want to dwell on it, didn't want it to be the focus of her time with you, of her Christmas. She was afraid you'd pity or judge her for getting dumped—though frankly, I say good riddance. That Pressley guy was a turd." He glanced around the table with pursed lips. "He's a personal injury lawyer for Bruce Kay and Associates."

A bunch of the men grimaced in understanding.

Zak didn't understand and his face said as much because Liam took pity on him and explained. "Notorious ambulance chasers in town. They're the scum of the earth. Nearly out of their cars before the paramedics are, hounding victims as they're being loaded onto stretchers and put in neck braces. It's disgusting how cut-throat they are. When her boyfriend told me who he worked for I immediately went and washed my hands after shaking his." He shuddered. "She's better off without him for sure."

"You said Dina hired Aurora?" Aaron asked, changing the subject and then raising the stakes by tossing more poker chips into the center, making all the other men's eyebrows lift.

Liam nodded. "Saw something in her. Passion and drive, integrity and a willingness to put in the long hours, in the grunt work to prove her worth. She's a determined thing, I'll tell you that. Smart as a whip and always willing to help out on a case. Works her fingers to the bone."

"Dina was always an incredible judge of character," Aaron said stiffly, the muscles in his jaw clenching and unclenching. "No-nonsense, but fair and kind. She knew a person's worth within minutes of meeting them. If she saw something in Aurora, she wasn't wrong."

Liam swirled the ice around in his glass of scotch. "She wasn't wrong. Aurora will be the first of the new batch of first-year associates to make junior partner when she's ready. If she continues to work the way she is now, she's going to go places. I plan to do everything I can to keep her at our firm."

Zak sucked in a deep breath, pushing a strange ache out of his chest.

He felt proud of Aurora as he heard Liam and Aaron go on about her. Because he knew everything they'd said to be true. He hadn't known her for very long, but what he did know, he'd fallen hard for.

"You know you overreacted," Adam said, resting a brotherly hand on Zak's shoulder and giving him an affectionate squeeze. "We all overreact from time to time. And a good woman will see that you were being a pretentious ass and hopefully forgive you ... " He grinned and released Zak's shoulder. "If you're willing to grovel, that is."

Aaron and Mark snickered and nodded.

Mitch's bugged-out eyes said he'd groveled a time or two in his day. "No shame in groveling when it's a good woman you want to forgive you," he said. "It's when you let your ego and your pride get in the way that you lose out on the good things in life. The good people."

Emmett turned to face Mitch. "Fortune cookie?"

Mitch shook his head. "Horoscope app on Paige's phone."

Emmett nodded. "Wise words no matter where they came from."

"Look," Liam started, "do you want her back or not? Are you able to get over the white lies and start fresh? Start your relationship open and honest?" He lifted a shoulder, then drained his scotch before standing up and heading to his leather-top bar to refill. "I mean, if you guys *do* get together and things go south, I can't represent you. She works for my firm. It'd be a conflict of interest. She's also a great lawyer, so she'd take you to the fucking cleaners, just FYI." He grinned like an asshole as he used the ice tongs to grab a few cubes from the ice bucket and drop them in his glass. He poured himself the scotch, then wandered back to the table. "My money is on her leaving you though." He pointed his finger at Zak's chest and arms. "Muscles are overrated."

Zak snorted. "Says the man who is now seeing one of my personal trainers three days a week."

Liam sipped his scotch. "I'm looking to tone, not bulk up like The Hulk."

"What are you going to do?" Emmett asked. "I have her number if you want it. She didn't want yours though, didn't want to hound you. She's pretty resigned to the fate of your relationship, so if you want her, you have to go get her."

Did Zak want Aurora?

Was the Earth round?

Did beer taste good?

Was the Pope Catholic?

Of course he wanted her. He couldn't remember the last time he'd wanted anything or anyone so badly. He'd been a wreck all week, angry at himself, at Aurora, at Loni. His ex had made his ability to trust virtually nonexistent. He was unable to discern a forgivable lie from an unforgivable one. Because to him, a lie was a lie, and if you were able to lie once about where you worked, you were also able to lie about book club and orgies.

"Aurora is not Loni," Liam added. "You can't paint all women with the same brush. What if they did that to us?"

Fair point.

"I can see it on your face, bro," Adam added. "You miss her. You know you overreacted. You're just struggling with your ego to go to her and admit you were wrong."

"But she was wrong, too," Zak ground out. "She lied."

Nearly all the men around the table said "Oh for fuck's sake!" at the same time.

"Get over yourself," Mark said, shaking his head and tossing his cards into the pile. "I fold."

"Yeah, bro. We all fuck up. Even you," Aaron added,

tipping his scotch back and draining it. Liam angled his head, asking if Aaron wanted another one, but the big redheaded SEAL shook his head. "Gonna head out soon. You bitches gonna fold or play?"

Mitch stood up and tossed his cards down. "I'm tired of this, and I fold. Win her back. Don't. It's only your happiness on the line." He rolled his eyes, then took his empty beer bottle to the kitchen muttering things like "Christ almighty" and "what a moron."

The rest of the men followed suit, all of them but Aaron tossing their cards face-down on the table.

Zak tossed his cards down too. He had nothing in his hand.

Grinning, Aaron scooped all the chips toward himself, then stood up to go and collect his money from all the losers, leaving Zak sitting at the table alone with his thoughts.

"It's New Year's Eve tomorrow, dude. You going to start the new year off without at least seeing her? Without at least talking to her?" Emmett asked, returning to the card table and slapping Zak on the back. "Her car still in the parking lot at the gym?"

Zak nodded. "Yeah."

"Well, then you know where she'll be." He patted Zak's shoulder, and when he removed his hand, a piece of paper fluttered to the table in front of Zak. "Don't fuck this up, bro. She deserves a second chance. You both do."

16

ZAK WASN'T ready to go home yet. Especially since his house was now empty.

Loni and Craig—true to form—called him on December 27, saying that they left the cabin on Mount Baker early and were coming to pick up the kids. But, of course, because nothing was ever easy with his ex-wife and her small-footed lover, Zak had to take the kids again on New Year's Eve because Loni and Craig, the speedboat salesman, had tickets to a big party at The Ludo Lounge.

Zak hadn't had it in him to argue with the narcissists who figured nobody else had a life or any plans and that even if they did, they would change them up to accommodate Loni and pinky-finger-ring Craig.

His grandparents were over visiting Adam, Mira and Violet for a few nights, so now he was alone.

All alone.

No kids, no grandparents ... no Aurora.

And even though he normally had no problem arriving home to an empty house, tonight he just couldn't bear the thought of it. So he stuck around Liam's place, tying one on because it was the weekend and he was lonely and heartbroken.

Thankfully, his friend and the club founder didn't seem to mind the company.

They cleaned up the potato chip bowls, put the card table away and the beer bottles into the recycling. Mason stuck around too, as apparently, according to the baby monitor app he had on his phone, Willow was zonked out in her crib at home.

"So, whatcha gonna do about your lady love?" Mason asked, sitting back in Liam's brown leather couch, his ankle cocked on one knee, arms spread out over the back of the furniture like he owned the place. "You gonna go to her, tell her you fucked up, get on your hands and knees and grovel?" He tipped his beer up into his mouth, grinning around the bottle neck before he began to guzzle.

Zak's jaw clenched and unclenched. "I'm just struggling to get past the lying."

Liam sniffed, then leaned forward and knocked the ash from his cigar into the ashtray. They rarely smoked cigars around the table—because doctors Emmett and Mark would have conniptions, then proceed to lecture them—but once in a while Liam busted out a stogie. Zak never took part though —his lungs and mouth were clean and cancer-free, and he preferred to keep them that way.

Healthy body, healthy mind.

"You really think you have a right to be so high and mighty?" Liam asked, lifting his head slightly and cocking one brow before he sat back in his recliner. "I keep wondering when you're going to get a nosebleed from that mile-high high horse you're so precariously perched on and instead come down and join the rest of us average Joes who from time to time lie and screw up."

Zak's head reared back. "I don't fucking lie."

Liam's face held a peculiar look. He studied Zak for a moment, drew on his cigar, held the smoke in his mouth, then slowly released it, studying the cigar as if it were not just a nice Cuban from a grateful client, but a priceless artifact or the holy grail. "You sure about that?" he finally asked.

"What the fuck are you getting at?" All the hairs on Zak's arms rose to attention. An itch at the back of his neck grew practically unbearable until he was forced to scratch it, chasing it around the top of his spine and down his shoulders.

"You don't think I know?"

Zak lurched forward and stared Liam square in the face. "Know what? Fucking spit it out."

Unlike Zak, who was about ready to snap, Liam was as cool as a goddamn cucumber. That just made the whole thing worse. "That you threatened your ex-wife into giving you shared custody of your children."

"Dude," Mason muttered, his blue eyes darting back and forth between Liam and Zak. "Not cool." Then his face grew serious and he sat forward in his seat. "Like threatened to beat her up?"

Zak's body slammed back into the couch, his hands landing hard on his thighs. "How the fuck ... ?"

Liam simply lifted his brows. "Secrets have a way of coming out. Just leave it at that. I know you leveraged the video you had of her for a fair custody agreement. Even after you told me that you wouldn't sink to her level, you did anyway. You lied to me." He held up his hand, his cigar between his index and middle finger, the smoke curling up around his dark blond head like a gray-blue halo. "I'm not judging you, man. Loni was a bitch for what she put you through. The cheating, the lies. You deserved shared custody, don't get me wrong. But you're lying to yourself, and you're lying to everybody else, if you don't think you stooped to her level. You're a liar just like the rest of us."

Holy fucking shit! Liam knew.

Zak didn't think anybody but he and Loni knew.

Had she told her lawyer? She must have.

Liam swirled the ice around in his glass and stared blankly into the fire. "Had Cidrah done something like that to me and I was on the verge of losing Jordie, I probably would have sunk to a whole new level too." His gaze pivoted, and he pinned it on Zak. "But if you had come to me beforehand, we could have gone about it the right way. I could have gone to her lawyer. Instead I had to find out about it *from* her lawyer. It made me look like I didn't know what the hell was going on with my client—because I didn't. It made it look like you didn't trust me. It made it look like I don't know how to do my job—which I certainly fucking do. And, it made it look like you were threatening her."

Zak's gaze fell to his lap, and he stared at his drink as the memories of just how far he'd stooped hit him in the back of the head like a sucker punch.

"Fuck," Zak breathed.

"Dude, what'd you do?" Mason asked, his voice low.

Liam took a sip of his drink. "I'm not angry ... just *disappointed*. I'll always have your back, man. You should know that by now."

He did know that. He just didn't want anybody, not even Liam, to know how low he'd sunk.

So much for that.

It's surprising the lengths a person will go to when they think they're about to lose everything that means anything to them, when they think they're about to lose their children. He was ashamed of what his ex-wife had pushed him to do. He'd gone practically insane. He wasn't in his right mind, wasn't thinking clearly. He was blinded by the rage, the pain, the heartache, the fear.

The fear was the big one. The fear that after everything she'd done, she'd still win and Zak would lose his children.

And the thought of losing his kids, his business, everything he loved, everything he'd worked so damn hard to build, all because a woman who had lied to him since day one just continued to lie. She painted him out to be abusive and an alcoholic, and that had caused him to sink to a new low. A level so far below the surface, daylight was nonexistent. A place so dark and dismal, so void of any life, light or oxygen, not even maggots could survive. He'd found that dark place inside him, lurking, waiting for a moment when he'd been pushed beyond all reason, scared out of his mind. And that moment had come in the form of his ex-wife and her heinous lies. Only then did he reach inside, put a lock around his heart and another around his conscience, and then stepped directly into the darkness. He did what he had to do to ensure he didn't lose his children.

He blackmailed his ex-wife.

Somehow, Zak wound up with a video in his inbox one day from an anonymous email address. He never did find out who sent it to him. Not that it really mattered. What mattered was that in that video was none other than Zak's wife, Loni, doing three lines of cocaine off a glass table, naked, and then proceeding to get fucked—without condoms—by two men while blowing another. The music in the background suggested that it was some low-budget porno, and it very well might have been, but Zak would hedge to guess someone at one of the orgies was simply videotaping everything to use as leverage later.

And now that leverage belonged to Zak.

After he watched the entire video, he made sure the children were with Adam before he drove over to Loni's house and showed her what he had on her. Then, he gave her his conditions.

First, she would recant every harsh word and every lie she spewed about him, sign a letter stating that she lied in front of the mediator and that Zak was in fact *not* an alcoholic or abusive. That he had never raised a hand to her or the children.

Second, she would accept his terms for shared custody. He was just as much their children's parent as she was, and he would be with them an equal amount of time. They would decide on days and holidays at a later date, but she had no more power than he did when it came to the well-being of their children.

Third, he handed her a piece of paper with the amount he was willing to settle for in the divorce. She either had to accept it and not a penny more, or he'd have no choice but to give the videotape to Liam and tell him to file it with the court.

And fourth, if she so much as touched another drug of any kind during one of her fuck parties, he would make sure she never, ever saw her children again.

She'd forced his hand, so he had to force hers. She'd made him stoop to her level, made him play dirty. After she'd ruined their marriage, made a cuckold out of him, lied to him and their children for over a year, she still wanted more. She still insisted upon torturing him even more, on taking from him even more. And so he'd reached his limit.

He lifted his head and stared into the orange flames of the fireplace, watching them lick and flicker. All of his actions, all of his choices came back at him in full force until he felt like an anvil was perched on top of his chest and he could hardly breathe.

He blinked and swallowed. Suddenly, a short stocky tumbler of amber liquid was thrust in front of his face. He grabbed it and immediately brought the rim to his lips, letting the smooth bourbon slide down his throat. The slight burn at the end was most welcome.

"Figured you needed this," Liam said with a deep exhale as he wandered back to his chair. "Falling off a horse that high is bound to hurt. Drink up. It'll ease the pain."

Mason chuckled and finished his beer. "We all lie, bro. It's human nature. Most of the time it's for self-preservation, and it sounds like that's what this chick was doing too." He drew his free hand down his short, dark beard, his blue eyes glimmering in the muted lighting of Liam's living room. "I mean, fuck, I lie to myself every goddamn day when I look in the mirror and say I know what the fuck I'm doing with Willow. That being a dad is easy and I'm rocking it." He shook his head, pulled harder on his chin and made a noise in his throat. "I'm up to my neck in baby shit, man. Spit-up and sleepless nights. And I'm raising a *girl*. I don't know the first thing about chick shit. About periods or hormones, training bras or tea parties. I'm royally fucked." He closed his eyes for a moment and swallowed. "When I decided to go the surrogate route, I knew that it was obviously a fifty-fifty toss up— boy or girl—as it is with any pregnancy. But anytime I pictured holding my baby or playing with my kid, I pictured that kid being a boy. I figured I could handle being a father to a boy. Teach him how to write his name in the snow, throw a football, walk on the street side of the sidewalk when he's with a woman—you know manly shit." His blue eyes went wide with terror. "What am I supposed to teach Willow?"

Zak could remember having similar feelings shortly after Tia was born. He loved Aiden with all his heart, but with Aiden he felt more prepared. He would teach his son the things that Zak's grandfather had taught him. But what would he teach Tia?

His little spitfire of a daughter had quickly shown him

though that it wasn't *he* who would be teaching her, but *she* who would be teaching him. Every day, every moment he spent with his daughter he learned something new about himself, about who he was as a man, as father, as a person.

Liam tilted his head, his smile small but also kind as he focused on Mason—their newest single dad recruit. "Boy or girl, we're all treading water with weights on doing this whole single parent thing. All Willow really needs right now is to know that her daddy loves her and will always be there for her. The rest will sort itself out. Don't beat yourself up."

Just when you thought Liam was a giant dick with a shriveled prune where his heart should be, he surprised them all with his compassionate side and his words of fatherly wisdom and encouragement.

Liam shrugged, then tucked his cigar between his teeth. "Besides, enough of these fuckers are getting pussy-whipped, you can always get one of their women to give Willow the period talk and take her bra shopping."

Shit, Zak spoke too soon.

Liam chuckled and sucked on the tip of his cigar, his dark eyes holding that devilish gleam they all knew too well.

Mason didn't seem overly reassured. Instead, he stood his big frame up off the couch with the grunt normally reserved for a septuagenarian, stretched his tattooed arms and glanced at his watch. "And on that note, I'm going to go see my baby and let her know how much I love her. Maybe I'll see if I can find a good picture book on puberty that I can buy her. If I start reading it to her now, perhaps I won't have to have the talk with her when it happens." He lifted his eyebrows in hope, then dropped them as he stopped in front of Zak, his blue eyes laser-focused. "Aurora sounds like a great woman, and even great women make mistakes. If I were you, I wouldn't let my biggest mistake be letting her get away." Then he took his leave, promising to see Liam the following night at some New Year's Eve party.

Zak focused back on the dancing flames in the fireplace.

He was a fool.

He'd lived his life so strictly, so scheduled, so ... rigid. He even demanded rigidity from his kids. His house had rules, and everyone was expected to follow them. No sugar besides special occasions, no screen time besides the weekends, daily exercise, thirty minutes of reading before bed, integrity, compassion, honesty, transparency—always.

It was how he functioned. How he'd managed to become a success. By demanding excellence from not only himself but from others as well.

And yet, when threatened with his biggest fear—losing his children—he lost all composure, all integrity and had gone and blackmailed the mother of his children. Then he lied about it. He lied about it to everyone. Hell, in some ways, he'd even lied to Loni, because getting that video filed with the courts was the last thing he ever wanted to do. Not when it meant his children could have access to it later. She was, after all, still their mother. He only wanted her to think he would so she'd let him keep his kids—and his business.

But no matter which way you looked at it, he'd lied.

He boasted, even. Told anybody he could that Loni had dragged him through the mud, yet he'd kept his hands clean, refusing to stoop to her level. Only he had.

He was a liar.

He'd made a mistake.

"Having some epiphanies?" Liam asked, flipping the lever on the side of his chair so the footrest popped up. With an *ah,* he leaned back, brought the cigar to his lips again, shut his eyes and inhaled. "You did what you did to keep your kids. Nobody is going to fault you for that. It's not like you leaked the video, and I think I know you pretty well to know that you never would leak it. But you put the fear of God into Loni, and that worked in our favor." He lifted his tumbler of scotch in his other hand and offered a small toast, still not bothering to open his eyes. "Nothing wrong with using the leverage that falls in your lap to your advantage." He finally opened his eyes, pinning them on Zak as he lifted his glass higher. "To leverage. To liars and, most of all ... to forgiveness." Then he tipped his tumbler back and finished his drink.

Zak slammed his drink, stood up and wandered over to the leather-top bar to pour himself another. He'd been a right fool. Not only for believing that he was better than he was, thinking that if he told enough people that he hadn't sunk to Loni's level that in some way it would eventually be true, but for thinking that he was better than Aurora. That he was above lying to make himself look better in the eyes of people whose opinions he valued.

Because she obviously valued his opinion, otherwise she wouldn't have let him believe the things she did. She'd protected her pride and her heart. He didn't want him to know she'd just been dumped by her boyfriend, who then ran back to his ex and proposed. That had to hurt. It'd hurt Zak if he were in her shoes. He'd have done his best to keep that news under wraps too.

She wanted him to see her for more than her deficiencies, more than her shortcomings, but for the incredible, beautiful person that she was inside. And he did see all of that—and more. She was amazing with his children, his grandparents adored her, and Zak ... Zak hadn't been able to stop thinking about her since the moment she left on Christmas. Not since Loni—hell, possibly not even Loni—had Zak been so taken, so smitten with a woman like the way he was with Aurora. She was smart and sweet and funny. And when he'd laid his heart bare, telling her about his childhood and his divorce, she hadn't recoiled in judgment or looked at him with pity.

Instead, she'd curled up tighter against him and, without any words, reassured him that there were still good women out there. Good, loving women.

And he'd gone and fucked it all up with the best, most loving woman of them all.

He was a class-A idiot who needed to learn to be flexible and forgiving. He only hoped Aurora could forgive him, because he'd certainly gone and made the biggest mistake of them all—letting her get away.

"Yep, there it is," Liam said, one eye open as he lounged in his chair, his cigar between his fingers, his empty glass in his other hand. "Just figured out you can't live without her. That you've fucked it all up and you need to go beg for forgiveness."

Zak slammed back the full glass of bourbon, sucking in air as it burned its way down his throat. He poured another and did the same.

"Slow down, bro. Bourbon is meant to be sipped. If you're going to do shots, there's Patron in the cupboard," Liam said, standing up from his chair with grunts similar to those they'd heard earlier from Mason. He approached the bar, setting his glass down on the leather top and pointing to the bottle of scotch next to Zak's wrist. Zak unscrewed the lid and poured Liam three fingers.

Liam thanked him, lifted his glass in the air and waited for Zak to do the same. "To epiphanies. May you remember yours in the morning."

17

It was the morning of December 31st when Zak's phone ringing on his nightstand woke him up.

Having taken an Uber home from Liam's, Zak drank a couple more beers before he retired to his cold, empty bed, passing out more than he fell asleep. Needless to say, the ringing in his ears, combined with that of his phone, sounded more like a fire alarm going off inside his brain.

The call display said it was Loni.

Oh fuck.

He did not want to speak to his ex-wife right now.

But there might be something wrong with the kids.

Groaning, he slid his finger across the screen and put on the speaker option.

"Hello?" he croaked

"Dad?" It was Aiden.

Zak's eyes widened, and he sat up in bed, knuckling the last bits of his restless sleep from his sore eyes, his head pounding with every movement. "Buddy, what's wrong? Everything okay?"

"Have you talked to Aurora?"

Zak scrubbed his hand down his face and pulled on his chin. "No, buddy, I haven't."

Aiden sighed. "I know she lied, Dad. But they weren't like Mom's lies. Please don't dump her. Tia and I really like her, and she makes you happy ... at least she did."

He already planned to go see Aurora today, to apologize and ask for forgiveness, to grovel if he had to. He just needed to shower, pop a couple of Tylenol and down a gallon of coffee before he saw her. The woman deserved an apology by a man who didn't currently have a meat cleaver severing the two halves of his brain.

He blinked a few times, saw spots and then decided that keeping his eyes closed was probably better. "Buddy, these are grownup issues," he finally said, the words in his head sounding like a Slipknot record being played backward.

Aiden growled on the other end. "No, Dad, they're not." His son's words were heated, full of frustration and pain. Zak wanted to reach inside the phone and draw Aiden into his arms, absorb his hurt. "Learn how to forgive, Dad. Learn that people make mistakes but that we can learn from them, that we can be better people. Isn't that what you teach us? It's okay to make mistakes as long as we learn from them?"

"Even you make mistakes, Dad," Tia yelled from the background. "And we forgive you for them. Like when you accidentally stepped on my papier-mache bunny that I made at art camp. I forgave you."

Zak's body slowly sank back down into the pillows. "Where's your mother?" he asked, hoping that Loni wasn't right there snickering with Craig.

"Mom and Craig are still sleeping. We're in the basement so they can't hear us," Aiden said.

Smart move.

"Please, Dad," Tia said, her voice closer to the phone now. "We really like Aurora. Doesn't our opinion mean anything?

You can't just break up with her without our input. We're all in this together, right?"

Zak's head throbbed.

"We'll be very disappointed in you if you don't at least talk to her, Dad," Aiden said, adopting his best Zak voice. "And as you know, disappointment is worse than being angry."

"That's right, Dad. We'll be *very* disappointed in you," Tia added.

He knew his words would come back to haunt him one day. Be thrown in his face. Bite him in the ass. He'd known it the moment he'd spouted them off the first time to his children. But it was what parents said. His grandparents had said the same thing to Zak and Adam when they were kids, and he was sure that cavemen and cave-women were grunting similar things to their cave-children back when they were inventing the wheel.

I'm not angry you left the mammoth meat out for the saber-toothed tiger to steal, son, I'm just disappointed. Or something like that. He wasn't a history nerd like Adam.

"We like Aurora. More than we like *Craig.*"

"Nobody likes Craig," Aiden said to his sister.

Zak's chest shook on a laugh, which only made his head hurt even more.

Nobody liked Craig.

"You're coming to get us later, right, Dad?" Tia asked. "Can we all go see Aurora together?"

Zak wasn't awake or sober enough to think clearly. But the one thing he did know, and had passed out last night knowing, was that beyond a shadow of a doubt, Aurora Stratford was worth fighting for, and damn it, hangover or not, he was going to do his best to win her back.

"I like that plan," Aiden said. "Dad?"

"Hmm?" Zak groaned.

"So that's the plan then, right? You'll come get us, and

then we'll go see Aurora. Apologize and say that everyone makes mistakes, including you," Aiden said, his voice sounding a lot more chipper than a moment ago but still with that fatherly bite to it at the end.

Zak swung his legs over the side of the bed and scratched his balls with his free hand, holding the phone out in the other one. He needed a shower. He needed coffee. He needed Aurora.

"Okay, Dad. We'll see you soon," Aiden said into the phone. "Then we'll go see Aurora."

"Wear something nice, Dad," Tia called. "We need to win her back. We should go get her flowers too. So she really knows you're sorry."

Zak stared at himself in the bathroom mirror.

Win her back.

He needed to go win her back.

He was ready.

He pulled on his chin—well not *quite* ready. Shower, Tylenol, breakfast, coffee, *then* win her back.

"Dad?" Aiden asked.

"Hmm?" Zak groaned again.

"We forgive you for breaking up with Aurora. Everybody makes mistakes."

Zak slowly blinked a few times at his reflection in the mirror, his eyes widening. He planted his hands on the bathroom counter and took a long, hard look at the man who gazed back at him.

A man who made mistakes.

A man who asked for forgiveness when he made those mistakes.

A man who forgave others when *they* made mistakes.

When had he become such a stickler to the rules? Unwilling to bend and compromise. Unwilling to forgive.

When Loni started fucking half the neighborhood?

But Aurora wasn't Loni.

Aurora wasn't Loni.

He knew that now without question. Aurora was the antithesis to Loni. She was kind and sweet, honest and compassionate. He doubted the woman had a mean bone in her body—well, unless she was dealing with Shadley Taylor, but he wouldn't even call that mean so much as just a real strong spine.

"That's right, Dad. Everybody makes mistakes," Tia said, interrupting his thoughts.

"You can say we're right, Dad," Aiden said. "Because you know that we are."

"He's just being stubborn," Tia murmured.

Zak blinked at his phone, then let out a long sigh. "You're right. You both are. Everybody makes mistakes."

"Including you," Tia added.

"Including me."

Both kids made *phew* noises on the other side of the phone.

"Didn't think we were going to get through to him for a moment there," Aiden muttered.

"Me either," Tia whispered.

Zak rolled his eyes. God, how he loved his kids.

"Are those Craig's footsteps upstairs?" Aiden asked, his voice an even lower hush.

"I think so." Tia grumbled. "He sounds like an elephant."

"Ah, crap. Okay, Dad, we gotta go. But we'll see you soon, and then we'll go get Aurora back." Then the phone went dead, and Zak was left staring at himself in the mirror, seeing for the first time in a very long time a man who had sunk to a low he was ashamed of, who had lied, who had made a mistake and who now needed to own his faults, ask for forgiveness and win back the woman who made him believe that he could indeed be happy again. Not only for the sake of his kids, but for the sake of his family.

For the sake of his heart.

Because he was only lying to himself—yet again—if he claimed that Aurora hadn't taken a huge piece of his heart the moment she walked into his life. She filled up the hollow in his chest left by Loni and her deception.

And now he had to go get that piece back, go win back the woman who made him feel whole again. Who made him wish for a partner, a person, a love he could come home to and share his life with.

She wasn't Loni. She was Aurora, and she'd made a mistake.

Now, he only hoped she'd forgive him for his.

"WE'LL FIGURE IT OUT, Mom, don't worry," Aurora said, wiping away a tear as she spoke with her parents over the phone.

After arriving home on Christmas, she was barely able to make it inside her sorry excuse for an apartment before she crumpled to the floor behind the door in a heap of tears. Only when she was severely dehydrated and in desperate need to use the bathroom did she pry her broken-hearted butt from the floor and schlep her way into her home.

She could have sworn her dead cactus was laughing at her.

She didn't bother to eat—she wasn't hungry. But she did unwrap the parcel from her parents to find a beautifully hand-knitted scarf and hat. Her mother was such an accomplished knitter, could do it without even looking. Aurora always wanted to learn how to knit. Needing to feel love, even if through the phone from thousands of miles away, she called her parents immediately and spoke with them for hours. They'd since spoken on the phone every day, and it felt really good. It eased the aching hollow in her heart that threatened to consume her whole every time she thought about Zak and the way he'd looked at her, the way he'd spoken to her.

She hadn't deserved his ire, but she also knew why he'd been so mad in the first place. She should have known. The man was jaded. The man was hurt. The man hated liars.

And Aurora had lied.

They were small lies in comparison to his ex's, but they were lies nonetheless, and Zak had a strict no-lies policy. Which she'd violated.

Since leaving the warm family environment at Zak's, she'd been overcome with a sense of loss and loneliness, particularly since she'd only left her house once, and that was to the corner store to get food. But of course, the corner store prices were double that of her regular grocery store, so she only bought the basics and had been living on cereal and milk for breakfast and lunch for the last week. Dinners were ninety-nine-cent Lean Cuisines she'd found in the back of her freezer. She forgot she'd bought about ten of them when they went on clearance.

Once you scraped off the freezer-burned parts, they were palatable.

So any time she wasn't working on cases emailed to her by the senior associates, she was on the phone with her parents. Her heart grew just a touch lighter, because it was back in New Hampshire, with people who loved her for who she was—lies, mistakes and all.

"I think we're going to have to sell the house," her mother said, emotion choking her words. "Your father's medical bills are just piling up too quickly."

Aurora clenched her jaw tight. "Just wait, okay? I'm due for a raise soon, and that should help."

Her mother let out a rattled breath. "I hate that you're having to take care of us. That's the not the way it's supposed to go. Parents take care of their children, not the other way around."

"And then children take care of their parents. Yes, that is the way it's supposed to go. It's okay, Mom. We'll sort it out."

"Maybe if we moved out west, got a place with you. I could work. We could share the responsibility of caring for your dad."

That was actually a fairly decent plan. She would love to have her parents closer. To have family and a support system.

"What does Dad think of that?" she asked.

"He misses you," she said. "We both do. Sure, this is our home, but it's empty now. We want to be where our daughter is." Aurora's mother didn't have to say it to know that she was thinking about Brecken. With him gone, all they had left was Aurora, and they didn't want to spend their last remaining years away from her.

Aurora didn't want to be away from them either.

"Let's look into that possibility more, Mom. I like that idea."

"You'd be okay living with your parents again?" she asked, a tense chuckle in her voice. "We wouldn't cramp your style?"

"What style? I work eighty-plus hours a week. I have no time for *style*."

Her mother's laugh was filled with hope and, in turn, filled Aurora with hope. The first bit of hope she'd felt since she walked out of Zak's home and into the cold and unforgiving winter wind that made icicles skitter down her back. "I'll talk to your dad about it, and then we can take the idea to his doctors. They'd need to sign off on him leaving as well."

"Right, that makes sense." Noise outside drew Aurora's

attention. Lots of clunking and beeping. She stood up from her spot on the couch, walked over to the window and pulled back the drapes. She had to squint through the blurry plastic she'd put up over the single-pane windows to trap some of the heat. Otherwise, her electricity bill would be through the roof, trying to heat the place. Not that she turned the thermostat on much—she just put on another pair of socks and a sweater. Slept in her winter coat if she needed to.

But it was easy enough to see what was going on, even through the plastic, and what she saw made her nearly drop the phone.

It was her car.

It was being offloaded onto the side of the road by a big, red tow truck.

"Mom, I'll have to call you back," she said quickly into the phone, rushing to her front door and sliding into her winter boots.

"Everything okay?" her mom asked.

"I don't know. I'll call you back." Then she hung up, grabbed her coat off the hanger and threw it on, slipping her phone into her pocket. She raced down the hallway of her apartment building and nearly fell down the single flight of stairs.

Bursting through the front lobby doors, she didn't have time to shiver from the intense gust of icy wind that hit her face and chest. She waved her arms to get the attention of the tow-truck driver. "Sir, sir, I can't pay for this. I'm sorry, but I can't pay for this."

This wasn't normally how tow-truck companies worked, was it? She thought they were called by the owner of the parking lot and the car was impounded until the owner of the car could pay to get it released.

Was Zak the owner of the parking lot?

"Sir, I'm sorry, but I think there's been some mistake," she said, coming to stand in front of the man who was currently working to unhook her car from his tow hitch.

"This your car?" he asked, not stopping what he was doing.

She zipped up her coat. "It is, but I can't pay for your services."

"Don't have to. It's been covered. All fixed, new winter tires. Your baby is running like a dream now. I towed it here because it's just me working tonight and I wouldn't have had a ride home."

Aurora's bottom lip dropped open. What?

All fixed. New winter tires. Running like a dream.

But who?

Just then, a truck she recognized pulled up along the curb behind her car.

A man she recognized and had cried millions of tears over the past week sat behind the steering wheel, his eyes sad.

He'd barely shut off the truck before the two back doors of the cab flew open and two smiling, gorgeous redheaded children ran toward her.

Tia and Aiden launched themselves at her, causing them all to fall back into a big snowdrift.

The kids giggled.

"We've missed you," Tia said, reaching into the neck of her coat and pulling out her friendship necklace, holding it up to show Aurora. "I haven't taken mine off."

Aurora reached into the neck of her coat and pulled out hers as well. "I haven't taken off mine either." She turned to Aiden. "And I found the perfect frame for your painting. It's already on my wall. Right in my living room so I can see it every day."

Aiden beamed.

"We came to say we're sorry," Tia said. "Well, more like

Dad needs to say he's sorry. He needs to gravol—I just learned that word from Grammy—and Dad needs to do it."

"It's *grovel*," Aiden corrected.

Tia scrunched up her face, relaxed it, then shrugged. "Well, whatever. Dad needs to do both, *gravol* and *grovel*. We just came here because we wanted to see you."

Aurora squeezed both kids tight. God, she loved these two.

The truck door shut behind them, and Aurora lifted her head, watching Zak as he slowly made his way around the front of the truck to stand in front of them.

Aurora stood up, leaving the children in the snow behind her. She blinked back tears. "I'm sorry I lied."

He swallowed as he shoved his hands into the pockets of his jeans and rocked back on his booted heels. "I'm the one who needs to apologize."

"Dad, you need to grovel," Tia interrupted. "Grammy says on your knees. You need to crawl toward her on your knees to let her know you messed up. That's what Grammy said you should do to get Aurora back."

Aurora's chin and bottom lip jiggled.

Zak rolled his eyes, but he was smiling.

"On your knees, Dad," Tia repeated, she and Aiden still sitting in the snow behind Aurora.

With his chest shaking, Zak did just that. On his knees, in only jeans, he sank into the snow and shuffled toward Aurora, taking her hand. He was smiling, but his eyes held so much more than amusement. They held sincerity; they held hurt ... they held hope. "Aurora ... Rory, I'm *really* sorry for how I reacted. It was uncalled for, and it was cruel. I never should have said the things I did or let you leave. It was a painful fall from my high horse, but one I needed to make in order to see how much richer our lives were in the few short days we got to know you."

Aurora let out a shaky breath, her eyes stinging when the chilly wind hit fresh tears.

Zak went on, taking her other hand as well and squeezing them both in his, keeping her warm. "We all make mistakes, including me."

"You make a lot, Dad," Tia said behind him. "But this was a big one."

"Thank, T," Zak ground out. "I'm beginning to regret bringing them," he said under his breath.

"I'm not." Aurora chuckled, her heart finally beginning to feel light again.

Zak's face sobered. "You are not *her*. You are not my ex, and I shouldn't have lumped you in with her like that. Her lies and your omissions could not be more polar opposite. Emmett and Liam told me the rest of your story ... " His mouth dipped into a frown. "I hope you don't mind?"

She shrugged. "It's my story. I should have just owned it instead of try and run from it. Try and hide it."

"I want to help you," he said. "Help your parents."

She was about to shake her head and say that she wasn't a charity case when Tia sprang up from their spot in the snow. "Dad, you forgot the flowers!" She raced back to the truck, heaved open the door and climbed in. Moments later she returned with a big bouquet of what looked like dark purple lilies and bright pink roses in her arms. She handed them to Aurora. "Dad picked this out."

Aurora smiled as she released Zak's hands and accepted the bouquet, bringing it to her nose. "It's beautiful. Thank you." She glanced at her car. "And thank you for getting it fixed and for the new winter tires. You really shouldn't have. It's too much."

Zak shook his head. "No, it's not. I owe you for how I treated you, for how I behaved. Helping you with your car is the least I could do. It's a start."

"My butt's wet," Aiden said, standing up.

"Mine too," Tia agreed. "Can we go into your house?"

Still on his knees in the freezing snow, Zak rested his hand on his daughter's shoulder. She was now the same height as her father. "Aurora might not want us in her home, honey."

Tia gave her dad a confused look. "Why not?"

"Because she hasn't taken Dad back yet," Aiden said, brushing snow off his pants.

"Well, why not?" Tia asked. "What's the problem? We brought her flowers. Dad apologized. He got her car fixed. What more is there to do? Is he not groveling enough? What does groveling look like? Should be on his stomach? Grammy said on his knees."

"Maybe they need to kiss?" Aiden asked, making a grossed-out face.

Zak's lips twitched, and a small smile crooked up at the corner of his mouth. He released his daughter's shoulder and reached for Aurora's hands again. She tucked the flowers into the crook of her arm and let him take her hands, loving his warmth and finally getting to touch him again. It'd only been a week, but it had felt like a lifetime.

"Tell me what I can do to make this right," he said, his dark blue eyes beseeching and earnest. "I'll strip down naked and roll around in the snow until I'm blue if it means you'll give me another chance."

"Gross," Tia muttered.

Aurora laughed through her nose.

Zak rolled his eyes again at his daughter before focusing them back on Aurora. "I'm really, truly sorry, Rory. I was an idiot. A self-righteous jackass. Blinded by my need for perfection and order, unable to see the mistake I was making, because in my head, I don't make mistakes. But I do. I make *a lot* of them, according to my kids. And treating you the way I did, letting you leave, was the biggest mistake of them all. I overreacted, and I'm so incredibly sorry."

"Like *way* overreacted," Tia said, rolling her eyes.

Zak shot his daughter a look. "Thanks, T."

She grinned at him.

"We'd love it if you came back to the house and spent New Year's Eve with us. As a family. We're going to have nachos, watch movies and drink sparkling apple juice when the clock strikes twelve."

"We never get juice, so it's a big deal," Tia added, her eyes going wide.

Zak's eyes twinkled. "It's a pretty big deal." He cleared his throat and squeezed her hands. "I've refunded your gym membership."

She jerked free from his grasp and took a step back. Her fingers tightened around the bouquet, which had now fallen to her side. "What? Why?"

He took an awkward knee-shuffle step forward, his eyes pleading with her to give him back her hand. "Because I told you I want to help you. I had no idea you were a lifetime member. That's an insane amount of money. Whatever possessed you to—"

She lifted her eyebrows, hoping he caught her drift and she didn't have to spell it out.

His own eyebrows nearly shot off his forehead. "Oh!"

"Call it a guilty pleasure—the only one I allowed myself." *More like an obsession, but we're not going to argue semantics.*

His grin turned boyish and cocky. "Okay, then."

Tia and Aiden's eyes bounced curiously between Aurora and Zak.

"Do you know what they're talking about?" Tia asked, wrinkling her nose.

"No clue," Aiden said, his tone almost bored. "I know I'm hungry though."

"Me too," Tia added.

"Clif Bars are in my glove compartment," Zak said, not taking his eyes off Aurora. He reached for her hand again. This time she let him take it. "And grab some towels to sit on. I don't want your wet asses on my seats!"

She hadn't taken her eyes off him either, but she heard the kids run through the snow and open up the truck doors, then slam them.

Her eyes slid to the side. When had the tow-truck driver left?

"I never cheated on anyone," she whispered, not quite ready to look him in the eyes again and instead glancing down at her snow-covered boots and his now soaking-wet knees. "I *was* with someone, like I told you, but he dumped me. I was ashamed. The problems in my life just kept piling up, and for a few short days, I just wanted to forget they existed. I didn't want him to ruin my Christmas. To ruin *our* Christmas. I'm sorry. I should have been honest from the beginning, honest about everything."

Zak shook his head. She helped him to his feet, and he cupped her face in his palms. There was nowhere else to look now but into the deep, fathomless pools of his crystal-blue eyes. Eyes that had captivated her from day one, eyes that had stolen her heart and looked at her in a way that made her feel like the most beautiful woman to walk the Earth. His lips brushed against hers. "It's I who needs to apologize," he said. "Say you'll give me another chance." It wasn't a question.

He released her face and tugged her against him, wrapping his arms around her waist until there wasn't even room for air between them. His mouth once again hovered over hers, their breaths mingling.

She blinked up at him. "I don't want to be a charity case," she said. "I don't want you to just *fix* all my problems with your checkbook. I want to pay you back for the car and the tires."

He shook his head. "That's not necessary. Call it a belated birthday present. But I promise that I won't just fix everything with money." His lips lifted into playful, lopsided smile. "Only some things."

She rolled her eyes and smiled, glancing back at her car once more.

He chuckled and tugged on her hands to get her attention again. "But please let me help you in different ways, then. You don't have to weather the storm alone anymore. You don't have to carry all your baggage by yourself anymore." He released her for a moment and flexed his arm muscles. "Have you seen the guns, lass?" he asked, adopting the brogue that made her swoon every time. "I can lift so much baggage with these things and not even break a sweat. Let me carry your luggage for you, lassie." He lifted his eyebrows up salaciously as he wrapped his arms around her waist again.

She tossed her head back and laughed. She loved the way he pulled laughter from the deepest depths of her belly. Made her whole face smile and her heart feel lighter than air.

"Only if you promise to *always* talk in a Scottish accent and only wear a kilt."

He dipped her low. "Och, lassie, even in the snow? My balls will freeze." His lips hovered just over hers, and his tongue darted out and slid across her bottom lip.

"You just offered to roll around naked in the snow for me, and now you're worried about wearing nothing but a kilt?" She cocked a brow at him. "Something seems fishy."

His wicked smile caused heat to flood her veins. "I'll do anything you ask, lass, just say you'll be mine. Say you'll give me another chance."

She wrapped her arms around his neck. "I'll give you

another chance, but you have a lot of groveling to still do. A lot of *apologizing* to do." She bit her lip. "With your tongue."

His smile was wicked. "I'll apologize to you all day, every day if I have to. Until my tongue cramps and falls off."

"Oh, well, we can't have that."

He swiped his tongue over her lip. "I'll never stop showing you how much you mean to me. How sorry I am for being such an inflexible, pretentious jerk."

She smiled against his mouth. "Okay. I like the sounds of that." She tightened her grip around his neck and hummed in thought for a moment. "Maybe I won't make you wear a kilt in the snow ... shrinkage and all that. But when we're in the bedroom, definitely." She nipped his bottom lip.

He growled. "Aye, I can do that. I can do that for you." His eyes darkened to the color of the night sky just before the stars came out. "I'll do anything for you." Then he sealed his mouth over hers, banishing the misery of the past week and filling her heart with hope for the future.

The horn of Zak's truck behind them began to honk incessantly, and they heard the cheers and whoops of Tia and Aiden inside.

Zak chuckled against her mouth, his teeth knocking hers before he pulled away. "You ready to take all three of us on?"

She glanced behind him and smiled. "I wouldn't have it any other way."

EPILOGUE

One year later ...

"OPEN OURS NEXT!" Tia beamed, bouncing on her knees in her plaid penguin Christmas pajamas. She exchanged looks with her father and brother as they all slid four shoebox-size boxes in front of Aurora.

Aurora pursed her lips and glanced at Zak. "You guys, we agreed to not go crazy. One gift each. This looks like more than three." She tapped each beautifully wrapped box. "I count four."

Zak rolled his eyes. "Just open them, will you?"

"Yeah," Aiden agreed. "We all went in on the gift. It's from all of us. We just needed four boxes to make it work."

Tia's amber eyes glittered as she nodded, barely able to contain herself from spoiling whatever was inside the boxes. The kids had already unloaded their stockings and the majority of their gifts. Aurora's gift for them and Zak remained unopened beneath the tree. She hoped they liked what she picked out for them.

"Pleeeeeease," Tia begged. "Open them."

Aurora set her coffee mug down and glanced up at the three people in her life she'd come to love more than anything. "But you guys have already given me so much, I don't need anything else."

"Will. You. Open. It!" Aiden ground out, an edge of frustration to his tone.

He was so much like his father, right down to the temper.

Zak's hand landed on his son's shoulder. "Easy, buddy."

Aiden glanced up at his father. "But Dad ... "

"It's not like we've got a hamster in each box and if she doesn't open the lid soon, they're going to suffocate. Patience, son."

Aiden let out an exasperated huff, then sat back and crossed his arms. "Sorry, Aurora."

Aurora's eyes softened as she looked at the boy she'd come to love like her own son. "It's okay, Aiden. I know you're just excited. But I'd actually really like it if you three opened your gifts from me first." Her gift from them was obviously going to be superior to whatever she got them, so she wanted to end it all on a high note rather than their disappointment.

Aiden sat up and was about to protest, but Zak rested his hand on his son's knee. "Sure. If that's what you'd prefer, we can open your gifts first."

"But Dad—"

Zak gave his son a stern look of warning.

Aurora reached for the three gift bags beneath the tree and passed them out to each of them, her gut spinning like she'd just stepped off the Tilt-a-Whirl at the fair.

"They're nothing big," she started, watching as they each opened their bags. "I've taken up knitting. A way to disengage from work and de-stress. It's been helpful. And then I thought that we could each do something special together, which is why there are gift certificates in each bag as well."

Aiden pulled out the dark gray and black knit cap she'd

knitted him, along with the pass for two people to the brand-new indoor rock-climbing gym downtown. He'd been making noises about wanting to try it out.

His smile warmed her insides, and the last of his frosty exterior and frustration seemed to evaporate. He lunged at her off the floor, wrapping his arms around her neck. "Thank you, Aurora. This is awesome. I've wanted to try that bouldering gym forever."

She grinned back at him, pecking him on the side of the cheek. "I've heard you. I've always wanted to try rock climbing too. Figured we could go together."

His smile grew even wider. "That would be great." He sat back down next to his dad and pulled his knit cap on over his wild red bedhead.

Zak pulled out a larger, matching knit cap to his son's and immediately tugged it over his hair. Then he drew out a gift certificate for the two of them to go on a brewery tour in Portland—something he'd always wanted to do but never found the time for it.

He glanced up at her, his eyes sparkling. "Thank you, Rory. This is really thoughtful. I love the knit cap, and I'm so excited for the tour. We've been looking at expanding Club Z to Oregon anyway, so it'll give me a chance to scope out some potential sites."

Tia, Aiden and Aurora all groaned.

"No work talk, Dad," Tia said with exasperation in her voice. "You promised Christmas would be work-free."

Zak's lip jiggled before he smiled and wrapped his arm around his daughter. "Right. Sorry. My bad. No more work talk, I promise."

Tia nodded, then pulled out her own dark green and light purple knit cap and a matching scarf. They also matched the scarf and knit cap Aurora had knit herself earlier and Tia had admired.

"I love them," Tia said, pulling the knit cap on her head and wrapping the scarf around her neck. "They're just like yours."

"There's more in there," Aurora said, her eyes flicking up to Zak's for just a moment. She'd cleared it with him before she bought Aurora her gift certificate for her first ear piercing. She'd also cleared it with Loni, as she didn't want to take that milestone away from Tia's mother if it was something Loni wanted to be a part of. Loni couldn't have cared less.

Tia pulled out the gift certificate. Her eyes squinted and ran across the piece of cardstock before they flew up to Aurora's face. Now it was her turn to lunge herself forward and into Aurora's arms. "Oh my God. Thank you, Aurora. I've wanted to get my ears pierced for so long."

"We can go grab lunch after if you like," Aurora offered. "And I figured, while we're there, maybe I'll get another piercing."

Zak's eyes went wide.

She gave him a sarcastic eye roll. "I've always wanted one in the top of my ear or my nose."

"I vote for your nose," Tia said, sitting back next to her dad. "When I'm eighteen, I'm going to get my first tattoo and my nose pierced."

"I know it's not much," Aurora started, "and I'm sure whatever you got me is going to be ten times more amazing, but, well—I hope you guys like your gifts." She knitted her fingers together in her lap and twisted. This family of three had embraced her like one of their own. Later today, they were going to embrace her parents as their own as well, when they arrived from New Hampshire and moved into the apartment over the garage.

Zak had done exactly what he'd promised. He took care of her. He took care of her family. Her parents had finally agreed to move out west. They sold their home (though it took a while), her dad's health got to a point where his doctors were comfortable with him flying, and now they were going to be living in the same household as Aurora—because she'd also moved in a short while ago.

"Aurora! Earth to Aurora!"

A light touch on her thigh brought her back to the moment. All three of them were looking at her funny.

"You okay?" Zak asked. "We thought we'd lost you there for a minute. Where'd you go?"

She blinked back tears and shook her head. "Just thinking about all the things I have to be thankful for this year. All the amazing things, amazing people in my life." She leaned forward and touched each of their knees, giving them a gentle squeeze. "I honestly don't need any gift, you guys. I have everything I've ever wanted."

Their smiles were all so similar, so genuine and kind.

"Your gifts were amazing, too," Tia said. "I love my hat and scarf, and I can't wait to get my ears pierced."

Zak and Aiden both nodded.

"Your gifts came from the heart," Zak said. "And you have the biggest heart we've ever met."

"Can she finally open her gifts?" Aiden asked, the impatience back in his voice.

Zak rolled his eyes, but he pushed the boxes closer to Aurora, nodding. "I'd say it's about time. Go on, open them." He tapped the one on the left. "Open them left to right, though. There's a method to our madness."

Chuckling, she carefully untied the red satin ribbon on the first box, then lifted the lid off. There was a piece of cardstock paper inside that said *Will*.

That was it.

Her eyes drifted up to the faces before her. Each held a different look.

Zak's was calm. Tia's anxious. Aiden could barely contain himself.

"Next one," Aiden said, bouncing up and down where he sat. He tapped the next box.

She did the same thing as before, untying the ribbon, then lifting the lid.

There was another piece of paper. This one said *You*.

Butterflies began to wildly beat their wings in her belly.

She moved on to the next box.

This one said *Marry*.

All those butterflies began to prepare for liftoff.

With slippery fingers and her pulse racing and her chest practically heaving, she untied the final ribbon and lifted the last lid.

Us?

Will You Marry Us?

On top of the last piece of paper was a small wooden ring box.

With shaky fingers and tears blurring her vision, she lifted the box up and opened it.

She was near blinded from the sparkler inside.

"We love you," Zak started. "You're already a member of the family, the most incredible stepmom to the kids, the most supportive and amazing partner to me. Let's just make it all official. Become an Eastwood. Or a Stratford-Eastwood, if you want to hyphenate. But marry us."

She lifted her head. Hot tears now teemed down her cheeks.

"Because you're not just marrying me. You're marrying us. I'm a package deal."

"Three for the price of one," Aiden said, his face now as radiant as the north star on a clear night.

"We helped Dad pick out the ring," Tia added. "Do you like it?"

Like it? She loved it. She was afraid to touch it.

She inconspicuously pinched the top of her wrist, just to make sure this was all still real.

She shut her eyes and waited for the walls to come crashing down around her, for the dream to finally end.

Nothing.

"What's she doing?" Tia whispered.

"Meditating?" Aiden asked.

Aurora opened her eyes and smiled at them all, blinking away fresh tears. "Just taking it all in," she said. "Had to pinch myself and make sure this was all real."

All three of them smiled back at her in understanding.

"Put it on," Tia encouraged.

"She hasn't said *yes* yet," Aiden whispered through the side of his mouth. "Why hasn't she said *yes*, Dad? Did we propose wrong?"

Aurora hiccupped a sob before reaching into the box and plucking the ring from its soft velvet bed. "You did it perfectly," she said. "It was best proposal I ever could have imagined."

"What's your answer?" Aiden asked. "It's *yes,* right?" He turned to face his father. "Why wouldn't she say *yes*? She lives here. She loves us. Getting married just makes sense, right?"

"Of course my answer is *yes*." She chuckled, wiping the tears from beneath her eyes. "A thousand times yes."

Aiden and Tia's smiles threatened to meet their ears.

"Dad, maybe she's waiting for you to put the ring on her finger," Tia offered. "Like they do in the movies."

"That must be it," Aiden agreed. "Why else would she still be holding it if she just said *yes?*"

Zak's chuckle was warm and throaty as he repositioned himself on his knees and took the ring from Aurora's still trembling and now very sweaty fingers. His eyes spoke of promises and passion that made those butterflies in her belly do loop-the-loops and figure eights until they were all dizzy.

"Aurora Stratford," he started, "will you marry us?"

She nodded and sniffed as more tears raced toward her chin. Then she held out her hand so he could slip the ring on her finger. "Yes, I'll marry you. I'll marry all of you." She lowered her eyes and her voice, focusing solely on Zak. "We'll get Liam to take care of the prenup."

His grin made goosebumps break out across her arms. "God, I love you."

Aiden and Tia both cheered, stood up and tackled Zak and Aurora until the four of them were in a hug pile on the floor, giggling.

Tia clasped her hands together and brought them beneath her chin, tilting her head to the side. "Sleeping Beauty is going to marry Prince Charming," she said whimsically. "We need to have a *huge* wedding." She grabbed Aurora's hand and held it up to the light, studying the ring. "Like hundreds of people, three dresses—a Kardashian wedding."

"How the heck do you know about the Kardashians?" Zak asked, adjusting himself so he was now flat on his back next to Aurora.

"The tabloids at the grocery checkout," Tia said blandly, linking her fingers through Aurora's so they were now holding hands. "And TMZ."

"Don't watch that crap," Zak said. "It'll rot your brain."

"Let's fly to Mexico like Mom and Craig did," Aiden offered.

Aurora felt Zak tense up next to her. That'd been a real sore spot for him for a while now. His ex-wife had had a destination wedding to Mexico with Small-Feet Craig, and she'd tried to make Zak pay for the kids' flights.

Uh, fuck no.

"I think we'll do it somewhere else," Zak said. "Seattle in the summer is gorgeous."

"Oooh, a summer wedding," Tia cooed.

"And you'll be one of my bridesmaids, right?" Aurora asked.

Tia's honey-colored eyes went as big as dinner plates. "Yes!" She hugged Aurora so tight, Aurora thought she might crack a rib.

"And you and Uncle Adam will be my best men, right, dude?" Zak asked, playfully pulling the knit cap down over Aiden's eyes.

Aiden pulled the knit cap back up. "Of course, Dad. Tia and I just want to see you happy."

Zak turned his head to face Aurora, then linked his hand with her free hand. "I'm the happiest I've ever been, buddy. I'm with my family."

NEW YEAR'S WITH THE SINGLE DAD - SNEAK PEEK

SINGLE DADS OF SEATTLE BOOK 6

Chapter 1

Coffee!

He needed coffee.

He needed to hook himself up to an espresso IV or at the very least put his large black coffee into a camel pack on his back.

How in the world was he going to get through this day? This night?

Stomping off the snow from his black dress shoes, and loosening the collar of his coat, Dr. Emmett Strong stepped toward the front counter of the downtown Seattle coffee shop. What were the odds he'd managed to arrive at just the right moment and miss standing in line for twenty minutes?

Were things finally looking up?

It was about time.

He walked up to one of the two barista's standing there waiting to take orders.

"What can I getcha?" the barista with the goatee asked him, his red tie just slightly crooked.

"Large coffee with two shots of espresso, please. And an everything bagel toasted with cream cheese, lox and cucumber slices." His brows instantly furrowed as he heard his order come out of his mouth, but then realized it was somehow said in stereo.

The two baristas behind the counter at the side-by-side cash registers gave him an equally surprised, almost spooked look, as well as the person next to him who had apparently ordered the exact same thing at the exact same time.

What were the odds?

He turned to see who shared his taste in breakfasts to find a very attractive woman laughing. Her light brown hair was cut in a sleek bob that fell just beneath her chin and her sky-blue eyes sparkled.

"Good choice," she said, continuing to laugh. "Just know that if they only have one bagel left, it's got my name on it. I'm running late for work and I'm freaking starved."

"You two don't know each other?" the male barista asked.

Emmett shook his head, so did the striking woman beside him.

"Just kindred breakfast spirits," she said lightly.

"We have enough bagels for both," the female barista said, her chipper tone indicating she'd probably had a shot or two—or three—of espresso herself that morning. "Though we've never had the exact same order at the exact same time like that. It was spooky."

The two baristas continued to ring up Emmett and this mystery woman's breakfast. They both pulled out credit cards and paid, then moved to the side like well-trained cattle so the next hungry Seattle caffeine addict could pump ethically traded Arabica into their bloodstream and make it through the day—and what was inevitably going to be a long night for everyone.

Even though it was now New Year's Eve day, Christmas

decorations still hung from the ceiling and painted the coffee shop windows, and the radio station over the speakers continued to blast out tunes like Mariah Carey's *All I Want for Christmas*. He would be glad when they could get back to the regular scheduled programming of tasteful classic rock and no sparkly shit hitting his head as he waited for his bagel.

Until Valentine's season hit them like that fat winged-baby's arrow that is, then it'd be all red and pink hearts and more glitter—AKA the herpes of craft supplies. His almost six-year-old daughter, JoJo, loved anything and everything sparkly. He was always finding glitter in the laundry, his shoes—his food.

She needed to keep that crap at her mothers.

He glanced at the woman beside him. She was tall. Not super tall, not taller than his six-three frame, but taller than his ex. Taller than most women.

She held her chin up with a confidence he admired, her eyes laser focused forward, her full lips resting in a kind line. She had a great profile and an air of ease and sureness surrounded her like a soft glow.

He must have been staring too intensely because her eyes slid to the side and she turned to face him. "Think they'll put the orders up at the same time or are we going to have to duke it out for the first one?"

Emmett's lip twitched into a small smile. "You can have it."

Her light blue eyes squinted just slightly and she made a fist with her hand and flexed her coat-covered arm. "You sure you don't want to arm wrestle for it?"

Emmett chuckled and scanned the coffee shop. "Afraid there are no empty tables." He snapped his fingers. "Shucks. And I was *so* looking forward to kicking your butt."

He'd been in a crappy mood this morning—too much beer at poker night last night—combined with the fact this past year had been complete shit. But this woman's smile pulled him from the dark place he'd woken up in. In fact, her wide smile made his stomach do a somersault and caused heat to began to pool in various places in his body—various *intimate* places. "Oh, that's some ego you got there," she said, her carefree attitude causing his own shoulders to shake off some of their tension.

"I prefer to simply call it confidence," he stated, matching her smile.

She stuck her hand out. "Zara Olsen."

He took her hand. It was soft, but the shake held strength. "Emmett Strong."

She tossed her head back and laughed. She had a great laugh. "Your last name is *Strong*?"

He knew his grin was goofy, but he didn't care. He liked how he felt around this woman. He liked her. "Yep. Told ya, I'd whoop you at an arm wrestle. My name doesn't lie."

"Well, if that's what we're doing here, my last name isn't Olsen, it's *Brilliant*. Zara Brilliant," she thrust her hand forward once again, "pleased to make your acquaintance."

Oh, yeah, he definitely liked her. Pretty and witty—a winning combo if ever there was one.

Twenty years ago, when he was an undergrad on the prowl in a hopping night club, he would have been a drunk idiot and thrown out a line like *"Your last name should be Gorgeous."* But he was too smart for that shit now. He shook his head at the memory of how much of a pussy-obsessed beast he'd been. He'd do his best to keep JoJo away from guys like him. His ego back then could have eclipsed the sun.

He fought the urge to shudder at the embarrassing memories.

He wasn't that guy now.

He'd grown up. He'd matured. He'd become a father to a

beautiful little girl who he wanted to wrap in bubble wrap and shield from any and all heartache.

Zara lifted a dark eyebrow at him. "You okay there, *Mr. Strongman*?" Her very full lips wiggled at one corner as she tried not to smile.

Emmett's chest shook and he grinned back at her. "Yep, just telling the twenty-year-old in me to *not* say the line I would have said two decades ago." Oh, why did he reveal that? Now she'd want to know what he was thinking.

Curiosity stole across her features and she opened her mouth, but they were saved by the barista. "Extra large black coffee, double espresso shot and an everything bagel with cream cheese, lox and cucumber," the male barista said, interrupting their banter.

Oh, thank God.

Emmett inclined his head forward to offer Zara the coffee and bagel first and was about to say something like, "After you," when the barista plunked the duplicates down and said, "times two."

They each reached for their coffees and breakfasts. Emmett's knuckles brushed hers just as they wrapped their fingers around their enormous to-go coffee cups and a surge of something he could only define as electric attraction sprinted from his hand straight down between his legs.

"Enjoy your breakfast, Mr. *Strong*," Zara said, once again tossing her head back and laughing as she made to leave. She shot him a smile over her shoulder and shook her head, chuckling as she heaved the door open and headed down the sidewalk.

Why hadn't he asked her to sit and have breakfast with him? Why hadn't he asked for her number? Why had he just stood there like an idiot and smiled like an idiot and flirted like an idiot, allowing the most beautiful and interesting woman he'd met in a long while walk right out the door?

Because you're scared. You thought Tiff was the love of your life, your soulmate, and she fucking ripped your heart out and stomped on it. You don't want that to happen again.

Fuck you. I'm not scared.

Well, you're talking to yourself ... so you're at the very least a little crazy.

Grumbling, he brought his coffee cup to his lips and took a sip, allowing the caffeine to flood his veins and wake him up. He made his way through the throng of people to the front door. The wind was strong, but thankfully it was only a hop, skip and a five-minute walk to the hospital. Hopefully, he didn't get blown away on his way there. Hopefully, he ran into Zara again.

And what are you going to do if you do see her? Challenge her to an arm wrestle?

Maybe. Was that such a bad idea? At least he'd get to touch her again.

Emmett groaned. Now he was behaving like a love-sick pre-teen. He wasn't sure if this was better or worse than the horny twenty-year-old.

He zipped his winter coat all the way up to his neck, put his head down and took off in the direction of work. Maybe sewing people up and treating broken limbs for the next nine hours would put him in a better mood, keep him from thinking about his lonely life and his ex-wife off with Huntley the Moron.

It was New Year's Eve, and the ER was going to be crazy.

It was New Year's Eve and Emmett had no one.

It was New Year's Eve—next year had to be better.

Tomorrow had to be better.

IF YOU'VE ENJOYED THIS BOOK

If you've enjoyed this book, please consider leaving a review.
It really does make a difference.
Thank you again.
Xoxo
Whitley Cox

ACKNOWLEDGMENTS

There are so many people to thank who help along the way. Publishing a book is definitely not a solo mission, that's for sure. First and foremost, my friend and editor Chris Kridler, you lady are a blessing, a gem and an all-around amazing human being. Thank you for your honesty and hard work.

Thank you, to my critique groups gals, Danielle and Jillian. I love our meetups where we give honest feedback and just bitch about life. You two are my bitch-sisters and I wouldn't give you up for anything.

Andi Babcock for her beta-read, I always appreciate your attention to detail and comments.

Author Jeanne St. James, my alpha reader and sister from another mister, what would I do without you?

Megan J. Parker-Squiers from EmCat Designs, your covers are awesome. Thank you.

My Naughty Room Readers Crew, authors Jeanne St. James, Erica Lynn and Cailin Briste, I love being part of such a tremendous set of inspiring, talented and supportive women. Thank you for letting me learn, lean on and join the team.

My street team, Whitley Cox's Curiously Kinky Reviewers, you are all awesome and I feel so blessed to have found such wonderful fans.

The ladies in Vancouver Island Romance Authors, your support and insight have been incredibly helpful, and I'm so honored to be a part of a group of such talented writers.

Author Cora Seton for your help, tweaks and suggestions for my blurbs, as always, they come back from you so sparkly. I also love our walks, talks and heart-to-hearts, they mean so much to me.

Authors Kathleen Lawless, Nancy Warren and Jane Wallace, I love our writing meetups. Wine, good food and friendship always make the words flow.

The Small Human and the Tiny Human, you are the beats and beasts of my heart, the reason I breathe and the reason I drink. I love you both to infinity and beyond.

And lastly, of course, the husband. You are my forever. I love you.

ALSO BY WHITLEY COX

Love, Passion and Power: Part 1

The Dark and Damaged Hearts Series Book 1

Love, Passion and Power: Part 2

The Dark and Damaged Hearts Series Book 2

Sex, Heat and Hunger: Part 1

The Dark and Damaged Hearts Book 3

Sex, Heat and Hunger: Part 2

The Dark and Damaged Hearts Book 4

Hot and Filthy: The Honeymoon

The Dark and Damaged Hearts Book 4.5

True, Deep and Forever: Part 1

The Dark and Damaged Hearts Book 5

True, Deep and Forever: Part 2

The Dark and Damaged Hearts Book 6

Hard, Fast and Madly: Part 1

The Dark and Damaged Hearts Series Book 7

Hard, Fast and Madly: Part 2

The Dark and Damaged Hearts Series Book 8

Upcoming

New Years with the Single Dad

The Single Dads of Seattle, Book 6

Valentine's with the Single Dad

The Single Dads of Seattle, Book 7

Neighbours with the Single Dad

The Single Dads of Seattle, Book 8

Flirting with the Single Dad

The Single Dads of Seattle, Book 9

Falling for the Single Dad

The Single Dads of Seattle, Book 10

Lost Hart

The Harty Boys Book 2

ABOUT THE AUTHOR

A Canadian West Coast baby born and raised, Whitley is married to her high school sweetheart, and together they have two beautiful daughters and a fluffy dog. She spends her days making food that gets thrown on the floor, vacuuming Cheerios out from under the couch and making sure that the dog food doesn't end up in the air conditioner. But when nap time comes, and it's not quite wine o'clock, Whitley sits down, avoids the pile of laundry on the couch, and writes.

A lover of all things decadent; wine, cheese, chocolate and spicy erotic romance, Whitley brings the humorous side of sex, the ridiculous side of relationships and the suspense of everyday life into her stories. With mommy wars, body issues, threesomes, bondage and role playing, these books have everything we need to satisfy the curious kink in all of us.

YOU CAN ALSO FIND ME HERE

Website: WhitleyCox.com
Twitter: @WhitleyCoxBooks
Instagram: @CoxWhitley
Facebook Page: https://www.facebook.com/CoxWhitley/
Blog: https://whitleycox.blogspot.ca/
Multi-Author Blog: https://romancewritersbehavingbadly.blogspot.com
Exclusive Facebook Reader Group: https://www.facebook.com/groups/234716323653592/
Booksprout: https://booksprout.co/author/994/whitley-cox
Bookbub: https://www.bookbub.com/authors/whitley-cox

JOIN MY STREET TEAM

WHITLEY COX'S CURIOUSLY KINKY REVIEWERS
Hear about giveaways, games, ARC opportunities, new
releases, teasers, author news, character and plot
development and more!

Facebook Street Team
Join NOW!

DON'T FORGET TO SUBSCRIBE TO MY NEWSLETTER

Be the first to hear about pre-orders, new releases, giveaways, 99 cent deals, and freebies!

Click here to Subscribe
http://eepurl.com/ckh5yT

Made in the USA
Las Vegas, NV
04 October 2021

31710694R00166